TYCE

BY
SHAREEF JAUDON

{WRITE NOW BOOKS}

LOS ANGELES CALIFORNIA   DENVER COLORADO

WRITE NOW BOOKS

First Paperback Edition: March 2011

Jaudon, Shareef, 1978-
TYCE : a novel / by Shareef Jaudon.---1ˢᵗ ed.

Summary: A gritty coming of age story about a young man who was found in a dumpster as a baby. Growing up on the streets of Los Angeles, he matures and sets out to find money by staging three heists with new and old friends. He's blindsided by trouble and love as he battles to get the upper hand on his life and his enemies.

Printed in the United States of America

~For everybody that had to be cold sometimes to survive but always kept a warm heart~

Me

Nobody ever gave a fuck about me. Who's my momma? Where's my daddy? That's what I would ask myself when I was old enough to wonder. I was pushed out my mother's warm womb and abandoned. A female police officer was chasing a purse-snatcher down an alley one night, when I announced to the world, that I was here. She was sprinting as if she was the one being chased down the dark alley, when she heard my cries bouncing off the high brick walls of the buildings. I must've been sounding off something fierce, 'cuz she forgot about the nigga she was after and stopped dead in her tracks. The officer shifted her attention to the direction of the high-pitched screams and approached with curiosity her gun leading the way. My cries were pulling her toward the back of a Chinese restaurant. Her blue eyes danced back and forth, as she scanned the area for any signs of danger. She finally found the source of the noise and peaked over the crusty edge. She was horrified as she saw a heavily soiled used to be white pillowcase wiggling and moving. The officer immediately holstered her weapon and started swatting away greasy take-out cartons and thick slimy noodles and then she snapped the rubber band that was clinching the dingy pillowcase closed. With trembling hands, she reached inside and lifted me out of the filthy dumpster.

When she found me she immediately began checking me over to make sure I wasn't injured. Pamela was a nurse before she decided to become a cop, so she had a quick career relapse right there in that shadowy alley. Pamela had just returned to active duty after being pregnant. Unfortunately her son died inside of her at six months...she had to deliver and bury him in the same week. Therefore, when she held me in her arms, she just couldn't bring herself to let go. In some ways, I think we helped each other, I feel like we saved each other. She wrapped me tight in her police issued coat and put me on the floor of her patrol car. Pamela kept me in her home for two weeks before turning me over to social services. Nobody claimed me...there was no picture of me on the back of a milk carton. No missing persons report filed with my description on it. During that time, she gave me my name. While giving me a bath in the kitchen sink one night she said to herself,

"He is a tough lil' boy, he's so young and cute," She gazed at me lovingly, "Listen lil' man...a million dollars in a trashcan is still worth a million dollars, you are exceptional, and don't you forget it," Tears slid down her vanilla cheeks.

She washed my tiny brown body and dressed me in the clothes meant for her son. She prayed silently while she fed me from his never used bottle, tears continued to fall and she made no effort to wipe them away, she just let them run.

"You're a miracle baby." She declared. "You are tough, young, soooo cute and exceptional!"

"Tough, young, cute, and exceptional TYCE!"

When I was child, the state was my mom and the county was my dad. I liked it that way tho, 'cuz couldn't nobody take credit for shit...I was a self-made man. Foster homes and substitute parents couldn't hold me for long, at 15 I hopped the fence of the boy's group home I was in and landed on the streets. I had one pair of jeans, and an Addida's jacket stuffed in a backpack. I had 300 hundred dollars in my front pocket that I'd won playing pool and shooting dice. It was me against the world, and I held a record of 1 and 0. I was supposed to die in that fucking dumpster...but I didn't. One thing I knew about me was that I hated losing. I found my new home in a boarded up warehouse. I bought the most expensive space heater I could afford, a cot from the army surplus store, and a two-burner hot plate. I lived there for a year, just the mice, my thoughts, and me.

Like I said…nobody gave a fuck about me.

Fresh Out The Gate

"What up my nigga?"
"Aint shit, was hatnin?" I reached out and gave Omar a pound.
 "Man it's hot as a mafucka out here, I'm sweatin' n shit." He huffed as he grabbed a white towel hanging from his back pocket. He wiped his black beaded forehead and draped the towel over it. "Ay, when this nigga said he gon be here?" He asked looking down at the hot sidewalk.
"Biz told me he'd have his man here round four." I said scanning the block.
I looked down at my watch it read 3:55p.m.
"What man?" Omar asked suddenly irritated.
"What happened to Scoop?"
I glanced over at Omar, "Scoop had a hot

date".

Omar slowly nodded, he knew what that meant. Scoop's hot date was a bullet, that nigga was a memory. Omar pulled his 9mm from underneath his *"Lakers"* jersey and tucked it behind his back so he could sit on the steps in front of the corner store. Omar was the kinda nigga that stayed ready; he blocked the entrance on purpose. He was secretly wishing somebody would tell him to move. A fine ass female or an old ass woman got a pass, but niggas would have to show some respect to get by. That's just the way he was, and that's why I hustled with him. Omar squinted from the sun as he looked up at me,

"That nigga Biz is cold, I'm sayin' how tha fuck you kill ya nephew?" He asked as he spit out sunflower seeds. "That nigga Scoop aint know 'bout Angelique. All he did was push up on her...and shit, who wouldn't...she a bad ass bitch! Shit, every nigga I know wanna fuck her."

I nodded in agreement, "Yea, you right...but niggas know to keep tha dick zipped when Biz is playin' with his new toy".

Omar and I been hustling together since we was 16. I met him when I was jacking gear at the *"Crenshaw Mall."* I was being chased all through the mall by security. I was leaving them fat ass niggas in the dust til' I had to avoid a damn baby stroller. My legs were pumping as I sprinted toward the escalator. Omar was talkin' to some girls when he noticed the commotion coming his way. As I raced by him, we made brief eye contact. He saw they were gaining on me, so he stuffed the phone numbers in his pocket and stood by a trash barrel. As the two officers sped by him, he picked the barrel up and hurled it. The full trashcan smashed into one man knocking him down, the other tripped over him, and did a face plant on the newly waxed floor. As I reached the bottom of the escalator and jumped over the side of the stairs, I looked up and gave him a nod, silently thanking him. Omar said he kicked the dudes front tooth as he ran away laughing, he caught up with me a few blocks later.

"Wait up nigga!" He shouted after me, "You a fast ass mafucka, but you was 'bout to get got when you almost hit that stroller!"

I just calmly stared at him. He pointed his finger at his chest.

"What I wanna know is...why you stealin' from *"Foot Locker,"* when you work there?" He said between laughs.

I grinned at him and shook my head; he was talking about the black and white striped shirt I was wearing. I had an official *"Foot Locker"* employee outfit on.

"Man I don't work there! I got hired jus' to get tha outfit." I schooled. "I been to seven different malls in tha last two weeks, havin' this outfit on makes it easy to slip in tha back and jack em." I held up the black trash bag full of new "*Jordan's.*" "Here," I reached in the sac and handed him a pair, "You look like you a size 12, good lookin' out my nigga." Silence replaced the giggles as he recognized my young genius.

He held up the shoes, "Yo how much you be sellin' these shits for?"

"Seventy five dollars and I got eight pairs in here." I answered.

"I sold a hundred pairs in tha last two weeks." I said still grinning.

"Niggas be callin' me "*Jordan.*"

Omar was impressed. Shit all the niggas he knew was trying to sell dope to get paid, including him, and here I was slanging shoes, making the average corner nigga look broke. Omar said to himself,

"This dude can sell his shit on the blocks and not give a fuck about the holice!"

After putting Omar up on game, he and I became tight and we started slanging shoes together. I had him go cop a "*Foot Locker*" outfit the same way I did, and we got busy. We were making over 10g's a month, and we split the money 50/50. Couldn't nobody tell us shit, we was 17 years old pushing brand new *"Acura Legend"* coups. Our pockets had a constant case of the mumps, we was little thousanairs. However, with the money, came bitches, and with the bitches came niggas. In my eyes, niggas fit the bitch profile better than women did most times.

Our activity caught the attention of one of the neighborhood bosses. Biz was a slick ass nigga whose stock was on the rise. He was looking for some solid soldiers to hold down a few spots he wanted to control. Biz didn't want some dumb ass greedy niggas; he needed some mafuckas with intelligence and heart. He knew everything that went on in the hood, and little did we know he'd been secretly watching us for months.

I sold my last pair of *"Air Force Ones"* to a single mom with a teenage son, put the 50-dollar bill in my pocket, and headed up the block to my whip. Omar's car was parked in front of mine. He was sitting on his hood talking to a chick that made herself comfortable between his open legs. I walked up on them and the girl began grinding on him when *"Adina Howard's,"* *T-shirt and My Panties On*, blasted from his speakers. While she was winding and rolling her body to the beat, she used a cherry flavored blow pop as a mic and sang the words. Omar was too busy enjoying the free concert to notice the pearl white *"Mercedes Benz"* 500 pull up next to us. I stopped and eyed the car; my right hand was already obeying my brains order to grab my piece...so I was ready for whatever! A big Debo looking dude got out the driver's side and just stood there in the street.

"Tell dat lil' nigga to turn dat shit down!" He barked.

That finally got Omar's attention as he turned around to see who said it. He grabbed the girl by her waist and gently pushed her away from him. He hopped off the car and never took his eyes off the giant as he moved toward me. Omar pressed the volume button on his stereo remote, placed it in his back pocket and slowly pulled out a 9mm. Omar cocked his bald head to the side and glared at the linebacker. I however had my attention on what I couldn't see.

"Nigga who tha fuck is you?" I said evenly.

"Mafucka, don't worry 'bout who tha fuck I am!" The linebacker shouted.

I gave him an easy grin, "I wasn't talkin' to you".

I shifted my eyes to the back door and waited for the person behind the black tint to join the party. The back window slid down silently and a shadow leaned forward. "Relax ya back fellas, we don't mean no harm." It said.

The door opened and almost in slow motion, a cream-green alligator shoe pressed against the street.

"Yo cat daddy, we aint got no gators." Omar joked.

The stranger got out, stepped around the door, and walked easily toward us. He wore a beige sharkskin suit and a butter cream silk shirt with no tie. A green handkerchief peeked out his coat pocket.

"I jus' wanna talk to you fellas for a few ticks if that's alright." He extended his chocolate brown manicured hand, "I'm Biz. The large man over my left shoulder is Bruce."

Biz stood about 6.2, if I had to guess, I would say he was about 45. He had short black wavy hair and a smooth goatee. His deep tanned complexion was absent of any bumps. Everything about him said...money. When I shook his hand, I could tell he never worked a hard day in his life; he had hands as soft as surgical cotton. Biz looked us up and down and side to side. I was beginning to get agitated with this whole scene, when he spoke again.

He nodded in my direction, "You must be Tyce? And I don't buy my gators off the street...Omar." He said narrowing his eyes at him.

I always like to listen as people talk, 'cuz when your mouth opens your brain is on display. Omar on the other hand wasn't as patient.

He blurted out, "What tha fuck are you a stalker?"

"Naw young blood, I jus' recognize good shit when I see it." He responded calmly. "Listen, ya'll wanna make some money? I'm 'bout to get into some shit, and I could use some young brothers like you." He cut to the chase.

Right on cue, Omar spoke while I just listened. I was always cautious when somebody said they could "use me."

"Man we makin' money, do we look hungry to you?" He bragged.

"I aint talkin' 'bout no sneaker doe, I'm talkin' 'bout so much money you get tired of countin' it. I'm setting up shop in San Diego; ya'll can give them shoes to the niggas you'll be runnin' down there. I got mafuckas weed wackin' niggas right now, makin' room for my shit." He paused checking my reaction.

Now I'd heard of Biz from a few niggas I knew in Oakland. They said he was on the rise and moving down south...guess they was right.

"You said ya name was Biz, right?" I asked making eye contact.

"That's right." He confirmed.

"Look Biz...if ya "bizness" is dope, you talkin' to tha wrong two niggas. We aint got time for that shit!"

He leaned in a little closer to me, "What you mean you aint got time?"

"Holice givin' niggas all day for that shit, we aint got time to waste sittin' in a cell tryin' to play catch up when we get out." I leaned in a little closer this time, "You gotta come with somethin' a lil' better than that to fuck with us." Omar shot me a quick look of protest, which I ignored. Biz noticed it, but didn't say shit. I never liked the dope game it was over crowded with bitch ass niggas. Fake ass niggas that claim to be solid, but would fold up like lawn chairs under pressure. I wasn't trying to be locked up 'cuz another mafucka was afraid to be. Biz smiled and stroked his goatee; he strolled back to his Benz and put his hand inside. A petite feminine hand placed a pager in his palm. The diamond tennis bracelet she was wearing winked at me as the sun hit it. He walked up and gave me the pager,

"Get back when I hit you...I think I might have a lil' somethin' better."

That was nine years ago, Omar and me had been working for Biz ever since. Now here we were both 26 years old posted up on a California block. We were waiting for Biz's new man to show up with some money Biz owed us. Yeah, we were hanging on a street corner but understand we weren't your average everyday corner niggas.

All Grown Up

I walked in my kitchen holding a bag of take-out from Shabazz restaurant. I ate my dinner on a 5,000-dollar mahogany table that was placed on top of a 40,000-dollar marble floor. I had a two-foot shark swimming in a 500-gallon fish tank in my bedroom. I sat on heated toilet seats with built in air suction when I took a shit and wiped my ass with 20-dollar toilet paper...yes there is 20-dollar toilet paper. Life was good. I had no kids and no wife. You don't lose bitches chasin' money, but you lose money chasin' bitches. I believe that shit. Now don't get it twisted; I love the ladies! I just don't get side tracked; I put business first. I mean what woman wants a broke ass nigga. Shit, I was far from broke and I love being wanted.

My wet feet pressed against the slate tile as I walked out the shower room, and looked in the bathroom mirror. I got some baking soda out the medicine cabinet and started brushing my teeth. That white powder kept my shit gleaming even though it tasted like feet. I was what old people called "paper bag brown" not to dark and not to light. However, I had the dark features of a

Dominican or Cuban nigga. I kept my hair short and faded up...'cuz afro's was outta style and braids were for girls. I had a solid frame from eating well that was nicely cut up. Being 6.1 and weighing 190 looked good on me. I didn't want to be all buff and shit...I liked being underestimated. I enjoyed seeing the surprised look on niggas faces when I flashed on em. I was the nigga you didn't see coming. I kept a low profile and stayed in the shadows. Yeah, I got loud and live at times but I kept that shit to a minimum. Shit, the *"IRS"* used new potential employees to get info on tax dodging niggas. They would post up at the local clubs and write down the license plate numbers of expensive cars, so the *"IRS"* can run the info and see who was legal and who wasn't. So I wasn't trying to get a letter in the mail talking some bullshit about tax evasion. I got dressed and drove into the city. I was passing by *"Marcus Garvey's"* school when I seen Lil' Flash. Niggas called him that 'cuz he'd get the crack to the fiens in a blink, and holice couldn't catch that nigga on foot. I pulled over and honked the horn.

"What up Flash?"

He bent his knees a lil' bit to get a better view, "Washatnin' Tyce!"

He jogged over and leaned in the window.

"I didn't know it was you nigga, where the

Range at?" He asked.

I was rolling in a new "*Jeep Cherokee*" with straight factory equipment.

"It's at tha house; sometimes you gotta know when to dim the lights...you feel me?" I schooled.

"Yeah, fa sho." He replied.

"You on the job?" I asked.

"You already know my nigga!" He answered raising his hands.

"How much you finna' make in the next two hours?" I questioned.

"Shit, 'bout three hundred...why?"

"'Cuz I need you to run this package over to the "*Mosque*" for me, and time is money. I'll give you four hundred if you handle that for me."

He playfully punched me in the chest, "Hell yeah I'll drop that shit off for you!"

I gave instructions, "Look, it needs to be there this morning by ten...ask for Cory, and give it to him. Wait inside for Cory to bring you another package and bring that shit back to me. When you get the package from him, you get paid, but don't forget to bring me my shit."

Flash pulled his jeans up from around his ass and adjusted his wife beater. He snatched his hat down low on his head, college boy style and looked from side to side. Flash was 15, the same age I was when I bounced from the group home. He had a dark baby face with a long scar on the right side of his forehead. The white T-shirt he wore contrasted with his black skin and hugged his broad chest.

"That aint shit man, I got you." He said confidently.

I reached under my seat and handed him a box wrapped in brown paper, "Hit me when you get that, and I'll meet up with you." I looked in his speckled brown eyes, "Don't tell anybody I sent you!"

"Bet!" He said and dashed off.

Flash made the ten block walk and rounded the corner walking briskly up to the front door of the Mosque. He stepped inside and was immediately met by a tall man in a blue suit. Flash sized the dude up and gripped the package.

"Ay 'cuz, I'm here to see Cory." He announced.

"Alright young man, just hold here a minute." The clean cut man stood back and began to search Flash's body for weapons. His body tensed up when the man's hands got close to the gun that was tucked in his back. The man's hands landed on the weapon, and Flash jumped back.

"You can't come in here with that young brother," the security guard told him.

"I'm going to have to take it for now, but I'll

give it back to you when you leave."
Flash wasn't comfortable with that idea at all, but he trusted Tyce not to send him into some bullshit. He reached behind his back and handed the man the gun. The brother nodded in appreciation and allowed Flash to enter into the next room. He followed closely behind him and motioned to another man sitting in a corner. The man stood up and started to approach the two of them.

"I'm Brother Cory, what can I do for you?" He asked Flash politely.

"Yo, I got this package for you and you only." Flash handed the beige skinned man the package and waited for his response.

"I see, well feel free to have a seat, and I'll get back with you shortly."

"Naw, I'm good, I'll jus' stand in the back."
Flash moved to the rear of the room and leaned his back against the wall. Although he wouldn't admit it, he felt safe in the room, even without his gun. He began to relax and his ears tuned in as a young bold man preached to the full audience seated in front of him. Inside the privacy of his office, Cory opened the package. He pulled back the flaps and seen a stack of hundred dollar bills in a rubber band. The box also contained an envelope. Cory opened the envelope and read the note inside.

Thought you might be able to put this 10,000 to

good use. Keep doin what ya doin'. Watch the dude that brought this to you, if he stays for the entire service...give him 400 dollars. And yo, please put a bean pie in a box, tape it up and give it to him.
*   -peace*

Cory smiled at the anonymous package. He removed four hundred dollars from the stack and placed the rest of money in an office safe. He buzzed the secretary and informed her they had a donation. Cory let his curiosity take lead as he watched Flash lean against the wall listening intently to the student minister speak.

I was on my way to Omar's spot two hours later when my cell phone rang. I turned down *"Young Geezy's"* vocals and grabbed the phone.

"What up Flash...you got my shit."

"Nigga you know me, when have I ever slipped up?" He challenged.

"Yeah, you right my nigga that's why I sent you," I agreed.

"You get ya money?"

"Yeah, good lookin' out Tyce."

"Yo meet me at Omar's crib so I can get that from you." I told him.

"Bet." He shot back.

I mashed on the gas and sped toward Omar's house. Man, I hope he hurry up 'cuz a nigga was straight starvin'!

Time To Go To Work

I pulled in front of Omar's crib and hopped out my jeep. His two huge Dobermans Bonnie and Clyde immediately greeted me. I tussled with them for a minute and walked up to the oversized door. Before I could knock, Omar swung the door open. I lowered my hand and looked at him like he was crazy.

"You alright?" I asked looking him up and down.

"Yeah, I'm straight." He sighed scratching his head. "Come on in, I jus' heard the dogs barking that's all."

I walked in the living room and sat on the leather sectional. I leaned my head back against the cool leather and closed my eyes. My thoughts were interrupted by the sound of high heels clapping on hardwood floors. Omar's most recent girlfriend, Tasha was coming up the hallway. Tasha was a beauty queen; she was all legs and ass. She didn't mind showing off what her momma gave her. She had on jean boy shorts that let the bottom of her ass escape and a tight yellow wife beater with no bra. Her long jet-black hair swooped behind both ears and cascaded down her back, my mouth watered because of the way she was chewing her damn gum.

"O, baby have you seen my yellow earrings?" She sang, "I thought I left them on the coffee table last night."

Omar was in the kitchen grabbing two beers, and didn't see what I saw. Tasha stepped right in my view, turned around and proceeded to bend over to look for her earrings. She did this while keeping her long legs completely straight.....stripper style, less than three feet from my face. I closed my eyes and leaned my head back continuing my train of thought. She strutted off before Omar could witness the flirtation. He walked in and handed me a *"Heineken,"* and a pink box.

"Lil' Flash left that shit for you earlier."

Just then, the doorbell rang, "Yo that must be Bruce". He said.

Omar disappeared and returned with Biz's right hand man, Bruce. We exchanged mutual glares as he sat in a chair across from me. He must of thought I was a muthafuckin' sunset 'cuz he just stared at me.

"You niggas ready to punch in?" He finally asked.

"We stay ready so we aint gotta get ready." I came back at him.

"Yo, let's go to the pool house, 'cuz I don't want Tasha all in my business." Omar ordered. Once the three of us were behind closed doors, Bruce gave me and Omar the details of the next hit; it was a drop house in Riverside. Some mid level nigga was getting too big down there. His business was beginning to sip profits from Biz's cup, and that shit couldn't happen. Biz stayed on top of the dope game because of us. Me and Omar were the two most efficient jack boys in the dope game. We controlled the competition. We robbed and bodied niggas all over the west coast. Only those niggas that Biz saw as a threat got the pleasure of meeting us. Biz already sent the messenger boys to help this new nigga see the light, but that shit aint work. Bruce informed us that those niggas was three weeks missing, so we were up next. Niggas feared us in the streets, but the trip thing was they didn't even know who we were. Omar and I weren't known in the dope business 'cuz we never sold the shit. All niggas knew was that Biz had a jackin' crew that you aint wanna fuck with. It was just me and Omar, 'cuz we aint trust nobody else. We ran up on niggas while they was fucking bitches, getting high, playing *"Madden"*, or eating Christmas dinner; we aint give a fuck. This shit wasn't some smash and grab random shit...naw; we studied these niggas.

We knew they habits, what they drove, what spots they partied at, what ho's they fucked with, every fucking thing. The split was 70/30 on the cash and Biz kept all the dope we found. We'd offer the niggas a deal but if they wasn't with it...then we'd fill em with some hot shit! Simple.

I insisted on just getting the loot and leaving the dope to the rest of the niggas. Yeah, some might say I was leaving money in the streets, but fuck what they say. I hate losing and too many niggas was losing in the drug game. Getting locked up, set up, flipping and spitting out names for fake ass detectives. Shit, I made sure my name wasn't part of a bitch ass plea bargain...............I didn't fuck with them niggas...period.

Look But Don't Touch

Booom! Booom! Bap Bap Bap Bap! Me and Omar hit the shooting range at least twice a week. I wasn't with that sideways shooting-hit a nigga four times before you kill him shit. Hell naw two shots, center mass or in the dome! Simple.
"Tyce, how much Biz say them niggas is holdin'!" Omar yelled over the gunfire.
"300,000 at least." I shouted.
Omar stopped shooting and faced me, "You know we could turn 210,000 into a half a mil if we flipped that dope."
"All money aint good money my nigga." I schooled.
"Whatever you say Tyce."
He turned away and kept shooting at the distant target. I made a mental note to talk to him later about his attitude. I was focused in on my target, when I felt a tap on my shoulder. I turned around slowly and grinned when I saw Angelique.
"You know you can't shoot Tyce." She teased.
"If you want I can show you how it's really done!" I stepped aside and said, "I don't mind a woman teaching me a thing or two."

She smiled unclipped her *"Gucci"* purse, and pulled her pink pearl handle 9mm out. She opened her stance, squared her shoulders, and squeezed off five perfect headshots.

"Damn, remind me never to piss you off."

"You could never do that." She replied making eye contact. "Maybe next time we'll work on the...or two." She said with a wink.

Angelique was off the pillow fine. She could easily have been a model but she was to gangsta. She had brains and beauty. She had a degree in communications from *"USC"* but her high street IQ is what got her paid. She had the kind of body that made niggas write...pay to the order of Angelique, on their paychecks.

"When you're finished here, meet me outside ok?" She said leaving.

Omar didn't pay Angelique no mind. He wasn't trying to end up like Scoop. So when she left he put his brain on display.

"I keep tryna tell you, that bitch is trouble Tyce. You know what happened to Scoop and I don't know how many other niggas behind her ass!"

"Dog, I don't mix business with pleasure, you know that shit." I reminded him.

As we walked out the building and into the bright sun, we saw her leaned up against her Jag. She was parked next to Omar's *"Escalade."* I took a mental picture of her tight white leggings and gold fitted shirt that gripped her hips. My eyes followed every dip and curve of her body like a roller coaster.

I walked up on her and asked, "What did you want to see me about?"

"I got you two some gifts." She answered.

"What kind of gifts?" I asked curious.

"Nothin' much, jus' a little somethin' I thought you could use."

"Thanks. If you woulda told me I would have came by and picked em up." I offered.

"No problem, gives me a chance to get a little me time." She said rolling her eyes in her head.

"Plus I like to know you guys are safe."

I just laughed a little after she said that. She popped her trunk and pulled out a large box. I took the box from her and tossed it to Omar.

"Ay how you know where I was anyway?" I wondered aloud.

She grinned, "You always get a little practice in before a job."

And with that, she walked back to her car jumped in and sped off.

Jack Boys

We'd been in Riverside for about two weeks checking up on this nigga Ash; we knew every move this fool made. He had a small but loyal crew. His main man was a hotheaded essay nigga named Chico. Ash had two main spots he hustled out of. He had an apartment where he cooked and bagged the product up and a little house on the east side of town that served as the drop. This niggas shit was sloppy though, he spent too much time chasing pussy and blowing money. It was easy to get up on him, whenever the drop was made only him and Chico were there to meet the bagman. We planned to hit the house fast and hard when the delivery was made.

We were sitting at a booth in the back of a spot Ash and his crew hung at. We stayed low key and just blended in with everybody else. Ash and his boys were acting a fool in the club as usual. They were at a round table throwing money at a female while she danced in the middle of their table. Ash opened a bottle of Champaign and sprayed the girl's chest hoping to get a better view of her titties. The amateur stripper screamed with delight, putting her hands up to shield her eyes from the spray.

"What you drinkin' tonight fellas?" A cute waitress asked me.

"Two double shots of *"Bacardi"*...light." I responded handing her a 50-dollar bill.

She weaved her way through the crowd and moments later returned with the drinks. She set the drinks down and started to hand me the change. I raised my hand in protest and told her to keep it. A huge smile spread across her face as she leaned closer to me. I felt a faint tap in my lap and looked down as she dropped a folded napkin on my crotch.

"That's my number feel more than free to use it." She whispered in my ear.

"Damn you aint shy at all huh?" I asked.

"Not really my style, I like what I like and I let you know." She said smartly.

"Well Ms. Bold, I aint shy either." I came back.

"Well call me and prove it, the names Angel."

"Well, you are definitely blessed." I complimented.

A sly smile spread across her dimpled cheeks as she turned around a let her ass wave goodbye.

"MAN... How coulda' nigga be gay with bitches like that around?" Omar asked pounding the table with his fist.

"Shit I can't call it my nigga….pussy feel too good to throw it away." I cosigned putting the napkin in my back pocket.

"Hell yeah!" He agreed.

"Shhiiitttt!" We said at the same time laughing at each other's expressions.

It was 12 midnight. The bagman arrived at the house between two and three in the morning. We watched as two of the four niggas from the crew left with the wet dancer, leaving only him and Chico. As usual, on drop nights, Ash and Chico sent everybody else on their way. We downed the shots and left out the back exit. We hopped in the rental car and headed toward the house. Before we got there, we pulled over in a dark alley to grab a case we'd hidden earlier. Omar opened the case full of equipment and we both suited up. Exactly 15 minutes later, we were posted under the wooden porch of the drop house waiting on the bagman.

Devil nThe Flesh

Biz pulled his cell phone out and dialed slowly. He was sitting across the table from some bosses he'd flown in from D.C. He held his hand up to excuse himself before he spoke into the phone.

"Tyce; I was jus' checkin' to see if you gonna make it to that party tonight?" He paused while he listened, "Good, good, well I hope you two have a blast, hit me later, and let me know how it went. Give my regards to the host." He said coldly.

He returned his attention to the guest in his office. Orlando and Marcus were two major hustlers from the east coast. They were looking to expand to California and Biz was the nigga to see. In exchange for a piece of his pie, Biz wanted a slice of theirs. The deal was already set; all that was needed was a few details and handshakes. One detail the D.C. niggas were concerned about was how Biz handled resistance in his organization.

"I'm lovin' what I see; you got shit tight out here." Marcus confessed. "But...how do you deal with hard head mafuckas? Too much blood is bad for business, but I'm sure you know that."

Orlando cosigned, "Yeah nigga we rest in Washington, we can't afford to be wrapped up in bullshit in California."

Biz stroked his salt and pepper goatee. He knew this was a concern for them. Shit, he asked them the very same question and was satisfied with their operation. So how could he blame them for wanting that same sense of security the phone call in front of the men was a deliberate move to answer that very question.

"The man on the other end of that phone call is my problem solver. He and his man keep unruly mafuckas in line. Between my rep and their perfect record, don't nobody fuck with me for too long" Biz assured;

He leaned back in his chair and sipped his drink. "Now, to show my appreciation...I arranged to have ten kilos dropped off tonight as a personal parting gift and a lil' sumthin'... personal."

Biz pressed the intercom button and told Angelique to come in. She walked in with a train of beautiful girls trailing her. Angelique stood next to Biz's chair as the women made a circle around the desk and stood in a row beside the two men. It was a pussy parade and Orlando was in heaven. He hungrily eyed the young gorgeous women stopping his gaze on every curve. They may have looked like grown women, but these girls were no older than 17. Angelique studied the scene and felt a wave of sadness come over her. She saw her reflection in those wide-eyed girls. She remembered when Biz first climbed on top of her and snatched her virginity. She had been the same age as they were; he was 44 at the time. Orlando chose three girls for himself and graciously allowed Marcus to make his selections. Marcus placed a hand on his stiff dick and licked his lips.

"I want her," he said pointing at Angelique.
Biz raised his eyes and looked up at Angelique. He motioned for her to go over to Marcus.

"I see you recognize good shit when you see it." Biz complimented.
Angelique's mouth opened in shock at what she was hearing.

"Fuck that, and **fuck you muthafucka**!!!" She shouted at Marcus.

"I aint the bitc....."
Biz sprang to his feet and backhanded her across her cheekbone, slamming the brakes on her words of protest. The unexpected blow made her take a bow in the opposite direction. He snaked his hand around her slender waist and helped her stand up straight.

"That was so disrespectful baby. You should be

honored the man chose you in a room full of beautiful younger ladies."

Marcus watched silently still holding his dick. He was getting more aroused by her feisty attitude. Biz pinched her side tightly twisting her flesh in his fingers.

"I think you owe Marcus an apology." He said staring intensely in her eyes.

Realizing the situation she was in, Angelique regained her composure. The juvenile girls silently cheered her bravery as they waited for her next move. Angelique stood to her full 5.7 frame arched her back and smiled.

"You're right babe, I'm sorry Marcus. If you still want me...meet me in the guest house in five minutes, I want to change and freshen up a bit." She said seductively.

Satisfied, Biz released his grip on her rib cage. Angelique switched out the office and down the hallway. She slipped off her shoes and crept into Biz's master bedroom. Once inside she contemplated storming back in the office and letting her 9mm do the talkin'...thinkin' of something much better she went into the back of the walk in closet and eyed the safe. Her fingers obeyed her brain and moved quickly dialing in the combination. The safe door swung open and she filled a leather bag with stacks of money.

Angelique shut the safe, hurried to the open window of the room, and tossed the bag out. She quickly returned to the closet and began to pick through her lingerie. She walked out the closet holding a two-piece thong set as Biz walked in.

"Nice choice." He said noticing the underwear.

"Do you think he'll like it?" She asked.

He answered, "What man wouldn't?" He walked over to her and kissed her forehead, "Thank you for helping me seal this deal."

"It's in the bag baby...you know I got you." She said kissing his smooth cheek.

Biz was sure that once Marcus got his kilos and fucked Angelique, it was a done deal. Not many men could fight off the urge to fuck her and not get sprung. Angelique started toward the door when Biz grabbed her arm. He spun her around gently and put his face in front of hers. She could smell the cognac on his breath as he exhaled slowly.

"You *ever* disrespect me like that again...I'll bury you in the back woods bitch." He threatened. "Now go, he's waiting in the guest house."

Downstairs Angelique snatched her keys slipped on her shoes and stepped into the huge backyard. She looked toward the guesthouse and saw Marcus standing naked in the window. Angelique trotted over to the bushes and retrieved her money. She slid the steak knife she grabbed from the kitchen inside and tossed the bag over her shoulder walking casually toward the guesthouse. She gave Marcus a devilish grin and stepped inside the room.

"Sorry to keep you waiting so long baby. I wanted to freshen up for you. I'm sorry I was a bad girl earlier and now I wanna make it up to you. Now get on the bed and put ya dick in the air…..' cuz you 'bout to get the best ride of yo life baby!!"

Marcus smiled like a schoolboy and obeyed his new mistress. He laid on his back crossing his arms behind his head. His stiff dick bobbed slightly up and down to the rhythm of his heartbeat. His fantasy walked over to the stereo and pressed play. "*Toni Braxton's*" sultry voice filled the room, Angelique walked slowly around the bed undressing teasingly to the slow seductive beat. Marcus watched her every move as he licked his ashy lips. She grabbed four silk scarves from the nightstand drawer next to the bed. She expertly tied each one of his limbs to the bedpost. She made knots that the boy scouts would be proud of. Once she made sure, he was secure and not going anywhere, she dimmed the lights. From the nightstand on the left side of the bed, she grabbed a rubber ball gag and gently slipped it over Marcus's head. Biz would never admit it but it had been in his mouth more times than she could remember. As her sex slave opened his mouth to try to protest, she hushed him with one finger on his lips.

"Sshhhh baby, I jus' don't want everyone out there to here you moanin'. There will be no interruptions tonight. You have to trust me....remember *you* chose me."

"You a freaky ass bitch but that's cool with me. I could tell you was a handful when I first saw you, shit do what you want...jus' don't tell anybody." He instructed staring at her wildly.

After she placed the gag in his mouth so nobody could hear him scream like the bitch he was, she sat on top of his hairy stomach and asked,

"How bad you wanna throw that dick inside this pussy? Yeah, I saw you staring at me...you wanted to fuck me an hour before you even met me! You sure you can handle a bitch like me?"

Marcus shook his head up and down rapidly! Angelique leaned over the side of the bed while still on top of him, her hand found the leather bag and inside she retrieved what she was looking for. As he squirmed showing his excitement she let him see the knife as she waved it menacingly in the air. Marcus's eyes bulged and he muffed and growled in anger, spit leaking from the corners of his mouth. Marcus raised his hips in the air and tried to buck her off but Angelique tightened her thighs and rode him like a professional bull rider. The tip of the blade dug into his skin as he forced out muffled screams. Angelique continued to straddle him, locking his waist in her powerful thighs and performed her surgery despite the turbulent ride. When she was finished, Marcus lay on the bed exhausted with crimson puddles on the sides of his body. Sweat flowed into the river of blood oozing down his rib cage. Angelique stood up and admired her surgical skills. The words **FUK U** were jaggedly carved into his chest.

"See you one of those muthafuckas that think he can have what you want when you want it! Well sorry, pussy ass nigga...**I aint for sale!** Now you have somethin' to remind you of that shit everyday!"

As Marcus laid there bleeding and panting in pain, Angelique put on her clothes and grabbed the bag that held her punitive damages. She walked back to the side of the bed looked Marcus in the eyes and spit in his sweaty black face. Wasting no time, she ran to her Jag, jumped in and quietly rolled away. Once she was safely on the freeway, she inspected her face in the rear view mirror. She had a gash on her cheek and her lip was cut in the corner.

"*Fuckin' bastard*!" she spat. "Who tha fuck Biz think he is slapping me, I'm not that run to the shelter, file a restraining order type bitch! I'm the kinda bitch that will hit you where it counts, in the pockets! That was a two hundred thousand dollar smack...I hope he enjoyed it!" Then her eyes shifted over to the bag that held her parting gifts and she felt a little better.

The Hit

Hidden under the porch me and Omar waited patiently. We were dressed in all black and blended in with the shadows perfectly. I pulled the ski mask over my face and released the safety on all three of my guns. Omar did the same and handed me the silencers. He tossed me a pair of gloves and put his mask on.

"You want some *skittles*?" I offered pulling out a pack.

"Yeah."

We ate and crouched in silence, I turned my phone off after Biz called to check in on us, I didn't want Samsung giving away our position.

A white minivan pulled up in front of the house and a short Mexican got out. He walked briskly across the grass and approached the steps. I turned and nodded at Omar. We rolled out from under the porch, sprung to our feet, and aimed the guns at the drop man.

"Don't fuckin' move holmes!" I commanded.

Omar rushed behind the dude and quickly searched him. He was shook; we had caught him off guard.

"**Move!**" Omar said pushing the man to the side of the house. "Get on ya knees!" He ordered.

I shoved my gun in his right eye and Omar jammed one in his crotch.

"You droppin' tonight!" I questioned.

"Nnn no no, pickeen nup!" He stammered.

"Pickin up what vato?" I asked.

His left eye moved around rapidly as he talked.

"I'm pppickeen nup tha dinero, tha dinero!" He said in an accent.

"How much?" Omar asked jamming his gun in deeper.

"Two hunerd an fifteee!"

I snatched the man to his feet and put the barrel in his right eye again. His left eye was tearing up and bouncing around like a pinball.

"Look at me! You knock on that door and don't say a muthafuckin' word comprende!"

"Si yes yes yes!"

I took the gun barrel off his pupil, "Relax." I told him patting him on his back. I reached in his back pocket and grabbed his wallet. Shoving my hammer in the small of his back, I pushed him toward the porch. I stood on the side of the door and Omar crouched down. He still had the gun aimed at the dude's dick.

"Get cute and I'ma shoot ya balls off!"

Omar whispered.

The drop man took a deep shaky breath and knocked on the door.

"**Who izzit**?" A loud voice boomed.

I looked down at the drop man's driver's license to make sure he wasn't trying anything funny.

"It's Luis!"

"You late nigga!" The voice on the other side of the door said.

The clicking and pinging of several locks were heard before the door opened up. I didn't waste any time, I spun around and shot Ash in the thigh causing him to hobble backwards. Omar pushed Luis in first, using him as a human shield. He saw Chico on the couch; threw Luis on the ground and aimed his hammer at Chico's head. Ash fell to the floor screaming and clutching his leg. Omar kicked the front door closed and stayed on his man. Chico was high and didn't have the reflexes to get to his gun sitting on the make shift coffee table. Omar grabbed the piece and stuck it in his waist.

"What tha fuck Muthafucka!!!" Ash shouted in pain.

"Who tha **FUCK** is ya'll niggas?!!" Chico yelled now completely sober.

"Shut tha fuck up!" I ordered. "We tha bag men bitch!"

I walked over to Ash and put my foot over the bloody hole in his jeans. I leaned all my weight on his leg. "You aint gotta die tonight, that's why ya leg is fucked up. I informed him. "Biz wanted me to ask if you changed your mind."
He screamed from the pressure and grabbed at my boot.
  "Keep ya hands to ya self, I don't want you fuckin' up my shoes!"
  "Fuck Biz...and fuck you niggas! Tell Biz he can suck my dick!" Ash shouted.
He was much to pretty to be talking like that; he looked like an R&B singer instead of a drug slanging gangsta.
  "He speak for you nigga?" Omar asked Chico blankly.
  Chico spit at Omar and said, "**FUCK YOU** *'BIZ ASS NIGGAS!*"
Omar stiffened his wrist and shot Chico twice in the chest! His body lurched against the cushions and he slumped over on the arm of the couch.
Omar looked down at Luis."Stay." He ordered. I put my gun inside Ash's pretty mouth and rested the barrel on his back molars. Omar knelt down and put the hot barrel in the middle of his forehead.
  "My friend Luis came to get some money-where is it?" I questioned.

I pulled the gun out his mouth to hear the answer.

"I aint givin' ya'll muthafuckas **SHIT!**"

I wiped the spit off my gun on his shirt. I grinned at him through the hole in the ski mask and shot him in his foot. The bullet put a perfect circle in his *"Air Max's."* He rolled around in agony, screaming and banging his fist on the floor.

"Mutha Fuck, Shiiittt, shit shit *aight aight*...It's in tha closet in tha dryer!" He gasped.

"Now how hard was that?" I asked standing up. I walked down the hall to the laundry closet an opened the door. My eye caught the shimmer of a thin silky string as I heard the click.

"BLAMMM!!!"

Omar's head jerked up!

"**T!!**" He shouted! "**T!!**"

Ash was laughing on the floor, "Yeahhh, he don't hear you, that nigga dead!" He chuckled sadistically.

Omar ran down the hallway stopping when he got to me. The shotgun blast hit me in the chest and slammed me against the wall. I was struggling to breath and my head was spinning. Omar grabbed me under my shoulders and sat me up.

"That sneaky muthafucka." I said faintly. That nigga shot me." I said gasping for air.

Omar ripped my shirt open. "Damn nigga that
shit fucked yo vest up!" He said unstrapping it.
I felt my bare chest, searching for any wounds.
I looked at my dry hands and grinned. I thought
back to when Angelique gave the vests to us
outside of the gun range; her gift was right on
time. I intended to thank her personally for this
one.

"Help me up man."
I was still laboring to breathe as I stood up slowly
shaking my head to clear the cobwebs. I cautiously
approached the closet and inspected the inside. A
short barrel shot gun was mounted to the sidewall.
A string was tied around the trigger which
attached to the inside doorknob. It wasn't a
sophisticated boobie trap but it was effective. I
opened the door to the dryer and pulled out a blue
duffle bag. I handed the bag to Omar; he looked
inside and smiled. We walked back into the front
room. Ash's big ass smile froze on his face when
he saw me alive and well. Omar aimed his
hammer at Ash and I instantly grabbed his arm.

"Naw man...let him live." I said.
Ash's body relaxed with relief. He rested his
head on the wood floor and sighed.
"A few more seconds!" I added shooting him
twice in the head.
The bullets shattered his skull, leaving his blood

spattered eyes staring at the ceiling. We quickly headed for the front door. I snatched a stack of bills out the bag and tossed it at Luis. It landed in the middle of his back, 'cuz he was still laying face down.

"Gracias amigo!" I said.

"Denada." he said into the wooden floorboards. I felt the night air brush across my chest as I ran the two blocks to the car. We hopped in and hit the free way...I was thinking the whole ride back.

New Moves

We rode back to the city in silence. The guns and shit we used was at the bottom of the Pacific Ocean. The two dead examples we left in the house, would make niggas think twice before fuckin' with Biz. Our job was done as far as I was concerned; Omar however was dissatisfied.

"We should of went and hit that apartment Tyce, it wasn't nothin' but three niggas and some naked bitches in there baggin' up product!" He reasoned.

"You don't know that O." I stated. "I aint takin' unnecessary risks for no dope." I said looking out the window.

I grabbed my cell phone and dialed Biz's private number; he picked up on the first ring.

"HELLO!" He shouted.

I pulled the phone away from my ear and looked at it.

"What tha fuck you yellin' in my ear for?" I asked irritated.

"Nigga I aint got time for no games! Jus' bring me my shit...I got niggas waitin' on it." He spat impatiently.

Something must be wrong I thought to myself, he aint never this hype. I rubbed my sore chest and sighed, "Aight nigga...calm down. You jus' turned 75 years old, you can't be yelling like that."
I informed Biz in code, his cut was 75,000 off the hit. The phone went silent.

"Is that all?" He asked.

"Yeah, jus' the paper...nuthin' else." I said as Omar looked over at me.

Biz clinched his jaws in frustration. "What tha fuck you mean...nuthin' else!" Biz questioned.

"Jus' what I said man, NOTHING ELSE!" I said more clearly.

Omar pulled the car over to pay closer attention to the conversation. I reclined my seat back and lit a clove cigarette. I blew out the flavored smoke and waited for the bullshit to land.

"You niggas fucked up," he shouted." I might lose a deal behind you muthafuckas! So consider this a loss nigga, and bring my muthafuckin' money!" He demanded.

I took another drag off my cigarette and blew the smoke out the window.

"I don't work for free, and I don't take losses nigga! I think you may have forgotten who you talkin' to, but I can remind you." I warned.

"Look you parentless BASTARD, I'm not tha nigga you wanna fuck with!" He challenged.

I felt a quick surge of anger in my chest over that bastard comment but I kept my cool.

"Alright Biz, grab a pen and write this down." I told him.

Biz smiled as he opened his desk drawer and pulled a pad and pen out. He was all set to write down the instructions on how to get his money.

"Yo write this down...Fuck you! I aint givin' you shit muthafucka!" I shouted hanging up the phone.

Who the fuck he think he was? He must be getting crazy in his old age talking to me like that. He knew I wouldn't go for that bullshit; I don't let niggas run me. That's the very reason he recruited me years ago to be on his team.

"Yo, I told you we shoulda got that dope now this muthafucka trippin'. Why you aint ask me what I wanted to do?" Omar projected.

I turned and faced him, "Trust me on this. This workin' for Biz shit is runnin' out of gas. Aint no future in it for me and you, we can't keep breaking this nigga off 30 percent every lick. Plus shit aint poppin' like it used to, we only hittin' niggas once every two or three months, that aint shit! I been thinkin' on some new shit we can get off. If we do it right, we can both be millionaires."

"Yeah I feel you, so what's the plan?" He

asked.

"I got a few more details to work out first. Gimme' a few days, and I'll drop it on you. But yo, we need to stay ready case this old ass nigga wanna flex. Keep ya eyes open, aight?"

"Tyce, I wish that muthafucka would. I keep heat for situations like this!" Omar said convincingly.

I reached behind me, grabbed the bag off the back seat, and started countin' the stacks. It was an even two hundred and forty thousand dollars. I put a hundred and twenty thousand back in the bag and handed it to Omar, I put the rest in my leather backpack.

"Don't that shit look better than tha eighty four thousand you woulda got fuckin' with Biz? I questioned.

Omar raised a stack to his nose and sniffed it,

"Hell yeah, it smell better too."

We got back on the freeway and sped toward the city. Omar drove into an underground parking garage and stopped next to my Range. I gave him a pound and jumped out. Wasting no time, I got in and mashed out. I hit the CD button on the steering wheel, and *"Jagged Edge"* blared from my speakers.

"I love it when you grind on me. When you take ya time on me. When you put a little uummph

in it. That's when I lose control. When you put
a little uummph in it. Start squeezin' and you
won't let gooo!

I sang along bobbing my head, they was the only
singing niggas that got play in my rides. I wasn't
with that crying *"Keith Sweat"* type shit, niggas
whining about how much they love her and wanna
make love all night long...*please*. If it takes a nigga
all night long to satisfy a woman…he aint hitting it
right. I was feeling good despite my aching chest
muscles. I was about to make a move that would
set me up for life. It was three o'clock in the
morning but I was in the mood for some company.
I pulled my cell out and called Honey; she ran a
high priced escort service and was familiar with
my taste in women. Unlike Omar, I didn't want a
girlfriend. They took up to much time and energy.
I preferred a professional when I wanted some
pussy. I didn't have to wine and dine these women,
they didn't blow my phone up when I was taking
too long to get home, and I wasn't financing
shopping sprees every fucking weekend either. I
paid-we laid-she left. Simple.

I checked into a room at the *"Four Seasons"*
hotel. I took a long shower letting the hot water
soothe my chest and changed clothes. I always
kept a new outfit and an overnight bag in my trunk
just in case I needed it. I was watching *"Mike*

Tyson's" greatest hits on *"ESPN"* when the phone rang.

"Mr. Adkins, there's a lady by the name of Dallas at the front desk to see you."

"Okay, send her up." I said turning the TV down.

Moments later, I heard a soft knock at the door. I looked through the peephole just to make sure it was her. You can never be too careful. I opened the door and Dallas stepped in. She was 5 feet 4 inches of pure and uncut sexy. Her hair was black with caramel highlights; it was pinned up allowing one curly lock to fall on the side of her auburn face. The sea green dress she was wearing embraced her curves and stopped right below her round ass, a little black moe was perfectly placed above her succulent lips. Dallas was the type of woman that wore *"Victoria Secret"* period panties. She didn't fuck with low budget niggas. Her company tonight would cost me two thousand dollars.

My eyes moved slowly over her, "Thank you for comin'."

"You're very welcome. I don't normally come out this late, but Honey said you'd be worth it. I'll have to thank her in the morning." She flirted.

I shut the door as she made her way into the front

room. She sat down in the middle of the couch and stretched both arms across the top. She stared at me with a hint of smile in her eyes. I grabbed two small glasses and filled them with Remy. I gave her the drink and sat directly across from her on the love seat.

"Sooo, Tyce Adkins." She said slowly. "I've heard great things about you. Simone tried to switch dates with me when she found out I was seeing *you*. As you can see, I said no, I wanted to meet you myself."

I grinned a little, "Ahh, Simone. Yeah me and her got along well together." I thought about her and had a pornographic flashback.

"I *know*, she told me." She teased.

Dallas uncrossed her legs and stood. She took a sip of her drink and walked slowly over to me. Standing in front of me, she unpinned her hair, letting it tumble down. She licked the tip of her finger and pressed the off button on the TV remote. She slowly began moving to her own rhythm as she peeled her dress off. Her body was stunning. Her waist and hips formed a lazy S down her sides. The princess cut diamond pierced in her belly button matched the ones in her ears. She moved her hips left to right slowly wiggling out of her tight ass dress. Letting it fall to her ankles she stepped out and formed the letter A with her legs.

Dallas just stood there open for business and completely naked. She took a long sip from her glass again and pushed the dark liquor passed her lips using her tongue. A little stream of bronze liquor flowed over her chin and trickled down her neck. My dick was pushing against my zipper trying hard to escape. I stood up and placed my hands on her waist, the tip of my tongue was traveling to her neck like an arrow. I tasted the liquor as I worked my way up to her chin. I stood back a little and looked down at her face.

"Damn you fine! You look good as hell...but I can't do it baby." I said shaking my head side to side.

She gently grabbed the back of my neck, pulling me down to her and outlined my lips with the tip of her sweet tongue.

"Baby don't sweat the money, we'd be doing each other a favor. Shit I'd fuck yo sexy ass for free." She placed her hand on my chest.

"Excuse me baby, I'll be right back." I escaped from her sexy grip.

I walked in the bedroom grabbed a robe and three g's out my bag. I returned to a naked and confused Dallas still standing in the front room. I put the robe around her and gave her the money. I guided her hand inside my jeans and let her grab my throbbing and disappointed dick. I wanted to show

her that it wasn't her stopping me at all. Plus that's
how gay rumors got started!

She massaged my dick, "Well what's the
problem Tyce? I can tell you want me as much
as I want you. I aint met a nigga yet that can
resist me. And trust me baby...I won't let you
down." She said sarcastically.

I backed up and looked in her eyes. "That's
exactly why I can't fuck you. I don't mix
business with pleasure and I have somethin'
else in mind for you." I said calmly. "Since I
paid for your company tonight, let's talk. I want
your attention, not your pussy."

I grabbed my drink and lit a cigarette, offering her
one. She took it and leaned in my direction so I
could light it for her. She sat back down on the
couch and crossed her legs, ignoring her wide-
open robe. She put the cigarette to her lips, tilted
her head back, and blew smoke in the air.

"What's on your mind?" She asked smiling at
me.

Guess Who's Coming To Dinner

Angelique stood out on her balcony sipping a *"Corona."* When she was 18 years old she'd moved in with Biz, after learning more about his personality and herself, she decided to secretly rent a condo just in case she needed to get away. Standing there in the evening sun, alone, she was glad she did. However, she knew her name was in the streets. Biz wouldn't tell anyone what she did, for fear of losing respect. What he would do was have people looking for her. She had to figure out her next move. She had plenty of people too turn to, but none she trusted and not one that could handle a situation like this. There was one person that she thought she could trust. She downed the rest of her beer snatched her keys and left as the sun was fading; 20 minutes later, she was in front of his house. She reassured herself silently that this was the right move as she parked in the driveway. Angelique stood in front of the door, debating if she should knock, "Fuck it," She said knocking on the door.

"Jus' a minute." A female voice sang.
Moments later a woman wearing a G-string bikini

opened the door. The woman just stared at her with piercing eyes, bulging with attitude.

Amused, Angelique asked, "Is Omar here?"

"Who tha fuck are you?" The doorman snapped.

Holding back her laugh Angelique answered, "A friend."

"What kind of muthafuckin' friend!" She asked crossing her arms.

"Look bitch, I don't want him, I wanna see him. Now get ya fake *"Sports Illustrated Swim Suit"* ass in there and get him."

"Tasha, who is it?" Omar yelled from the back yard.

Angelique struck a model pose as Tasha stepped aside so he could get a better look. Omar instantly recognized the woman he dreamed about fucking since high school. Dreaming was all he would do; he still thought Angelique was bad news.

"Yo baby, let her in." He ordered.

Angelique walked pass Tasha looking straight ahead.

"Bitch." Tasha hissed.

"That you *don't* wanna fuck with," Angelique retorted.

Omar was sitting in the hot tub on the patio. Angelique spotted a chair and sat. Tasha threw her hips east to west harder than she had to as she approached the hot tub and slowly climbed in. She possessively rubbed Omar's chest and kissed the lion head tattoo on his neck.

"What brings you here girl?" He asked enjoying the attention.

"I need to ask you somethin'."

"Wasup?" He said curiously.

Angelique was suddenly nervous. Maybe it was because she didn't know what he would say after she asked.

She licked her lips, "I need to know where Tyce lives. I also need his phone number. Trust me, I wouldn't ask if it wasn't important."

Angelique was aware that Tyce never let anyone know where he rested. The only person that knew the address to the bat cave was Omar. Biz kept Tyce's phone number private, so she didn't have that either. Tyce was the only person she could think of when it came to trust and who she knew wasn't afraid of Biz. Therefore, she had to ask Omar and hope he cooperated.

Omar studied her, "You good?" He questioned.

"Yes, I jus' need to see him that's all." She offered.

"Ok...I was jus' askin' 'cuz you got a bruise on your face." Omar cocked his head to the side.

Tasha giggled, "Yeah bitch who whooped yo

ass?"

Angelique didn't flinch a bit, "It's nothin' I can't handle…are you gonna help me or not, I really need to talk to him."

"Yo, I can't give you tha spot, but I'll give you his cell number. If he wants you there, he'll let you know. That's the best I can do ma." Omar said sensing her drama.

"Thanks O." Angelique said relieved.

Tasha tried to kill Angelique with her eyes. How the fuck is this bitch gonna come up in here and get Tyce's number, just like that. She had been crushing on Tyce for months and he never paid her any mind. So she snagged the next best thing, his best friend.

The black Jag pulled up slowly and rolled to a stop in the circular driveway. As soon as she left Omar's, Angelique quickly dialed Tyce's number and asked could she come by. He immediately gave her directions without any questions. Now she was nervous as she looked out her window and seen him standing on his porch. Her pussy smiled as her eyes took in the gorgeous view; he was wearing red sweats and a red wife beater. The tattoos on his thick arms were highlighted by the overhead porch lights; it was like he was on stage in front of his own house. The tight fitting shirt grabbed his muscular chest and tapered along his torso. One-carat studs sparkled in his ears trying to compete with his smile. He walked down the steps and opened her door for her. As soon as she stood up, he gave her a huge warm hug lifting her off her feet.

"What was that for?" She asked pleasantly shocked.

"That was for the vests! That shit was a life saver...literally." He said sincerely.

"I aim to please." She said girlishly.

He grabbed her by the hand and walked toward the house, "You know you're the first woman to be at my crib." He said pointing at the house.

"I know." Angelique said grinning.

He looked at her once they were under the light of the porch and appreciated her sexiness. She wore tight ass jeans with slits in the back and front thighs. Her 34C's were covered by a blue and white shirt that said DIVA in rhinestones and her body was elevated by cream and blue stilettos. Sexy yet simple. He moved his attention upward and paused.

"What the fuck happened to your face?" He asked turning her cheek.

Angelique forgot about the bruise on her cheek and turned her head in embarrassment. She wasn't the type of chick to be abused and she was not happy about it.

"Biz had a pimp moment and hit me. I left his ass right after though. But not before I made his ass pay!"

"That muthafucka! What you do, stab his ass?"

"No I robbed his ass!" She said hatefully.

"That's what the fuck I'm talkin' 'bout. Don't hit him in his face, hit em in his pockets." I approved.

"So you kinda get why I'm here? I know he's looking for me, and I didn't want to be alone. Do you mind if I stay here for a few days to clear my head?"

"Naw I don't mind, take as much time as you want. As a matter of fact, I'm glad you came. I need to talk to you about somethin'."

"Okay." She said easily as they walked inside. Standing in front of him, she finally granted her pussy's request and kissed his cheek.

"Thank you Tyce."

"It aint nuthin' girl. Now let's put a beer in ya hand and one on ya bruise. We gotta get that swelling down. I got plans for you."

The two sat at the kitchen table eyeing each other admiringly. Deep inside his chest, he was pissed that Biz had hit her but his emotions were expertly concealed.

"So, you really left that nigga huh? You sure you aint jus' mad at what happened? Maybe

you still got your door open for an apology
with some shiny shit attached to it?" I tested.
"Hell naw! Fuck Biz, I **been** trying to shake his
ancient ass...he served his purpose, now I'm
ready for somethin' new." She shot back
flirtatiously.
"Alright then, that's good to hear. Listen I got
somethin' I been workin' on for a minute. I
think it might be that "somethin' new" you said
you ready for."

Angelique sat up in her chair with interest and
took a sip of her beer. Resting her chin in her
palm, she said "What you been plottin' on Tyce?"

He worked that sexy smile that made her pussy
twitch. "Money equals oxygen in my world, so
you already know what it's about. I'll give you
the details later on, for now the guest room is
in the back on the left, make yourself at home.
I gotta make a run tonight but I'll be back in a
lil' while. Stay here, but if you gotta leave take
my Benz, I jus' had it delivered and aint
nobody seen it yet." He instructed.

He gave her a look that lasted a second to long and
left the kitchen. Angelique took another sip of her
beer and sighed. She felt safe, and that felt good.

Omar

After Angelique left, Omar was hoping he and Tasha could pick up where they left off before the interruption but Tasha had other plans, she crossed her arms and put a screwed up look on her face.

"Who tha fuck is that and why do she know where we stay!" She snapped.

"Ay check this out she aint nobody, why we can't finish enjoying the rest of our evening?

"Oh what the fuck nigga, you jus' gonna ignore my questions and think it's all good! I don't know what kind of bitch you take me for!"

"Shut the fuck up!" Omar interrupted. "I don't know who you think you talkin' to, but you better find your memory and check your tone!" That said he got out the hot tub and went to the bathroom. Freshly showered and dressed Omar headed for the door passing a pissed off Tasha who was sitting on the couch.

"Where you goin'?" She asked irritated.

"Away from yo muthafuckin' ass." He spat grabbing his keys and slamming the front door. Tasha sat quietly and chewed her bottom lip in anger.

"Did he really jus' walk outta here like that over that fake "*Meagan Good*" lookin' ass bitch for real!? Hmmmm...It aint nothin' I'ma pop this x pill and get myself right tonight" She thought as she scrolled thru the contact list on her phone.

Her acrylic nails landed on the number she was looking for and tapped the call button.

"Shit any nigga would do, a bitch jus' need some attention...and maybe some dick." She said out loud.

"Hello." a man answered.

"Hey sexy, this Tasha." She replied casually.

"Long time no hear from." He said irritated.

"Don't be like that baby...I gotta leave you to be missed."

"Yeah whateva...what you want?"

"You."

The phone went silent as the voice pondered the answer.

"I want a little conversation and a whole lotta dick...can you help me out?" She asked bluntly. Remembering the way she sucked his dick upside down and squeezed his joint with just the right amount of pressure, made him stiffen instantly.

"I'll be home in an hour." He said defeated and hung up.Tasha poured a shot of vodka and swallowed an X- pill called the smurf berry and headed for her closet. Her girlfriend told her they were the shit, and she hoped she was right 'cuz she needed to roll hard tonight.

Mission accomplished. Fuck Omar...at least for now.

Tasha

Ace sat in his leather recliner enjoying the show and loving how the red light highlighted her body. With low eyes, he focused on Tasha's ass as she swayed back and forth to the beat. She had the kind of body that demanded attention. Anything she wore couldn't hide her gifts and Tasha never wore much. He'd been fucking with her for about a year now and she still excited and surprised him. Tasha peeled her fitted dress off like a banana, revealing her turquoise bra and matching G-string. She reached behind her back and unsnapped the bra that held her cantaloupe sized breasts in place. She walked over to Ace and put her knees on the arms of the huge lazy boy. The width of the chair made her thighs spread leaving her pussy wide open floating over his abdomen. He took full advantage of the view as her titties grazed the top of his curly head. She reached between his legs and pressed down hard on his big dick. As Ace's eyes rolled back into his head, he gave a soothed and refreshed *ummm* to his seducer.

"Are you ready?" she asked coyly.

"Girl you know I'm always ready for some of you."

Tasha leaned backwards like she was doing a back bend and did a perfect flip landing with her knees on the ground and her face in Ace's lap. She unzipped his jeans and fished for his dick, she had no trouble finding it 'cuz he always went commando. Her hands embraced his stiff manhood and she took him into her mouth slow and hard. As his body began to tingle and fall victim to the tricks of her tongue he uttered, "Damn girl ya head game is on point." Once Tasha was sure he was ready to explode, she stopped and stood in front of him. She bent down and removed her G-string, placing it over his head and letting it rest on his neck like a chain. The effect of the ecstasy she took was beginning to kick in making her temperature slightly elevated and her sexual desire hit its peak. With a swift hop, she was on Ace's lap. Her right hand slid his tool into the opening of her tight and warm juice box. Tasha grabbed the

G-string she'd placed around his neck as if it were a pair of reigns and began to ride him like his name was silver. She dragged her pussy along his flat stomach then back down on his dick over and over again. Ace pressed her titties together so he could suck both nipples at the same time. He thrust his rock hard dick inside her and tightened every muscle in his body so he could stay there; he wanted her to feel every pulsing inch of him. A piece of paper couldn't fit between them as his dick disappeared in her pussy. Tasha responded to his generosity and grinded her hips faster and faster as her slippery pussy lips gripped the base of his dick. She put her hips in fifth gear and road him like a jockey coming down the home stretch in the "*Kentucky Derby*!" In unison, they both moaned loudly in passion. Tasha knew how to work her hips to find her own divine pleasure. Not that Ace didn't know how to handle his business but Tasha was all about making herself feel good right now. She began to tighten the muscles in her core abusing an unprepared Ace. It drove him crazy…he rose to his feet with Tasha still grinding into him. He snaked his arms under her ass and up her back gripping her at the base of her neck. Her calves elevated to his broad shoulders and she crossed her ankles behind his head. Tasha let her body do the talking, without saying a word she told him, "gimme' what u got" He bit down on the inside of his jaws as he began to punish Tasha. Ace thrust his dick in and out of her pussy, drilling her like an oil pump in Texas. He pumped her faster and faster as he felt the pressure of his fluid surge up his shaft. As Ace and Tasha both gave into their climactic release, he began to ease up the grip he had on her neck. He placed Tasha back on her feet, gave her a kiss on the lips, and told her with his eyes she was the best.

Out of breath, Tasha stretched out on the suede sofa and lit a cigarette. The ecstasy enhanced her craving for nicotine and made her extra horny all over again. She was rollin' hard now, her girlfriend was right, these smurf berries were the shit. She slowly exhaled the smoke and put her right leg on the top of the couch. She used her fingertips and began strumming her clit like a guitar as she gave Ace another order.

"Daddy come here and lick my sweet pussy." His dick had fallen asleep but it was wide-awake now as he took in the sexy masturbation scene. He fell to his knees and crawled the ten feet it took to reach Tasha's wet center. The hair around her edges was starting to curl up from the beads of sweat on her forehead. She had a first class weave equipped with black Indian style hair so it still looked good. Tasha adjusted her hips and took another drag of her cigarette; she exhaled smoothly and prepared herself for a bumpy round two.

Angelique

When Angelique woke up after a sound night of sleep in Tyce's guest room, she had the appetite of a lioness. She hopped out of bed and walked down the long corridor leading to the master bedroom. As she looked at the walls she decided while Tyce had great taste she could tell his home lacked the touch of a real woman. When she reached his door, she knocked softly but got no response. She knocked again and still no answer, her patience switched off and curiosity came on as she grabbed the doorknob. The door opened swift and quiet. She gazed across the room...so simple but so elegant at the same time. The oversized room contained a larger than life bed with steps to lead you up to what seemed like a stage covered in cranberry and gold linens. The massive cherry wood posts that were as thick as her thighs took her mind on a brief erotic vacation.

"What up?" Tyce called to her.
She was so caught up in her erotic thoughts she didn't notice Tyce was awake and staring at her.

"My bad." She responded. "Didn't mean to wake you up or scare you. I knocked but you

didn't answer." She explained. "I jus' wanted
to know if you were hungry, I was gonna make
some breakfast."
"No…but thanks I gotta get outta here." He
said hopping out of the bed walking toward the
master bath.
"Aight" She said a little disappointed.
She exited the master bedroom closing the door
behind her. As she walked, back down the corridor
she remembered the image that she knew would
forever be etched in her memory. Yummy…she
thought, she'd witnessed Tyce shirtless and each
and every muscle in his chest made her want to
lick him like a *"Dove Bar."* The tattoo that spread
across his upper back spelled his name in letters
the size of black licorice sticks. The way his
basketball shorts strained to imprison his manhood
at a full morning attention made her want to put
her own hand to her forehead and salute! His swag
was the perfect balance between sophistication and
gangsta. She found her way to the kitchen and
tried to find something she wanted to eat. Tyce cut
thru the kitchen moments later to grab some
"Gatorade."
"Hey I gotta run to make you down to roll?"
"Sure she responded jus' let me grab my purse
from upstairs and I'll meet you in the car."
Angelique did a five-minute makeover and

hurried to the car. She hopped in and had one small request. "Hey I know you gotta be somewhere but can we stop at somebody's drive thru cause I'm starving?"

"Yeah girl." He chuckled back.

After stopping at *"Popeye's"* the two were on their way. Angelique knew better than to ask where they were going, she knew everything Tyce did was calculated and anything he invited her in on would make sense later. She just sat there and enjoyed the fried chicken, red beans and rice, biscuit, and strawberry soda. After a 30 minute ride on the freeway, they pulled up to a not so modest house in *"Baldwin Hills."* Angelique paid attention to everything address, street, house color...it was just what she did. Tyce noticed her concentration,

"You comin'?" He asked"

"Yep." She answered grabbing the door handle.

They walked up the tiki torch lighted driveway to grand French glass doors. Angelique was impressed even though she didn't know what to expect. Tyce rang the bell, when the door opened there stood a tall sun kissed tan colored woman. As they entered, Tyce introduced the woman to Angelique as Simone. After the introductions Simone gave Tyce one of those too long and too tight for them to just be homie hugs. Surprisingly it made Angelique a little uncomfortable. She studied Simone and it made her feel uneasy, she couldn't find one flaw. Simone was a bad chick and even Angelique couldn't deny her that. She had the perfect tall chick shape. She was curvy like a belly dancer, no stomach at all and enough ass to give Trina a run for her money. The ends of her hair brushed across the top of her ass. Her grey eyes were very seductive and shaped like tiny footballs. Her whole look was something straight out of Puerto Rican pride fest. She even had that Spanish accent that drove men crazy. Even her outfit was in good taste, she had on maroon stilettos, matching leather booty shorts and a cream tank top. Very fly, even though it was obvious she was just lounging around the crib...a woman after Angelique's own heart she noted.

As Simone and Tyce talked, Angelique remained quiet and took notice of the way the house was laid out. From where she stood, she could see this woman took pride in her home and the things she bought to furnish it. After about five minutes, Simone handed Tyce a manila envelope. He thanked her and in return gave her a thick white envelope. They exchanged familiar looks before Tyce turned back towards the door. Angelique said nice to meet you; shook her hand and they were back in the car. Angelique gazed out the window trying to figure out who this Simone chic *really* was. She didn't like her. It could have been a little jealousy on her part 'cuz from their body language she could tell there was something more between the two of them. However, she was much more woman than that...it was just something that rubbed her the wrong way about this chic. What Angelique didn't know was that Tyce was taking mental notes as well. He liked the way Angelique handled herself around other women. She wasn't the least bit intimidated and exuded a confidence that turned him on. Also, the fact she didn't speak unless spoken to while he handled his business with Simone was something he added to his mental rolodex. So he decided to test her.

"Hey what you over there thinkin' 'bout?"

"Nothin' jus' enjoying the scenery."

"No questions?" He inquired.

"Naw, I'm sure if there's somethin' I need to know you'll tell me." She answered still gazing out the window.

Tyce left the conversation right there. He respected her to the fullest. She was beautiful, intelligent and she knew how to play her position.

Back to Bizness

Biz sat in the back of his *"Bentley"* as Bruce drove through the city. His frustration and anger was growing by the second. His people were searching for Tyce and Angelique, but they were nowhere to be found. He was certain they were together, Biz always suspected her of having a little candle lit for him. That's the reason he kept her on such a short leash. All he wanted to do was talk to Angelique. He just wanted the chance to ask her why she stole from him, and then stab her two hundred thousand times! One for every dollar she stole. Tyce became the most wanted man on Biz's list after he disobeyed him. The two of them murdered the deal he'd been working on for months in one night! After Angelique sliced Marcus up and the parting gifts were delayed, the men's confidence in Biz went south. Orlando and Marcus thought he was soft and losing control of his squad. They backed out the deal and returned to Washington, taking his coke and their two million dollars with them. Marcus vowed to murder Angelique if he ever found her. Looking back on things, he should of gave the greedy niggas his coke in the first place, at least it woulda been on time. Instead, he relied on third party contributions. However, Biz was greedy himself and hated giving away his product for free, he'd rather steal some other niggas shit and pass it on. Biz gave strict orders to bring Angelique back alive and kicking. He loved the fiery blood that ran through her veins but he was looking forward to watching it drain out of her bleeding body. Tyce was being set up on a hot date that would blow his fucking mind; he just didn't know it yet. Bruce turned a final corner and pulled up in front of a battered apartment building. He blinked the headlights and two men appeared from the shadows. They walked over to the car and got in.

"Don't slam my fuckin' door nigga!" Biz shouted.

"My fault man." One apologized.

After apologizing the man opened the passenger door wider and slammed it shut again, rocking the luxury car. The disrespectful man then turned his attention to Bruce, who started to say something.

"What nigga!" What you gonna do? I'll fuck yo big ass up! He challenged.

The second man sitting in the back pointed a chrome gun at Biz and spoke slowly.

"Now Mr. Biz, we don't enjoy being yelled at. Now we understand you're big shit in

California but were from Detroit. Now in
Detroit, no one's heard of you. Now in
California, you still managed to hear about us.
So, don't make the deadly mistake of thinkin'
we pussy's...'cuz you'll be the one bleedin' for a
week."
Saving the fight for another day, Biz calmed
down. He instructed his driver to do the same. He
liked the style of the two men, and they came
highly recommended.

"Look, let's cut the bullshit. Two bitches: ones
a man, the others a girl. I want the girl alive
and the nigga dead. Now can you Detroit
niggas handle that?" Biz questioned.
"Indeed." The man holding the gun responded.
"We need pictures and any info you have on
em. We also need half now."
Biz told the man in the front seat to open the glove
box and get the key inside, two photographs of
Tyce and Angelique were there.

"Since you got so much energy, run upstairs to
apartment number 36 and open the door. The
money's in a black duffle bag inside the
freezer. Call my private line when you find em.
Now, get out and don't slam my door." He said
smoothly.
The two murderers got out the car and disappeared
into the darkness.

"Detroit my ass!" Biz laughed to himself.
"Let's get the hell outta here Bruce, I'm
hungry."
The black *"Bentley"* silently pulled away from the
curb and slid down the street. After entering the
apartment and finding the money, Lincoln and TJ
began to outline the plan.

"First we gotta hit the streets and find this cat,
with the info we got it shouldn't be hard. How
many niggas gotta a chameleon painted Range
in this town? You know he'll be strapped of
course but we jus' gotta catch him slippin'.
We'll body his ass right quick...then find that
bucket head bitch he want us to chase down. I
don't know what she did to tha nigga but
personally...she could get tha business!"
Lincoln confessed.

"I know what you mean my nigga, she is fine
as fuck! I'ma make that bitch suck my dick
before we hand her over." TJ planned.

After contemplating the groundwork, they grabbed
the bag of money and shook the spot. They drove
towards Santa Monica, Lincoln picked a low-key
hotel off the strip and checked in, they decided the
best course of action was to hit the hotspots cause
where there are half naked bitches there was
always flossy niggas. TJ studied the photos of the
Range and Tyce while Lincoln showered. He ran

his finger over Angelique's photos and thought to himself…

"Damn she a bad bitch, I mean from head to toe flawless…but pretty bitches get it too!"

Sure that they were dressed to fit in they grabbed the Intel on their marks and headed back towards LA. The first stop was a spot called Fury, a fine little fish at the gas station told them that was the hottest spot in town. They cased the parking lot looking for the "*Range Rover.*"

"This nigga aint here." Lincoln said. "Let's check inside, case he rode with his homeboy or somthin', back in the parking spot close to the back door."

They paid the hundred each it took to bypass the endless line. Once inside the packed club they posted up at a table in the corner. They took turns going to the bar and the bathroom so they could case the joint from two angles. It only took a few minutes for them to realize their mark was not in attendance that night.

The Draft

I pulled up to the small arena and valet parked my Cherokee. I stepped out and handed the young brother a 20. He thanked me with big eyes and jumped in my front seat. Once inside the arena I found my place ringside and relaxed. I was sitting next to a loud-mouthed Italian dude. He was leaning over talking to a girl half his age.

"Watch this baby; you see that nigger in the red trunks? He's gonna put that other nigger on his fuckin' back!" He shouted in her ear over the crowd noise.

As he talked he gestured wildly with his hand. I peeped the big diamond and gold rings that squeezed each of his sausage fingers. The flossy Italian was dressed in a five hundred dollar silk shirt and two thousand dollar slacks. He must of weighed at least two hundred and eighty pounds. The black slacks wrapped around his upper thigh, revealed a knot in his left pocket.

I grinned to myself and nudged him in his mushy shoulder.

"Yo, seem like you know your shit!" I yelled over the crowd noise.

"Yeah, I knocked a few motherfuckers out in my day…still will if I have to." he responded looking me up and down.

"I bet you will!" I said appearing to be impressed. "I didn't mean to ear hustle, I'm jus' trying to get some info on these boxers. I wanted to place a bet but I got here too late." I baited.

"Oh yeah…who'd you wanna bet on?" He leaned in.

"I was thinkin' the dude in tha black trunks. He seems like he can bang a lil' bit. I was about to put ten G's on him but the fuckin' window closed on me, damn LA traffic!" I complained. Out comes a sweaty wad from Italian Jonnies pocket and his barely legal date begins dancing in her chair anticipating him winning some money.

"How 'bout we make a little wager boy?"
I paused for a second then turned to the couple seated next me. I explained the situation and asked the man if I can borrow the services of his girlfriend to hold the cash. Obliged and intrigued the couple both agreed. I whipped out my money and handed it to the cute girl; Italian Jonnie did the same. Our new accountant placed it under her ass,

"I'll keep it warm right her boys!"
With the money secured, I relaxed and enjoyed the fight. As the fight began, the two warriors eyed

and circled around each other in a smooth bouncing rhythm. They measured each other with straight jabs and faints. My newfound friend jumped to his feet when his guy landed a solid body punch.

"Yeahhh!" He screamed.

My man danced back and smiled at his opponent, thanking him for giving him more of a reason to knock is ass out. He began to break down the defense of his opponent by timing his punches and countering with right hooks. By the end of the first round, my less enthusiastic friend was sitting down. He saw what I already knew...my ten thousand was bet on a superior boxer. The opening of the second round brought both fighters to the middle of the ring. My dude began to use heavy body blows to make his opponent drop his hands and set him up for a brutal head shot. His plan worked perfectly as he connected with a left hook that staggered the man. He pushed off his opponent as he attempted to hug him in an effort to regain his focus. Now with some distance to work with he hit him with a stiff jab and rocked him with a right hand lead. The ropes dug into his skin as he stumbled backward. The ropes pushed him forward just in time to meet an uppercut that almost decapitated him. His legs melted and he literally went to sleep standing up! The crowd erupted as the fighter hit the canvass and the ref began to count. One, two, three, four, five, six, seven, eight, nine, ten thousand dollars, YOU'RE OUT!!

This time I jumped up and yelled,

"YEAHHHH!!"

I turned to my Italian buddy, "Hey, you win some you lose some."

"Yeah that guy's a fucking bum!" He complained. "I could of done better than that!"

"Hey, I'd put money on ya." I encouraged.

I was politely interrupted by a soft tap on my arm. I turned my attention to the pretty lady holding 20 grand and giving me a congratulating smile.

"Here you go." She said handing me the stack.

"Thanks baby."

"No problem, it was a pleasure just to hold it!" She admitted. "Keep the hundred on the top...it has some extra numbers on it." She said with a wink.

"I'll do that." I responded. I peeled off five hundred dollars and put it in her palm. "Take your boyfriend out to dinner and buy yourself somethin' nice."

"Thank you...and he's NOT my boyfriend." She corrected.

I smiled and nodded at her date, thanking him for his services.

"You gotta good girlfriend here, you're a lucky
man!" I yelled over the cheers.

"You got that right! She's an angel! Congrats
on the win!" He shouted back.

I shook the loser's chubby hand and made my way
through the crowd toward the back of the arena. I
coulda' socked him when I heard him call the man
a "nigger" but what good would that do. I'd rather
hit him in the pockets where he'll feel it...I never
miss an opportunity to make some quick cash; that
shit was too easy. I walked into the back dressing
rooms and stood against the wall. The double
doors swung open as the next fighters made their
way to the ring. I slid in behind them as they left
and went into the locker rooms.

"Wasup Sway!" I said lifting my arms in the
air.

"Tyce Adkins, what up my nigga!" He said
giving me a pound.

"Yo, you gave that boy the bizness tonight!
Good to see you still knockin' niggas out!"

"Shit...that's what I do man!" He said
confidently.

"Yeah I know that's why I bet on yo ass
tonight. Right on for the knock out my nigga."
I said handing him a grand. "I know these bitch
ass promoters aint payin' you shit. That's jus' a
lil' somthin' I made about ten minutes ago,

thanks to you."

"Good lookin' out man. Yeah these white folks only paid a nigga three g's for this fight."

"Damn, that aint shit for risking ya life." I said shaking my head.

"Yeah tell me about it, that lil' ass money barely pays my house note. With Renae and the kids at the house...I need to fight everyday jus' to be comfortable...u know?" Sway said seriously.

I took a seat on the bench, "I feel you, that's kinda why I'm here." I informed. "I got this thing I'm workin' on and I need a man like you on the squad. I guarantee the pay will be more than this shit."

"I'm listening." Sway said tossing his gloves inside his gym bag. "You always up to somethin'. But, if it involves that nigga Biz, I aint with it." He warned.

I could appreciate the fact that Sway disliked Biz. Biz had a rep on the streets for being greedy and shady. I knew Sway from the boys home we grew up in, his mom was killed and he never knew his dad...so the state took him in. The military was the option he took as soon as he turned 18. He was a decorated marine and picked up boxing while he was Enlisted. Sway was a married man with two kids, his life was different from mine, but we shared a get money mentality. I never hustled with Sway before but we kept in touch and respected each other's individual lives and choices. He didn't look down at me for killing muthafuckas and I didn't hate on him for being a faithful husband and father. He told me one time, that he probably killed more people than I did but I got paid more for it.

"Naw, Biz is yesterday, I'm talkin' 'bout today." I reassured.

"Alrite." Sway said calmly. "How much we talkin' 'bout?"

"Shit...I'm talkin' 'bout Yusef and Ameenah's college education paid for. I'm talkin' 'bout you and Renae walkin' on the lot and buying his and her "*Mercedes Benz's.*" I'm talkin' 'bout finding somethin' else to argue with Renae about besides money, 'cuz that won't be an issue no more." I preached.

"Ha ha ha awwww!!" Sway chuckled. "You know her ass be on a nigga! But, yo, that shit sound good to me tho. So what's the plan Tyce?" He asked.

"What you doin' tomorrow?" I questioned.

"Shit...sleepin'."

"You think you can wake up and meet me at my warehouse around this time?" I joked.

"Yeah, I can do that." He agreed.

"Aight, I'll get into it tomorrow with u. You still got the same number?"

"Yep."

"Cool, I'ma hit you. Ay, you lucky I wasn't in the ring with you tonight...I woulda whooped yo ass like I did back in tha day!" I teased throwing punches in the air.

"Shit, what you waitin' on nigga a crowd and a bell? We can go right here!" He said standing up bobbing and weaving.

"Naw, I wanna get you when you fresh, you jus' had a fight and I don't want no excuses." I laughed.

"Yeah, that's what I thought." He laughed back.

"Aight, tomorrow my nigga, get some rest!" I said as I snuck a punch in his chest and jogged out the locker room.

Contemplation

The *"Cadillac"* slid through the city as Omar sat behind the wheel thinking. He'd been driving for over an hour with no particular destination in mind. He just needed to get away from Tasha's ass and be solo with his thoughts for a while. There were a few things that were fucking with him lately. Like why did Angelique need to see Tyce so fucking bad? Whatever it was, it couldn't be good, 'cuz she seemed like she was pressed about somethin'. He called Tyce to see what was up with her but Tyce just told him not to trip and that he had it handled. So just like always...Tyce had it under control. There was also no doubt in his mind that Tasha got into some crazy shit as soon as the door closed but he was used to that shit. He knew what type of bitch she was but her tight sex game is what had him hooked. As long as he didn't wake up with his dick leaking, he didn't give a fuck what she did. The shit that did bother him was how she tripped over Angelique so hard. Bitches will be bitches and always hate on each other but it was something else in the background of her reaction. Tasha's gaming ass had a problem with Angelique 'cuz she was getting close to his homeboy.

"Bitches aint shit," He proclaimed stopping at a
light.

He wasn't blind, he knew Tasha had an eye on
Tyce but so the fuck what, so did every other
bitch. What made him so easy about it was the fact
that he knew his man would never fuck with her
anyway. Tyce would never let pussy come
between the two of them, plus Tasha wasn't his
type of chick anyway. The spoiled, thick, pussy
throwing bitches was more *HIS* speed and Tasha
was sniffing up the wrong tree when it came to
Tyce. Since they was little niggas running the
streets he'd come to quietly admire the way Tyce
dealt with women. Truth be told if he were more
like his friend, his own life wouldn't be as
dramatic. The green light glowed as he continued
his personal therapy session. The *"Escalade"*
floated down the street like a cruise ship in a calm
sea. The dark tint mingled with the black body
making it impossible to peek in from outside. His
was one of the thousands of *"Escalades"* that
jammed the streets of L.A. The only thing that
separated his from the pack was the twenty
thousand dollar rims and the plates that read 'I
GET IT' those
words had gotten him a lot of attention. He
couldn't count the number of times bitches would

ask

"You get what?"

"Whatever **IT** is" was his usual reply.

That always led to a little more conversation and plenty of fucking. Omar knew the type of chick that responded to his plates was exactly the type of chick he was looking for. Shit, pussy was easy to get...just look like you getting money and pussy will be thrown at you like a pass from "*Mike Vick.*" Shit all these bitches was on the hunt for a meal ticket. Don't let em find out you really *is* getting paper, 'cuz that's when they really start trippin'! He could paint brush all women in that category as far as he was concerned...everyone except Angelique. She didn't need a nigga or his money but she wasn't stupid either. If a nigga was dumb enough to trick out then she was smart enough to treat herself. You couldn't be mad at her for that but in her case she was more than capable of taking care of herself and a nigga if she chose to do so. Shit Angelique was educated and fine. Rumor had it she was a silent partner in a few low-key sex clubs and she owned four semi trucks that she rented out to drivers who didn't have their own rigs. She definitely was a progressive bitch; Omar had to admit.

As he pulled into the "*In n Out*" drive thru and waited in line he stared out the dark window and continued thinking. He and Tyce had been hustling together since they were 16 and running with him had definitely paid off. But following the rules of his no dope policy left a lot of money in the streets for other niggas to get. Biz was all too happy to get all the work they passed up 'cuz he was basically getting free product to flip himself...that shit aint make no fucking sense to him! But Tyce wasn't trying to hear that shit, that nigga was so scared of being locked up it was ridiculous!

"Welcome to *"In n Out"* may I take your order please?" The speaker asked.

At the same time, the phone in his lap started vibrating. Omar lowered the window and picked up the cell looking at the bright screen.

"Hold on a minute baby." He told the speaker.

"No problem sir, order when you're ready."

Omar raised the window and hit the talk button.

"What up my nigga?"

"Aint nuthin' what you into?" Tyce asked.

"Shit, starvin'. I had to get out tha house for a minute, you know Tasha's ass?"

"Yeah I could imagine."

"So what's good with ya? Any word from Biz?" Omar questioned.

A loud horn blared from behind his truck and Omar squinted at the rear view mirror. A balding over weight white man was raising both hands in the air silently asking what was taking so long as he laid on the horn again.

"Hold up T." Omar said grabbing his door handle.

He got out the car and opened the back door of his truck. The man froze behind the wheel when he saw Omar get out. He almost pissed in his pants when he saw a horse like Doberman jump out the back seat unleashed! The fat man began to panic as he realized he was trapped in the drive thru line with no escape. Omar and Bonnie walked briskly up to the tiny "*Nissan Sentra*" that Mr. Fat was crammed into. With shaky hands, the frightened man fumbled with the handle trying to roll the window up but it was too late, Omar was already at the driver side door. Bonnie's massive head was level with the window and her eyes narrowed in on his face. The man's head instinctively backed away from the dog but he didn't dare make any sudden movements. Omar's face appeared next to his dog like they were taking a picture together.

"WHAT THE FUCK IS YOU HONKING FOR?!!" Omar shouted. Yo big ass don't even need to be her nigga! You need to hurry up and wait...now, honk that FUCKIN' horn one more muthafuckin' time and I'ma let my dog munch on yo greasy ass! You extra hungry ass

muthafucka! SPEAK BONNIE!" Omar
boomed tapping her on the side."
"RRROUUGGGHHH!!!
RRROUUGGGHHHHRRRR!!! Bonnie
threatened.
The man's eyes were as big as pool balls and his
face turned two shades whiter than it was before.
He'd raised his hand up to protect his face in case
the dog attacked him. Bonnie's breath shot at his
face and made his eyes water and blink rapidly.
His ribs were pressing against the armrest as he
leaned back almost in the passenger seat. His
obese body shook like a spin cycle as a dark circle
began to form and spread over his pudgy crotch.
Omar chuckled at his accident and pulled Bonnie
back by the collar. He stood up and walked
casually back to his truck letting Bonnie jump
back in her seat as he returned to his.
    "My fault Tyce." Omar apologized picking up
    the phone still laughing.
    "What tha fuck was that?" Tyce asked.
    "Naw, this fat bastard was honkin' and shit in
    tha drive thru. I had to get out and tell him to
    shut tha fuck up. Shit, Bonnie made that nigga
    piss on himself! That shit was funny as fuck
    tho!"
    "You crazy nigga!" Tyce added his laughter. "I
    bet he aint hungry now?"

"Hell naw!"

"Wasup tho?" Omar asked eyeing the man in the rearview mirror.

"Oh yeah, tomorrow night meet me at tha spot, we need to talk about that move." Tyce remembered.

"Aight, what time?"

"I need you there round nine."

"Bet." Omar confirmed.

"And naw, I aint heard shit from Biz but keep ya antennas up." Tyce advised.

"Always my nigga do tha same." Omar said lowering his window to place his order and hanging up.

Omar was ready to hear what is homeboy had in mind, whatever it was meant more money for him and he damn sure was ready for that shit!

The Meeting

Tyce was there an hour before everyone arrived. The warehouse was home to him; it was where he'd lived after he ran away from the group home. Later on he bought the abandoned building and used it as his head quarters, it wasn't much, but it was private and low key. The old home brought back memories, this is where he'd planned and plotted the moves that changed his whole life. This was the building where he ate countless cans of tuna fish and bowls of chicken flavored "*Ramen Noodles*" but he was far from that memory now. Tyce was dressed casually in a cream and red "*Michael Jordan*" jump suit as he walked around the open space. Three hundred dollar matching J's decorated his feet and his barber had just lined the edges of his hair making his points hit like a Chinese star. Angelique was the first to arrive walking in like she was on a runway.

"Hey Tyce." She said smiling.

"Wasup, thanks for coming." He responded giving her a warm embrace.

"No problem, you know you gotta girl curious. Is it jus' me and you tonight? She questioned.

"Naw, O and some other people will be here
shortly. He informed walking to the window.
"Oh ok." Angelique said now more curious.
Moments later, she heard the bass from Omar's
truck as he pulled up. Omar hopped out and made
his way to the familiar building. He spotted Tyce's
Jeep parked on the side of the warehouse but
wondered why his new Benz was there also. Omar
walked in and was surprised to see Angelique
leaning against a wall.

"What up my nigga." Tyce greeted his friend
with a pound.
"Aint nothin', wasup with you? Omar asked
shifting his eyes toward the female in the room.
"I'm good." Tyce reassured.
"Wasup ma? How you doin'?" Omar now
addressed Angelique.
"I'm straight O. It's good to see you again." She
answered thankfully.
Tyce stood in the background and observed the
exchange between the two of them. He knew
Omar was distrusting of Angelique but this was
his show and everyone had a role to play. The
sound of an engine and a car door closing
interrupted their little reunion as the third guest
arrived. Omar looked at Tyce showing his
confusion about the situation. Tyce nodded at his
partner with an "it's good" motion. Angelique just

relaxed and let the scene unfold as she popped a piece of *"Orbitz"* gum in her mouth. Tyce's phone rang and he told the caller he was inside and waiting, seconds later Sway came walking in. He wore blue jeans and a white v-neck shirt that showed his athletic physique. Sway had short curly hair and a clean-shaven face. Two platinum dog tags hung from his neck with the names of his children in the center. A serious yet calm look was in his deep brown eyes. On his left side a small band-aid was stuck to his cheekbone, besides that his face was smooth. Sway scanned the room, his gaze landed first on the beautiful woman chewing gum, then to the silent man watching his every move. He walked toward the only face he recognized in the huge room.

"Wasup Tyce?" He asked giving him a pound.

"I'm good, I appreciate you showin' up."

"Shit, I wouldn't miss it." He said cracking his knuckles.

Angelique and Omar were both wondering who the mystery dude that just entered the warehouse was.

"You seen him before?" Angelique quietly asked Omar.

"Naw you know Tyce really don't get down with nigga's like that so this should be real interesting." Omar responded in a low tone.

"A few more minutes and we can get started."

Tyce said interrupting their thoughts.

The agitation was beginning to spread over Omar's face. He tapped his hand on the side of his thigh as he stood against the wall. First Angelique shows up then this new nigga, what the fuck was going on. Omar was under the assumption that he and Tyce were getting into some new shit he wasn't expecting "*Kool And The Gang.*"

Tyce began to slide some chairs closer together, then moved to the window to look out front. Not seeing what he wanted to see, he turned around and smiled.

"Alright, I aint gonna keep ya'll waitin' no
more, I know everybody got shit to do tonight.
I've been thinkin' on this shit for 'bout a year
now." He paused and eyed Omar. "Me and O
been gettin' it in for a while now but it's time
for a new direction."

No sooner, had the words come out his mouth; there was a light tapping at the warehouse door.

Tyce turned his attention to the door and went to open it, leaving all in attendance confused. When he opened it, Dallas was on the other side.

"Girl you late." Tyce said."

"My bad." She smiled.

Dallas instantly made herself at home, as she sashayed toward the group of strangers. She grabbed the last empty seat and crossed her curvy legs slowly enjoying the attention she was receiving as the late comer. Angelique on the other hand was now chewing her gum extra hard, keeping her left eye on Tyce and her right eye on Dallas. She still was the picture of calm but inside she was impatiently waiting.

Tyce began, "Now that I have you all in the same place I have a proposition for you. I been thinkin'…all the work and shit we've done, why haven't we retired yet. I'll tell you why; 'cuz you can't get rich working for someone else. What I'm thinkin' 'bout will set us all up for retirement in a short matter of time." Tyce continued. "You see everyone in this room has talent. Sway you were in the military, so you're good with covert ops, weapons, and shit." Tyce shifted his eyes to each of the lovely ladies in the room. "Dallas and Angelique, you ladies have intelligence and a loyalty that most men lack. Omar and I, well, we the best jack boys this side of tha Mississippi." Tyce stated proudly.

Omar nodded in agreement while making strong eye contact with Sway. Unfazed Sway returned the brief stare then turned his head toward Tyce again. Angelique and Dallas smiled independently, flattered by the comments about them, but all were listening intently to the only man standing up in the room.

Tyce eyed each of them. "Now I aint gonna lie to you, this shit is dangerous, it could get you killed if you get stupid and reckless. If you take this shit serious and stay focused, it can also get you paid. Now this aint mandatory, so if anybody aint feelin' this so far jus' say so and you can leave before I lay my plans out." He said in a serious tone.

The four chairs remained occupied, Tyce smiled and happily continued. "Ok then, I'm talkin' 'bout three major hits and all of em are different. The first one is Diego Alverez. The second is an underground gambling spot and the third is a bank in China town. With all three combined we lookin' at twenty million dollars. I know ya'll can divide so twenty divided by five is what I'm talkin' 'bout." He joked. "Four million reasons to get down."

Tyce paused his financial sermon to get the crowd reaction; Angelique was the first to break the silence.

"That's wasup!" She excitedly approved.

"Diego Alverez! That nigga been running shit for decades on the west coast, I see why you want his ass. And if you talkin' 'bout tha Club House, that's a good move 'cuz everybody I know gambles up in there.

Tyce aimed that billion dollar smile at Angelique
as his attraction for her bubbled up. He looked at
Omar, Sway, and Dallas and waited for their
response.

"Shit T, you already know I'm wit' it." Omar
said crossing his arms across his chest.

"Hell yeah I know that shit O, I wasn't really
talkin' to you." Tyce assured his long time
friend.

Omar looked directly at Sway, feelin' good about
himself and his position. Sway cracked his
knuckles again and leaned back in his chair.

"I been knowin' you since you was shootin'
dice in the hallways at the boys home Tyce.
I'm honored that you even came to me with
this, 'cuz I know you coulda' found another
nigga if you wanted to. I done killed folks
overseas for the government-came home and
me and my wife arguing and stressing over the
light bill. You better muthafukin believe I'm all
in with this shit!" Sway said still leaning back
in his chair with his arms crossed.

"Alright then people guess it aint nuthin' left to
do but break down exactly how it's gonna go.
Now first......"

"Hold up T. We aint heard from Ms. Late yet."
Omar interjected.

Dallas shifted in her chair and grinned at Omar. She took a lighter out of her coach purse and looked at Tyce.

"Can I have one of those clove cigarettes you smoke Tyce?" She asked confidently.

Tyce smiled enjoying her swagger as he reached in his sweats to get his pack of "*Djarums*." He handed her one and stepped back a little taking one for himself. Dallas put the fire to the tip and inhaled the flavored smoke; she licked her lips tasting the clove spice and sighed.

"I already heard what Tyce had to say, that's why I'm here. So *actually*…I'm early and you're late." She finally answered never looking at Omar.

Omar shot Tyce a disapproving look as her words registered in his mind. "How the fuck did this bitch know what was up before I did." He thought to himself. Angelique was a little shocked at what came out of Dallas's mouth but she knew Tyce had a good reason for his actions. She trusted him with all her heart; he was a natural born leader and she'd follow him anywhere. Angelique put a lid on all the feelings stirring around inside her pot but it was beginning to simmer over. Right now, she had to focus and play her part on the team.

"Ok now that we all on the same page…let's talk about the work." Tyce stated flicking ashes on the floor. "All three moves gotta be made in the same week. The good thing about tha shit is two of these muthafukas don't even fuck with the holice but you already know the bank is a different story. Diego is a no joke, aint nobody bold enough to fuck wit' him, but that's what makes him vulnerable. He's too cozy, but don't sleep, he's a beast. The Club House is a ten man operation but only two niggas handle the money. The bank is the hardest one...it'll take all of us at the same time to get that shit off." Tyce lectured taking a drag from his cigarette. The oversized room was quiet as the crew listened intently to the plans. Each member contributed in his or her own way as the meeting went on into the early morning hours. They covered the details of the details and got familiar with each other. Angelique warmed up to Dallas, seeing bits of herself in her personality. Although she was young, Dallas could hold her own, she was no dumb ass bitch. Angelique also recognized why Tyce had chosen Sway. He possessed a quiet manly demeanor and he was a team player. She guessed that was from his time in the marines. Sway shared with her a little about his family and himself showing her pictures of his kids. He was vested in his family but still would take a risk to provide for them. Sway confided in her that if it wasn't Tyce running this shit he would have stayed at home. Angelique knew her roles front to back and what Tyce expected out of her. He kept an eye on her the whole night and seemed to angle his words in her direction from time to time. Angelique appointed herself the official look out of the crew and she was looking out for one person in particular.

Lil' Flash

Flash turned the bag of "*Doritos*" upside down letting the last few chips slide into his mouth. It was eleven thirty on a Friday night, and the block was jumping with fiens trying to get right for the weekend. He was drained...the heads had him running all day with no breaks, his clientele was steady 'cuz they knew his shit was legit. Just as he tossed the empty chip bag in the alley a blue Neon rolled up with the back passenger window rolled down half way. The car slowed as it went by but kept moving and turned right at the corner. That was the signal all his customers used to get his attention. Flash quickly prepared to make the exchange before the car came around again the second time. He snatched the shit from his stash spot and jogged to the sidewalk scanning the streets for anything that looked suspect. The "*Neon*" slid down the street again and stopped at the curb where he was waiting. Two barely legal white girls were inside with "*Mile Cyrus's*" voice blaring out the factory speakers.

"Yo, turn that shit down!" Flash ordered.

"Oopps, sorry Flash." The young girl

apologized.

He leaned a little closer to the door and pointed with his right hand faking as if he was giving directions. Flash had already tossed the baggie in the girls lap and opened his left palm to get his money. The whole transaction took less than five seconds and the teenyboppers sped off keyed up to have an out of body experience. The 40 dollars he snatched was quickly calculated in his head and it brought the days total to 1,265 dollars. The Paris and Nicole look a likes bought the last of his product, so Flash decided to bounce from the block. When he got to his crib, he took a shower. As he stood under the hot stream, he tried to filter his internal war. He didn't like selling crack. Ever since Tyce had him go by the Mosque that day he'd been back on his own several times. The more he attended the Mosque the more he realized what he was doing was wrong. He wanted out the dope game but hadn't found an income replacement yet. He prayed daily that it would come soon though. He didn't like assisting people with slow suicide but on the other hand, he still needed to eat and with his criminal record getting a job was nearly impossible. He decided all he can do was keep pushing towards his faith and hope that it would all balance out eventually. Allah knew his heart.

Lil' Flash heard his phone ringing so he turned the water off grabbed a towel and answered it. Some of his boys were going to Jim's Grill to shoot pool. He told his man to give him 'bout twenty minutes and he would fall thru. He hung up the phone and got dressed. A half hour later Lil' Flash walked up to his people in the bar. After dapping them all down he asked the waitress for a *"Disaronno"* and *"7-UP."* His homeboy Tony gave Flash the let me holla at you head nod so he walked around the table and sat next to him.

"Hey I need to holla at you"

"Wasup?" Flash asked as the waitress brought his drink over.

"Ya boy Tyce he cool?" Tony questioned with concern.

"Yeah he good why?" Flash asked defensively.

"Word on the street is he the HMW."

"Tony, what the fuck does HMW mean, who the fuck says some shit like that?"

"It means he the hood's most wanted…there's a price on his head."

"Where you hear that shit at?" Flash frowned.

"Where *haven't* I heard it, everybody askin' about him, especially since aint nobody seen the nigga. Nigga where you been, you aint heard that shit? I jus' thought you might wanna let him know if he don't already."

"Damn. Good lookin' out my nigga." Flash
said digesting the news. "Who has a hit out on
him?"

"That nigga Biz is what I heard." He stated
downing his shot.

Flash thanked Tony by buying another round for
them both as they talked about the same ole shit.
Flash was half listening…his mind was on the bull
shit that just came out of Tony's mouth. Twenty
minutes later Flash couldn't wait any longer, he
dismissed himself from the conversation with a
customary pound, and walked out the bar. Within
seconds his cell phone was out and dialing Tyce's
number.

No Sweat

I racked the weights and sat up on the bench. Flash had interrupted my work out but for what he said I was grateful. So just like I thought; Biz hired some niggas to take me out. That was just like his bitch ass to get somebody else to do what he was to pussy to do himself. There's no doubt in my mind that Angelique was also on the menu. I needed to find out who was looking for us, I hated not knowing my enemies. They had to be some niggas from out of town 'cuz Biz knew I was familiar with the people in the city and who would fuck with me in my own backyard anyway? I knew he was up to something especially after Angelique left his ass. But now the shit was real, this elderly ass nigga was actually trying to murder me! Biz and the fake ass assassins was just one more thing to add to my "to do" list. These days I was a busy man but I could make time to exterminate some roaches. Yeah he hired some niggas to kill me…it's a damn shame he wasted his money.

Feels Like Home

Angelique was starting to like being at Tyce's house. Her mind had picket signs of protest marching across her forehead but a window in her heart opened up, letting a cool breeze blow in. The past few days Tyce had been laying low. He instructed the crew to do the same and just focus on what was about to happen. Angelique and Dallas exchanged phone numbers and had talked a few times. Dallas was a lot like herself and she was highly intelligent. When you talked to her, you'd never guess she was an escort, more like a sexy lawyer or a fashion mogul. One thing for sure was that she was nobody's fool and was definitely not a punk bitch. Angelique could see why Dallas had been drafted. While preparing chicken Alfredo for her and Tyce to eat she went over the plans in her head and couldn't find one flaw. Angelique could tell Tyce had done his homework and then some extra credit shit on top of that. The shit was solid and well planned and she was more than ready to go. As she placed the garlic bread in the oven her mind rewinded back to Biz and the problem she'd drove away from. Her life was so busy with Tyce these days she hadn't even thought about Biz's abusive ass in days but she knew better than to get to relaxed; that's when your relaxation turns into a deep sleep that you never wake up from. Moving around the kitchen in a familiar way, she began to prepare the plates making sure to fix Tyce's plate first. She hit the intercom button to call him up from the gym. She knew he'd be hungry after his work out so she piled the plate high with creamy noodles and extra pieces of chunky chicken breasts. She wanted to show her appreciation for all he'd done for her and this was one way she chose to do it.

Angelique put her lips close to the intercom speaker and pressed the button, "I don't wanna have to come down there and pull a bar off ya neck!"

"Girl please!" Tyce said into the other speaker laughing out of breath.

"Are you done?" She asked amused.

"Yeah, I'll be up in a minute."

Angelique busied herself with the last preparations for their dinner. She poured ice-cold guava juice into some glasses and put the hot bread in a basket covered with a cloth towel. She snatched two pieces of paper towel folded them in half and placed the silver ware on top next to the steaming plates. Just as she finished setting the table up, she heard Tyce coming down the hallway.

"What the fuck!" She thought to herself, "Why am I so nervous it's jus' fuckin' dinner!"

Tyce took a detour to the guest bathroom to wash up, that two minutes was just enough time for her to pull herself together.

"Damn girl, somethin' smells good in here."

He said walking in the kitchen.

"Yeah jus' call me *"Marie Calendar"* tonight but my food taste way better. I hope you're hungry."

"Hell yeah, I'm starvin'. What you fix?"

"Chicken alfredo, salad, and garlic bread." She stated proudly.

Raising his thick eyebrows with surprise, "Girl I didn't know you could cook."

"There's a lot you don't know about me. I'm a woman of many talents Mr. Adkins."

Tyce wasted no time and sat at the chair in front of the biggest plate. He looked down at the food and realized that no woman had ever fixed him dinner in his own home before. His eyes took in the view of the sexiest chef he'd ever seen. This culinary cutie had her hair in a ponytail, a *"Betty Boop"* tank top on and black track shorts that were too tired to run down the rest of her thighs. Her skin almost perfectly matched the maple wood cabinets mounted behind her. Angelique grabbed some pepper out the cabinet and joined him at the table. She snatched her fork and started to dig in when Tyce stopped her.

"Why don't we say prayer first?"
Pleasantly surprised, Angelique released her fork and bowed her head.

Tyce cleared his throat, "Thanks for what you gave us to get here and what you give us to get a lil' further…Amen."
"I thank YOU for the food Angelique 'cuz God aint the one who turned my stove on." He joked.

Tyce began to eat silently, concentrating on each bite. He made sure to get the chicken, sauce, and noodles on the fork together. She watched him as he ate.

He looked up from his plate and smiled, "You know you don't have to bite your lip if you're hungry."

Angelique didn't notice that she had been nibbling on her bottom lip while staring at Tyce. He had a sexy frown on his forehead; the kind of expression a man gets when he's seriously eating. He stuck his tongue out to lick the sauce that had crept into the corners of his lips. His right bicep flexed a little as he took each bite making the tattoos on his arm do a two-step.

"I was jus' makin' sure you liked the food. It's

been a while since I was in the kitchen. How is
it?"

"This food is the bomb girl; I think you got
some Italian in you." He said grabbing another
bread stick.

After dinner, they sat on the sofa, sipping
"Corona's" and watching TV. Tyce was looking
at the screen but his mind was elsewhere. He
turned the volume down and faced Angelique. His
eyes locked in on hers as he spoke,

"I heard from my man that Biz got a hit out on
me. I'm willing to bet that you're on that list
too. They been all around the city asking
questions and shit. I know you probably
expected it like I did, so now it's official. But
don't sweat it; I got you and I'ma handle Biz
and his *"Labor Ready"* niggas."

That was the end of that conversation; Tyce turned
the volume back up and switched channels to a
football game. Angelique sunk back in the soft
leather couch, took a swig of her beer, and simply
said, "Ok."

Dissatisfaction

The *"Bentley"* looked like a black panther crouching in the shadows of the night. Biz and Bruce reclined in the supple seats waiting silently for their guests. A tan sedan pulled up next to them moments later. TJ and Lincoln got out the car, moving in slow motion toward the already parked *"Bentley."* Their molasses movements were a deliberate attempt to make them even later to the scheduled meeting. Biz took notice of their slow pace and became increasingly agitated. On cue, Bruce hit the unlock button as the two men approached nonchalantly. Once inside the whisper of the engine running and easy breathing was all that was heard, Biz was the first to speak, making his anger take a back seat; he spoke calmly,

"You know…I'm very disappointed. I'm used to high quality shit. I don't pay for something that isn't worth the money." He stared straight ahead and continued, "I expect to get what I pay for; and when I don't, it really pisses me off. Now for instance the sales men told me that *"Rolex"* made the absolute best timepiece available. He told me my hard-earned money

couldn't buy a better watch. Now I believe he
lied to me…'cuz this watch says it's eleven
thirty eight. And you niggas were supposed to
be here at 11. So I'ma blame it on this 30,000-
dollar piece of shit watch…and not you two.
So I'ma take this watch back to the sales man
tomorrow and shove it up his ass so he can take
a shit 38 minutes early from now on." Biz eyed
the two men in the dark.

Bruce grinned to himself, amused at his boss's
way with words. Lincoln shifted in the back seat
and faced Biz. Before he could speak Biz cut him
off,

"Why is that bitch not in my storage room tied
up naked and bleeding; and why is Tyce still
above ground?"

"Look man, if it was that easy to snuff the
nigga out you woulda did it ya self. If you
don't think we workin' then send us home boss
man. Personally, I don't mind a hundred
thousand dollar paid vacation to lovely
California. How 'bout you TJ, you mind?"

"Hell naw, it's a helluva a lot warmer than
Detroit." He smiled.

Lincoln reasoned, "Jus' be patient old timer,
we'll punch his clock soon enough and
"FedEx" your ex bitch to your front door."

Biz reached inside his jacket pocket and pulled out

a cigar. He rolled it around in his manicured hand, "I'ma have three of these next time I see you, we gon celebrate a job well done. Now let me get back to work, so ya'll can get back to work."

"You shouldn't worry so much Biz; it's bad for your heart." Lincoln joked. "Relax a bit...they aint easy to find but they aint hard to find either, we gettin' close."

The brief meeting was over and the hired guns exited the car. TJ started to walk away but turned around and motioned for Bruce to roll down the window. Bruce hit the button again and TJ poked his round head through the window causing his thick platinum chain to clink against the outside glass,

He smiled letting his gold tooth shine, "By the way...nice watch."

Bruce rolled the window up trying to catch TJ's neck but he was too fast. He ducked out just in time and jogged back to the *"Camry."*

"Jus' gimme' the green light boss and I'll choke the jokes out them muthafukas!"

"Jus' be cool. Save your energy killer, 'cuz you might have to choke out three niggas."

Both cars sped of simultaneously into the night. Once the *"Bentley"* was back on the freeway, Biz took his cell phone out and dialed a number.

"Hey babe, how you doin'?"

"Hey Biz…I'm good sweetie, and you?" The voice sang back.

"Oh you know me, jus' handling my business for a living. Speaking of business, do you have anything for me?"

"You jus' cut to the chase huh; a girl can't get no love?" She teased.

"You know I love you but there'll be plenty of time for that, I jus' don't like loose ends baby you know that." He reassured.

"Yeah yeah promises promises." She joked.

"I've been workin' on it for you baby. You should of hired me instead of those tourist niggas you got, I won't hold that against you but it's gonna cost you. I'm thinkin' a candy red convertible with a glove compartment full of green white men." She said with enthusiasm.

"Come by tonight and I'll tell you all about it."

Biz, permit a smile to stretch across his smooth lips as he instructed his driver toward their next destination.

"I'm on yo ass Tyce." He whispered to himself as he stared out the window admiring the twinkling city lights.

Instigation

The vodka bottle sat empty on the coffee table. Tasha was patiently waiting for Omar to return from where ever he was. She'd been missing in action for about a week and now it was time to check up on things. She stretched out on the lengthy couch and accepted the buzz the alcohol was offering. A half hour into her high the front door opened as Omar walked in. He took off his leather jacket and draped it on the back of the dining room chair. He had a lot on his mind and wasn't in the mood for Tasha's tantrums tonight. He grabbed a beer and prepared for the drama.

"Long time no see." He started, "You done fuckin' with them play ground niggas, now you wanna come back and holla like shit is all sweet. Why don't you U turn yo ass back around and tell that nigga you on your way."

"Don't start O. I wasn't with no nigga, I was at my girl's house! I only left 'cuz you left. You know not to bring no disrespectful ass bitches up in here!" She yelled sitting up.

Omar took another long sip of his beer and sat directly across from her. His diamond studs glittered as he shook his head from side to side. He wiped the beer from his thin mustache and licked his dark lips.

"First of all, stop yelling in my shit. And second, stop lying in my shit. I don't give a fuck who you was wit', jus' be real about the shit. If you gonna be here then be here! Aint no back and forth shit jus' 'cuz you irritated over a bitch!"

Tasha stood up like a mannequin in a display window letting Omar get a first-class view. She purposely wore his favorite outfit, a tight see through dress with a matching thong minus the bra. She let her titties do as they pleased as she moved closer to him. She expertly used her body to diffuse the bomb in the room. Tasha knew Omar was weak when it came to pussy, all she had to do was show him the present, and he was happier than a boy on Christmas morning.

"Look baby, I don't wanna fight…I miss you. I jus' got upset when that Angelique bitch showed up. You know I can get a little possessive when it comes to my man. I'm sorry O." She said putting her foot in his crotch.

She made little circles with her toes and teased his dick. Omar relaxed a bit enjoying the feeling, Tasha knew how to handle him, but he would never admit it. He put his smooth head against the

cushion and finished the last of his beer. Tasha had
him right where she wanted him.

"You seem stressed O, what's wrong? I wanna
be here with you, I wasn't fuckin' with
nobody…you don't have to worry about that.
Baby the last thing I want to do is bring you
drama."

Omar caressed the back of her calf and looked
up at her, "It aint that Tasha, I jus' got some
shit on my mind."

"Some shit like what?" She asked repositioning
herself on his lap.

"Jus' some shit wit' Tyce. We workin' on
some new shit…well I thought *we* was workin'
on some new shit but he got some other
muthafuckas involved."

"He trying to cut you out!" She blurted.

"Naw, he aint like that, I jus' aint know it was
other niggas invited. He aint tell me shit. Tyce
jus' do what the fuck he wanna do and I'm jus'
sposed to ride with it; he don't give a fuck what
I think. I've been missing money for years
fuckin' with his no dope policy, a nigga
coulda' been extra rich by now." He frowned.

Tasha listened intently as he vented. She didn't
gamble but she knew better than to throw away a
lottery ticket. Omar tried to keep his business from
her but the voice recorder she'd hid in the pool

house kept her in the know. Plus she wasn't blind, shit she lived with the nigga she could tell he was tired of Tyce being *"Batman"* and him being *"Robin."*

"Damn, that's fucked up baby he didn't even ask if you was cool with the shit. I thought ya'll was supposed to be tight like brothers. You been having his back for years and he jus' gon add some new people to the mix! Fuck Tyce, he treatin' you like a stepchild baby. I didn't want to say nothin' 'cuz it aint my place…but he been holding you back for a while now."

She placed her mouth in front of his. Omar's full nostrils caught the scent of minty vodka as she slowly chewed her gum.

"You're smart and dangerous, now that's a helluva combination. I recognized that when I first met you. If Tyce don't see that…then that's his fuckin' problem." She sighed.

Omar kept his head steady as she lectured. She gently stroked his ego like a dick, causing them both to swell at the same time, "Baby if you wanna make some moves you can't wait for someone to let you by." Omar listened as Dr. Tasha spoke; he loved the psychology that spilled from her scarlet red lips.

"Hmmm, you right baby. I gotta do me…but I

need to be smart about it 'cuz Tyce aint retarded. I jus' gotta wait for the right time."
"Exactly O. You'll know when the time is right, when your opportunity comes…take it." Tasha coached. "Jus' promise me you won't forget about me when you all rich and shit." She seriously joked.
Omar traced his finger over her nipple, "As much as you trip on a nigga, if I was gonna leave yo ass I woulda done it already." He smiled.

The foreplay was over. Tasha loosened his belt and unzipped his jeans reaching inside for her friend. Omar put his hands in the air like he was being arrested. With her dress hiked up, she slid her thong to the side taking full custody of her prisoner. He surrendered as she handcuffed his dick with her tight pussy.

Mission accomplished, fuck Tyce…but not right now.

Did You See That?

Angelique opened the door for the gentleman from the rental car company. For a moment, he just stood there gazing at her. She was wearing a sexy orange two-piece Brazilian cut bathing suit. The young man wasn't expecting a model to open the door seeing as how the reservation was for a man. He regained his focus and gave his vocal cords a jump start.

"Ummm yes, is Mr. Adkins available please?"

"Sure come on in, I'll get him." Angelique replied flattered.

Angelique turned and walked away she could feel his young brown eyes staring at her assets as she climbed the stairs. The boy was struggling to remain professional so he switched his outlook and inspected the shiny floors instead. Angelique walked through the open door to Tyce's room.

"Hey, they rental car people are here." She reported.

"Cool, they right on time."

Tyce's eyes did exactly what the guest down stairs did as Angelique came in. He could also appreciate the site of a beautiful woman dressed to get wet. The messenger pretended not to notice and just continued switching her ass as she left the room. Tyce grabbed his bag and was happy to follow her out.

"Wasup man, how you doin'?" Tyce asked coming down the steps.

"I'm fine Mr. Adkins, thanks for asking. We have the car you reserved outside I just need your signature on a few pages here."

Tyce noticed that the young man appeared a little nervous. He was not making eye contact for very long and kept looking at the floor like he dropped something.

"You ok?" Tyce asked with concern.

Surprised by the question he answered, "Yes sir, I'm fine."

Tyce took the clipboard from the boy and signed on the highlighted areas. The boy was handsome and looked like he just turned 18 an hour ago. His eyes just kept moving to Tyce's face, then back to the floor.

"Thank you Mr. Adkins, if you don't mind we can step outside to look the vehicle over before I leave."

Tyce gave the dude a confused look then he put two and two together. He could hear Angelique behind him moving about the house. The young man was trying not to look at her for fear of being disrespectful. Tyce smiled at him and admired his mannerism.

He placed a hand on his shoulder, "It jus' means you have good taste man...relax. Shit I was lookin' jus' like you a minute ago, shit I couldn't help it." He confessed. "Now let's go outside and both look at this car."

Tyce returned from outside ten minutes later and made his way to the pool. The California sun was beaming and the pool looked especially inviting but not as inviting as Angelique. The pool and the weather paled in comparison to Angelique's honey brown body gliding through the water. She swam to the edge and lifted herself out. Her birthday suit had a million beads of water on it like a windshield on a rainy day. The bikini was dismissed and laying on a patio chair. He'd never seen her naked before. One thing was certain...Angelique wasn't shy and she had every reason *not* to be. She walked over to Tyce letting the breeze dry her body.

"Well well well happy birthday." Tyce said hugging her damp body.

"You're crazy, and today's not my birthday." She giggled.

"It should be." He replied.

Neither Angelique nor Tyce moved an inch; they just stood there and looked at each other. Tyce placed his hands on her hips and tightened his grip bringing her body closer to his. He couldn't resist anymore, he gently grabbed her bottom lip with his teeth. He sucked it soft and then harder as his passion grew. Their mouths opened up and their tongues fought like *"Ali"* and *"Frazier"*. Her tiny hand cupped the back of his neck as she tilted her head to the side. Warm air from his nostrils brushed her cheek as Tyce exhaled deeply. Their kiss intensified as Angelique worked her moist tongue like a ceiling fan on high. Their lips instantly became best friends who hated to be apart, seconds grew into minutes as the two continued to passionately assault each other. Their lips finally parted and they just stood there staring at each other, at the same time they both smiled like they were taking a school picture and started to laugh.

"Uuummm yeah I'll jus' ahhh...see you later." Tyce stammered.

"Yeah, I'll be here...soooo yeah...ok." Angelique uttered still holding the back of his neck.

Tyce walked toward the house and looked back like he was leaving his new car in the parking lot. Angelique looked at him like a picture in an art gallery...taking in every square inch.

Thinkin' Of A Master Plan

Things were about to change for me. They were changing because I wanted them to. I was about to jump into some heavy shit, not that I wasn't in deep shit before but this was a little different. I robbed and merked niggas that wouldn't call the holice for nothing. Now with taking a bank the law was definitely involved. Sitting in the barber's chair my mind was working overtime. On top of that, it wasn't just me and O this time, I had a whole crew depending on me. My plan was tight as frog's pussy, and that shit was waterproof, I was just praying my crew could handle it. As Malik expertly lined up my edges my thoughts took a right turn in Angelique's direction. I smiled to myself as Malik nudged my head down so he could get the back of my neck. I replayed the pool episode in my mind like an old favorite movie. Now I'd seen more naked women than a gynecologist and turned down pussy like a white banker looking at a black person's loan application. But for some reason I had virgin pupils when I looked at Angelique's wet body. Trying to play it cool was not an option at that moment; I just let it do what it do. I was beginning to get real comfortable around her. The shit that tripped me out was the fact that she'd been there for a while now and I wasn't the least bit tired of her. In fact it was the opposite...I actually looked forward to seeing her every day. We didn't have to be in the same room and shit, 'cuz a nigga still needs space but just knowing she was in the house gave me comfort. I never felt that shit before and to be honest it kinda fucked me up...but in a good way.

Malik tapped me on the shoulder and unsnapped the collar from my neck. I stood up and gave him a pound thanking him for his services. I didn't need the mirror 'cuz Malik always did me right. The shop was quiet that day, just a few niggas I aint never seen before. But one grimy dude in the corner was looking like he had something to say,

"Yo Malik, you charged me 15 dollars last week for my edge up! And I know this nigga aint have an appointment 'cuz you told me you wasn't even gonna be here today. Why this nigga jus' give you a pound and you all courteous and shit!" He challenged.

I started to say somethin' but Malik cut in front in my words,

"When **you** start paying me three hundred

every month whether you're in my chair once or five times, you won't hafta ask those dumb ass questions!" My barber yelled back.
I adjusted my shirt and put on my sunglasses, I chuckled at Malik and walked toward the door but I just couldn't resist,
"I woulda charged yo ass a thousand dollars to cut that nappy ass lawn. You need to fertilize that shit." I advised playfully.
The whole shop erupted in laughter as I stepped through the door. Niggas are funny I thought to myself. I hopped in my rental car and sped off from the curb, rental cars helped me blend in when I went into the city, especially when I knew niggas were looking for me. I was heading toward the heart of the city to see if I could spot Lil' Flash doing his thing. I wanted to thank him personally for looking out for me. I rounded the corner of Slauson and Cimarron and saw Flash walking across the street; I beeped the horn to get his attention. Flash slowed up and turned around squinting to see who I was. His eyes relaxed when he realized it was me in the *"Dodge Charger,"* I pulled up close to him and motioned for him to get in.
"What up Tyce, good to see you still here!" He said as he slid inside."You been alright?"
"Always my nigga. That shit aint nuthin' I can't

handle but thanks for pullin' my coat tail to it."
I said.
Flash sat back in the seat and raised up his shirt
revealing the handle on his gun, "Jus' holla if
you need us."
I smiled at his bravery but knew he was
serious, "I appreciate that, but this shit is
personal. You played your part and I'm
thankful. Anyway wasup with you these days?"
I asked changing the topic.
"Shit, I'm good, jus' runnin', you know how it
is.
"Yeah I know, you look a lil' stressed youngsta
you sure you ok?" I quizzed.
He sighed and adjusted his hat, "I jus' been
thinkin' and shit lately. Man it's getting harder
and harder to hit these blocks, I'm startin' to
look at shit differently; I see these niggas out
here workin' hard as fuck for nuthin'...and I'm
one of em. It aint no 401k in this line of work
and I'm startin' to see the effects of this shit on
people. I noticed it before but the shit never
bothered me." Flash confessed.

I turned down the volume on *"Steve Harvey's"*
radio show and listened as Flash aired out his
feelings. I'd never seen him like this but I could
definitely relate. I just noticed early in life that the
dope game on the street level was a dead end for

most niggas. Yeah, people bump the music of ex-
hustlers but those niggas were the exception...not
the rule.

"I blame yo ass for this new found conscience I
have. He joked.

"Me?" I asked pointing at my chest.

"Yeah you-ever since you had me drop that
package off at the Mosque I been poppin' in
ever since. I even joined the study group!"

"That's beautiful man...I know a lot of Muslims
and they good people. I thought about checkin'
more into it myself but a nigga like me gotta
sin to win...at least for now. I still got some shit
to do that God aint gonna like; I gotta fight fire
with fire and be hotter than hell in the summer
on these niggas. But keep ya head in that
Mosque and watch ya ass on these streets." I
warned. "If you need my help...jus' let me
know."

"No doubt Tyce. I been talkin' with Brother
Cory down there and he got me thinkin' 'bout
makin' a move. I been takin' some classes to
get my GED and he said he got a spot for me at
his insurance company when I finish. He said
he'd train me to be a financial planner and help
get me certified and shit when I turn 18. Corey
said it's basically the same shit I do out here
but legal." Flash laughed.

I nodded in agreement. I was proud of the way he was thinking. I sent him there on purpose 'cuz I saw a lot of me in him. Flash just needed a little direction, his mom died of breast cancer when he was ten and he wouldn't recognize his daddy if he walked right by him 'cuz he never even seen the dude. I could definitely relate to that shit!

"Yo, that's wasup. When you become an advisor...I'll be your first client." I smiled.

"I'm thinkin' on it, but it's easier said than done, a nigga still gotta eat you know?"

"I feel you but your head is in the right place...jus' pray on it, 'cuz I know you been doing that shit to, them Muslims pray five times a day in shit!" I teased.

Flash laughed at my accurate statement and shook his head. I reached in my pocket and handed him a piece of paper, "If you can't get a hold of me call this number, and ask for Angelique. This number is for you only." I said focused.

"Bet." He said pushing the paper in his front pocket. "Yo Tyce, there is one thing I wanted to ask you. I got a little female hangin on these days and I wanna shoot down to Vegas for the weekend. I wanted to know if I could twist one of your rides, she like that flossy shit." He grinned.

"Yeah that's cool, jus' don't wreck my shit or

leave some coochie crust on my seats." I joked.
"Naw man, I'ma take care of your whip, good
lookin' out tho. Let me get on down the street,
I got some impatient ass people waitin' on me.
I'ma call you when I'm ready to leave...I'm gon
my nigga."
Flash gave me a pound and hopped out the car. I
watched him adjust his Raiders hat again and pull
his black jeans up just below his hips. Now I didn't
pray five times a day but I was gonna get at least
one in for Flash...me and God would settle up
later.

Dallas

Dallas walked to the kitchen and opened the refrigerator. She was on the hunt for her turkey and avocado sandwich. White tube socks were pulled up past her calves and she had on red boxer shorts. She wore a black tank top with the words "Open Late" written in neon green. This was the complete opposite of her work attire but since she had a new job, she could afford to relax a little. The condo she stayed in was borderline luxury. She filled it with all the things she loved...if she didn't absolutely adore it...she didn't buy it. So every room was her favorite for a different reason. She made her home her sanctuary, a place where she could escape from the demands of her career. Dallas was completely at ease with her job title. Being a call girl was different than walking the corners. For one thing the pay was different...she wasn't giving up ass for 50 dollars, her time and pussy demanded four figures per hour. She didn't care if some women considered her a hoe...fuck them simple bitches. She would counter, how many men have you fucked for free? If you woulda charged their ass, you'd be at the car dealership with my hoe ass buying a new *"BMW"* too.

Excitement had moved into her life ever since she'd met Tyce, he was the kind of man that could make her a monogamous woman. Knowing men was her specialty and she knew Tyce was not like the rest of the tricks she met. Sure, he paid for sex but the difference was he didn't *have* to or *need* to. He preferred to have no attachments and zero drama from women. She could respect that, she couldn't stand women either. Dallas liked her new boss but she had a feeling she wasn't the only one catching feelings.

"Beep Beep Beep." The phone came to life on the counter top.

"Speak to me." Dallas answered.

"Hey lil' mama."

"Wasup Simone, what you doin' girl?"

"I'm jus' getting ready for my date."

"Oh…so you're working tonight?" Dallas questioned.

"No my dear, this is a personal date! All work and no play isn't good for a girl."

"You got that right." Dallas agreed. "So who is it this time some basketball player?"

"No, he's a player alright jus' not on the court." She joked.

Dallas took a big bite of her sandwich and sat
at her table, "Tell him I said to watch out 'cuz
he don't know what he's in for."
"I'll be sure to let him know. Speaking of
watching out...I haven't seen you around the
office lately. The boss lady told me you've
been MIA since you seen Tyce that night. I
gotta tell you girl I was a little salty with her
for not sending me. I love fuckin' his sexy
ass!"
Dallas sipped her tropical punch soda and took
another bite of her sandwich enjoying the
conversation. Maybe Simone had a thing for Tyce
outside of the bedroom as well.
"Well don't get to salty girl 'cuz I never fucked
him, we jus' talked a little. Not that I didn't
want to...it jus' didn't happen." Dallas
corrected.
"For real and he still paid you?" Simone asked
intrigued.
"Yep." Dallas answered licking crumbs off her
lips.
Impressed Simone commented, "Tyce does
know how to break a chic off, that's why I like
him. I seen him a lil' while ago and he had
some cover girl lookin' broad with him. She
was lookin' a lil' to hard at me, I started to say
somethin' to her ass!"

Dallas stopped chewing and turned her ears up.

The cover girl broad Simone was talking about had to be Angelique. Ever since the meeting at the warehouse, she and Angelique had gotten kind of close. She suspected her new friend had a thing for Tyce but that didn't bother her. After all, she was the one about to wear his dick out in a hotel bedroom not too long ago.

"Why did he come to see you?" Dallas asked.

"He asked me for a lil' favor." Simone chanted lazily. "I thought we could fuck like rabbits for the twentieth time but he was all business and I wasn't planning on a threesome."

Dallas listened as her co-worker fed her information. She couldn't help but wonder why Tyce needed Simone for something besides her pussy.

"Anyway lil' mama, I jus' called to check up on you since you all low key now. I gotta finish tweezing my eyebrows...I'll talk to you later."

"Ok Simone, have a great date! Talk to ya soon."

Dallas hung up and stared at her half-eaten sandwich thinking about the interesting conversation she just had.

Sway

Sway was busy doing what any man would do when he's about to get a large sum of money-decide what to do with it. Sitting on his back patio watching his kids play tag in the small back yard he fantasized about a better life for them. Currently there was no college fund set up for them. Their only hope for higher education was good grades or good athletic skills. Maybe they could secure some scholarships or something but that put the elite schools out of reach for them. The mortgage was being paid but many times that meant half ass paying other bills. He felt as if he was running faster and faster on a treadmill that he couldn't jump off of. So as his daughter caught up to his son and tapped his back, he imagined both of them graduating college, his wife instructing their private chef on what to cook for dinner, and himself sleeping peacefully without dreaming of bills. The vision made him smile, and all he had to do to make it real was follow a man he respected. He'd followed men he couldn't stand into combat, risking his own life. Killed men without knowing their names and didn't stay to watch the body fall. Now all he had to show for his services was a few medals, bad memories and a drawer full of late bills.

"Honey it's getting late, you should start the grill." Ranae said coming outside.

"Yeah, I'm starting to get a lil' hungry myself. After we eat I want you for desert." Sway flirted.

"I'm not on the menu…but I'll see what I can do." Ranae played hard to get.

They had a good marriage but it was infected with a financial virus. Ranae couldn't know what he was about to do. He needed a clear head and didn't want to deal with all the questions and concerns she would surely have. He would tell her after the jobs were done and they were in the clear. They had a no lie policy in their relationship, which he intended on honoring…just after he got the money. He ran his fingertips through his curly hair scratching his scalp. Ameenah's playful screams grabbed his attention as she ran from her brother. He noticed her worn out shoes; they were her play shoes but her school shoes weren't much better. Inside the phone rang and the answering machine picked up,

"Yes this message is for Mr. Daniels; my name is Rachael Montgomery calling from CTR collections on behalf of *"Ford Motor Credit."*

This is the fourth call I've made this week regarding your past due account and would highly appreciate a return call to discuss this financial matter further. My number again is 323 841-6982 extension 147. Avoiding my calls only makes your situation worse and my patience is wearing thin, the next step is to begin the process to garnish your wages. I expect to hear from you soon."

As they both listened to the message, Ranae looked down at her husband with tired eyes. She rubbed his back gently to show they were in this together. Sway stood up and walked toward the grill, "Fuck this shit." He whispered to himself.

All Aboard

I went over the plan for the hits in my mind for the hundredth time. I'd been planning this shit for a year now and it was finally time to cash in. What I didn't plan on was having to kill two extra muthafuckas along the way. But that's how it goes sometimes…shit happens and you just deal with it. I had to find out who they were first, once I did that stopping their heartbeats would be the easy part. I called each person in my crew; since the meeting everyone was doing exactly what I said to do and laying low. Although I didn't need to, I called Omar first to see if he was down. Just like I thought, he was still ready to get it in. I talked to Dallas and Sway and they both said they were more than ready. The one person I didn't have to call was Angelique, I just asked her if she was ready at the dinner table while we ate salmon and mashed potatoes, "of course" was her response.
Well, it was officially on baby, 20 million dollars in a week! I opened a bag of *"skittles"* relaxed on my Italian leather sectional and went over the plans again.

Vegas Baby

Flash drove his *"Cutlass"* to the parking garage where Tyce told him to pick the car up. It was located about an hour away on the edge of the city. All he had to do was park is ride; jump in Tyce's and hit the highway heading north. Bree told him she'd map quested the address to the garage and would meet him there after she left the mall. Flash was looking forward to getting out of the city for a while, he needed a change of scenery. Plus Bree was fine as hell but she lived with her strict ass grandmother and that made it real hard to hook up during booty call hours.

The Vegas strip was a long way from grandma's house so fucking at two in morning wasn't a problem. He liked Bree; he'd been seeing her for about six months but kept her away from his street life. He needed her to be his personal escape from the bullshit. She did more than take his mind off his stress; she made his dick and his spirit feel good at the same time. Flash had to practically force her to take a thousand dollars to buy some new outfits for the trip; she wasn't a gold digger by any means. With her being a sophomore in college, she was used to making what she already had work. But every woman liked to shop so she eventually gave in and hit the mall.

Flash pulled his gray old school cutlass into the underground parking garage and searched the aisles for his weekend wheels. He finally spotted Tyce's ride and his eyes widened with excitement. He parked a few rows down and grabbed the bags from his trunk. Flash walked to the automobile of his young dreams and searched for the key under the front fender, it was right where Tyce said it would be. His hand landed on the black key box and he quickly slid it open and poured the key in his palm. He hit the unlock button on the remote and got inside the cockpit. He took some time and admired the luxury as the scent of new car filled the interior. An envelope was on the passenger seat that had his name on it Flash started the engine and reached over to grab the white envelope reading the note inside:

What up Flash, I hope you like the whip I chose for your lil' vacation. Have a good time and do ALL the shit that I would do! I put a couple g's in the glove box for you and your lady...peace.
Ps. Don't wreck my shit, lol

Flashed laughed out loud, as he opened the glove box, 20 hundred dollar bills were sitting on the driver's manual. A smile spread across his adolescent face. He'd never told Tyce but he always thought of him like an older brother. He probably would never share that with him; niggas just don't say shit like that...they just watch each other's back. He would do anything for Tyce and he knew that Tyce would do anything to help him. They didn't need to have an express your feelings man therapy session, there was an understanding between them that didn't need mushy words added to the mix. Flash folded the note back up and raised his ass off the leather seat so that he could put it in his back pocket. Just as he grabbed his phone to call Bree, she called him,

"Wasup baby? You on your way here?" Flash said in a sexy tone.

"I was til' my raggedy ass car didn't start I'm still at the mall! I tried to start it a gang of times and the shit is jus' dead. I even got mall security to give me a jump but that didn't work either! I got all my stuff with me but you're gonna hafta come and grab me...is that ok?" She asked frustrated.

"Yeah, calm down baby, I'll be there in like an hour I'm a lil' ways out."

Bree sighed with relief, "Ok well I'll jus' go to the food court and get somethin' to eat...you want anything?"

"Naw I'm good. I'ma see you in a bit, I'll call you when I'm close."

"Ok, hurry I'm ready to hit the strip baby!" She sang.

Flash pulled out of the garage and headed to his damsel in distress, 45 minutes later the bass was knockin' as he entered the mall parking lot. He noticed all the double and triple takes he was getting from people as he crept through the rows of countless cars. He spotted Bree's *"Kia"* and snagged the empty spot next to it. Flash turned down the music and grabbed his cell phone, he hit the recent calls button, and the phone began to ring. Just as he heard Bree's voice over the speaker the passenger side window shattered into a million tiny pieces. Flash ducked his head down instinctively and reached for the gun in his waist. A hailstorm of bullets ripped through the tinted glass and body of the *"Range Rover."* As Flash reached for the door handle a bullet struck his wrist and another pierced his right shoulder. He screamed in agony as three more bullets entered his back; burning his flesh. His body nudged weakly against the door as he tried to escape the assault; he heard bullets whizzing past his ears before one hit him in the back of his neck slamming his head into the window. His lungs were trying their best to pump air but it was leaking out of his throat as bloody bubbles gurgled from his windpipe. He focused his eyes on Bree's car until the picture went black. The shower of bullets finally stopped.

"Flash! Flashhh! Flashhh!! Baby!!! Talk to meeeee!!! Flash say somethin'!! Flashhhh where are you?? Flashhh!!" Bree's frantic voice blared from the phone. "No No No Noooo baby!!! Oh my God!! Oh my God!! Nooo!! Flashhhhh!! Baby please say somethin'!!!"

Flash trembled as he struggled and tried desperately to hold on to life...his chest was heaving as he struggled to breath. His muscles relaxed and his body went limp...as death took over. Bree ran through the mall, crashed through the double doors and sprinted toward her car, while she was running she saw a tan *"Camry"* speeding away almost hitting a bus bench. Having kicked off her heels in the mall her bare feet pounded the pavement; she didn't notice the sting from hundreds of tiny pebbles stabbing her toes as she ran towards her man. Tears rolled from her eyes as she saw the horrible scene. Glass sprinkled the ground and the *"Range Rover's"* body was freckled with bullet holes. She snatched the car door open and Flash's head leaned out lazily. The white T-shirt he wore was soaked in blood; it looked like he'd taken a bath in cranberry juice. Bree tried to sit him up in the seat.

"HELP!!! Please help…somebody!!! She looked around wildly.

Bree silently prayed in her head as her shaky hands touched his smooth face.

A small crowd began to form around the scene as people started to realize what was happening. They watched with big eyes as they witnessed the horror.

"Flash! Baby please wake up!! Open your eyes baby, open your eyes!!" She screamed tapping his cheeks.

Flash's eyes were closed and his body was still. Bree cradled him in her arms like a newborn baby rocking him back and forth, her dress and hands were covered in blood. She squeezed his lifeless body tighter pressing his head to her chest and sobbed uncontrollably.

"No no no no no no!!!!" Bree shook her head side to side in disbelief.

The crowd was quiet as the sirens grew louder in the distance.

It's Quiet

The TV was black...turned off after the news reported on the drive-by shooting at the *"Crenshaw Mall."* The white female anchor explained what happened in a nonchalant manner. She broke down the details of the shooting and when she pronounced Flash's real name as the deceased victim...I turned the TV off and just sat in the dark. No tears slid down my face, I didn't punch the air, and I didn't need a hug to let it all out. My feelings were tightly capped inside, for the first time in my life I'd lost someone close to me. Before now, I was on the other side of death, now I felt the sting of losing a friend but rather than mourn-I was on some murder shit. The reporter said the holice had no suspects but I knew what the fuck happened, all those bullets Lil' Flash took were meant for me.

I had a wild caged lion inside of me! I was in pain but not the kind a pain *"Tylenol"* or morphine could take away; I wanted revenge! I felt responsible for his death. Why the fuck was he at the mall anyway? I told him just hit the highway and avoid the city streets, I put the car in a garage outside the city to keep shit quiet, I was trying to protect him. Anger and rage swirled inside my chest, I was mad at the fact that a young life was snuffed out over a mistaken identity. Them niggas thought he was me; well I'll be sure to introduce myself before I murdered them blind ass muthafuckas! I pulled my phone out the front pocket of my hoodie and dialed a dead man's number...Biz answered on the first ring,

"They missed. You should stop buying your hit men from the dollar store nigga." I stated calmly staring into the darkness of my living room.

"So you a comedian now huh? Don't you worry pretty boy; they still got enough bullets for you, as for Angelique, I'm going to fuck her one last time before I bury her fine ass, alive!" He threatened.

My jaws clenched without me knowing it, I wanted to kill this nigga so bad I almost couldn't breathe.

"Was that little crack star your friend Tyce, was his lil' black ass close to you? Shit, he had to be if he was driving your Range, either that or the lil' nigga stole it." He taunted.

I stood up and walked to the back yard to get some air taking the phone with me, "Thank you." I said enjoying the fresh breeze of the cool night.

"What the fuck you thanking me for?" Biz asked confused.

"I work better when I'm pissed off and I'm 'bout to work overtime on you. I was jus' gonna kill you before...but now I'ma get real demented on ya ass. So thank you for makin' this easy, I don't even mind that I aint gettin' paid for this one." I paced the patio slowly.

"I'ma deliver death like "*Pizza Hut*" nigga."
I didn't wait for his response; I hung the phone up in his face and continued to pace the patio trying to control my breathing.

Dumb and Dumber

The beach parking lot was empty, it was one o'clock in the morning, and the sound of the waves crashing repeatedly against the shore was the music of the night. The tan sedan sat in a dimly lit corner as Lincoln and T.J. argued back and forth,

"Nigga YOU said it was him! I was listening to your near sighted ass!" Lincoln yelled pointing his finger at T.J.'s head.

"Look man I fucked up aight, I saw the Range Rover with one nigga driving and I jus'
jumped...I been itching to plug that nigga and I jus' rushed that shit!" TJ explained.

Both men sat in silence as they stared at the black ocean. Biz had already cussed the men out and threatened to take the money back and their lives. To make matters worse they were now tied to a murder investigation. A murder of a known drug dealer who was also black, a common thing in Los Angeles but a murder investigation nonetheless. They didn't need that kind of attention, they needed to kill Tyce, find that bitch and get the hell out of town. Everything was amped up now; the luxury of time was no longer available and the welcome mat was gone from the front door. It was clear they'd underestimated Tyce but that wouldn't happen again.

"We need to drop this car and switch locations." Lincoln said breaking the silence. TJ nodded in agreement, "Yeah, and we need to step up the game and try something new. I think we need to make him come to us. Maybe shootin' that lil' nigga was a good thing, if he was close to him; he might want a lil' payback." TJ hoped.

Lincoln liked the way his partner was thinking, the old way of finding niggas on the street was obsolete in this case. Tyce wasn't on the streets now, so they would need to draw him out...then fill him with some hot shit.

Change Of Plans...Kinda

I was starting to lose focus. Flash's sudden death was running through my mind like a track team. I couldn't concentrate; it felt like I had some unfinished business to take care of. I stood in the steaming shower letting the water beat down on my shoulders. The shower had always been my personal therapy session, it's where I worked out my problems and planned shit out. Tonight, me and my problems could barely fit in my walk in shower room, I pushed the button on the wall activating all the jets; pulses and powerful streams of water gently attacked my body from every angle. My lungs inhaled the moist steam that was filling up the room like a thick "*London*" fog. The room was becoming cloudy-however my head was beginning to clear up. Over an hour of water therapy and reflection worked once again, I put shit into perspective and stepped out with a new outlook on things.

My reflection stared back at me as I confronted myself in the mirror, I took notice of a tattoo on my left arm that read "*ME vs. WORLD,*" that had been my attitude since birth. I could no longer completely think that way, not in this situation. I dried my naked body with a towel, closed the lid on the toilet, and just sat there. Before all this shit happened life was simple for me; I killed niggas and counted cash, now I had more complicated issues to contend with. I had a crew to look out for and on top of that, I had budding feelings for Angelique. She'd put her life in my hands and I couldn't live with myself if I had to attend her funeral. Sway, Dallas and Omar trusted me to hold shit down and lead the way, I didn't feel comfortable knowing trigger happy niggas could kill anyone of them to get to me. Flash had paid that price and I wasn't about to give Biz another sacrificial lamb. I had to take care of these niggas and do it before I made my moves. Looking over my shoulder while I was working wasn't good for business-or my nerves.

I put on black sweats a black T-shirt and finally stepped out the bathroom. As I made my way to the kitchen I was still forming the plan in my head, the last step in my private therapy session was cherry flavored "*Jell-O.*" I opened the fridge to find my sweet Dr. and noticed three cups were missing...I smiled at the fact that Angelique and I shared the same cravings. I grabbed a red cup and sat at the table, my spoon broke the smooth surface as I continued my thoughts. Four Jell-O cups later, I knew what to do and how to do it. Angelique's light was on in her room so I decided to stop by to see what she was up to. I knocked softly and listened for movement on the other side of the door. Her soft voice gave my body permission to move as she told me to "come in." Angelique was on her bed playing solitaire, she was wearing a yellow satin nightgown that ran out of material just passed her hips. The cards were spread out over the comforter and she was sitting Indian style as she played with herself.

"Who's winning?" I asked stepping in the dimly lit room.

"Me of course, I could use some competition if you're up for it?"

I eased onto the bed and sat across from her accepting the challenge. She began to shuffle the cards for an old school game of slapjack. Angelique stopped her dealer style shuffling tricks and just stared into my eyes and whispered to me,

"I didn't know Lil' Flash personally but I'm deeply saddened by his death. My heart is heavy for his family…and for you." Her eyes never blinked.

She stroked my knee as she gently asked, "Are you ok?"

I sighed heavily and smiled, "I'm ok now….thanks for askin'."

We broke eye contact finally and began to
play, "By the way, I need to ask you a favor." I
said repositioning myself on the bed.
"Ok…wasup?" She smiled.
I held my tongue and just looked at her pretty
brown face, "I'll ask you after I whoop your
ass in slap jack!" I promised. "And don't try
and distract me with your short ass pajamas
either."
"Pleasssse, I don't need to show you my cookie
to win; besides…I wouldn't let you eat it
anyway." She lied with a wink.

Foursome

The black on black *"Mercedes"* swooped toward the curb stopping in front of Malik's barbershop. The bass from the trunk vibrated the rearview mirror and made the street full of people turn and stare. I hopped out the car and walked into the shop not bothering to set my alarm.

"What up Malik." I said taking my usual seat.

"Same old shit jus' a different day Tyce, you seem a lil' up beat today...what you got goin' on?" Malik asked as he cleaned his clippers.

I smiled at him taking notice of all the niggas in the shop pretending not to eardrop on our conversation, "Yeah I'm in a good mood. Although my lil' man's life was cut short, I'm in good spirits. We having a party tonight to celebrate Flash's life, I wanted to extend an invite to you and your family."

Malik nodded his head sympathetically, "That's beautiful man. The whole neighborhood was hurt behind that shit. I'll definitely fall through, where you having it?"

"We throwing it over at Dizzy's club, it starts about ten, I'll hold a table and a bottle of

Goose for you." I offered while he pumped my
    chair up higher.
Underneath the drape cloth, I pulled out my gun
and let it rest on my thigh. The shop was packed-
typical for a Saturday morning. One by one niggas
started to talk about what happened to Flash. The
shop was buzzing with rumors and speculations
about the details of his murder. I just listened to
the chatter with my eyes closed as Malik cut my
hair. Some dude next to me finished his cut and
rose from his chair, he paid the barber and dusted
off his over sized white T-shirt. The young
stranger put his hat on and turned to me,
    "Ay yo man; where you say that party was
    gonna be at?" He continued, "I didn't know the
    dude personally but his girlfriend is my cousin.
    I'm sure she'd wanna go, she's been struggling
    with his death and maybe being around his
    friends and family would help her deal with
    shit." He said with concern in his voice.
    "Damn, small world huh? Flash told me he had
    a new lady but I never got a chance to meet
    her. Tell your cousin it's at Dizzy's club
    tonight; you know where that is?"
    "Yeah, yeah, I been there a few times, I'll let
    her know."
    "Tell her when she get there to mention my
    name and she won't have worry 'bout nothin'."

I instructed.

"Aight that's wasup man…what's your name?"

"Tyce." I answered taking my hand off the hammer under the drape cloth and shaking his.

"Curtis."

The stranger announced giving me dap, his iced out watch jiggled around his wrist as we went through the customary hood hand shaking motions. He passed out a few more handshakes on his way out; he paused to admire my ride and kept moving up the block disappearing from my view. I closed my eyes again letting my thoughts fast forward to tonight; I hoped this event would help people cope with Flash's death and give his family some closure. I was surprised at the response I got. The guest list was up to about three hundred and rising by the hour. Angelique was all in when I asked her to help me plan it out. She arranged for a limo to pick up Flash's family, I planned to order a dozen roses for all the ladies closest to him, I was happy to include his girlfriend in the plans since she was probably coming. The event company Angelique hired to handle the event was the best in the city, they planned a lot of "life celebration parties" so this one should be off the hook.

I was getting dressed as the evening transformed into night. Angelique was already at the club making sure all the details got taking care of. She took the rental car and picked up a few more people on the way. About two hours later, I was on my way to the spot; Angelique called me while I was driving and told me the shit was packed with people. I got there 20 minutes after we spoke and circled the block-I parked down the street and turned my headlights off.

Inside the club, there was a poster size portrait of Flash with thousands of red and white flowers around it. A gold treasure chest was placed in front of the shrine to collect donations from the over four hundred guests in attendance. The venue was a success and because the Nation of Islam was handling security, everyone felt safe to enjoy the party. With the function in full swing, Angelique was free to mingle a little bit. Both she and Dallas dressed to kill wearing outfits that looked like they were painted on. They worked the crowd like spokes models catching the eyes of every man there…including two men shooting pool quietly in the back of the club. The men stopped their game to gaze at the talent standing at the bar. As Angelique and Dallas turned around holding their freshly made martini's the men both agreed the view was even better from the front.

"That's what I'm talkin' 'bout! You see them bitches' nigga?" One man shouted over the music.

"Yeah I see em; shit every nigga in here see em." The other said licking his lips.

A young waitress passed in front of the men and was grabbed gently by the arm and given some instructions in her ear. Following the polite demands of the tall man she changed her route and headed in the direction of the bar, straight toward Angelique and Dallas. She gave a schoolgirl smile as she approached the extra sexy women. They both leaned in as the short waitress motioned for them to come a little closer to her.

"Whatever you ladies are drinking tonight is on the house, compliments of the gentlemen in the back. All they ask in return is that you play a game of pool with them." She said raising her eyebrows and grinning widely.

Dallas turned toward Angelique and smiled. At the same time, they both peered toward the back of the club but couldn't see the faces of their shy admirers in the low light.

"Tell em we accept." Dallas said not wanting to be rude.

"Yes tell em we'll be there in a sec. And since it's their dime, order four shots of *"Patron"* and charge em double, you keep the change for yourself sweetie." Angelique said finishing her drink and winking at the young lady.

Angelique lead the way, cat walking across the

dance floor toward the pool tables, Dallas followed behind her making her steps keep time with the beat of the music.

"Yo nigga here they come, that shit always works!" The tall man elbowed the other man in his ribs.

The ladies arrived at the pool table flashing million dollar smiles.

"Yo wasup, how you ladies doin' tonight? The shorter one asked holding his pool stick.

"We're fine, thanks for the invite fellas." Dallas said shifting her weight to one foot.

"This is my girl Kim and I'm Monique."

The two men looked at each other and grinned, "When you say your girl...do you mean *your girl*?" The short one quizzed sexily.

Dallas smacked Angelique firmly on her ass. Angelique did a little dance to show her approval then retaliated by giving Dallas a slow passionate juicy kiss on her bronze painted lips. After 15 slow motion seconds the two divas finally unlatched their lips and took a breather.

"I hope that answered your question but don't get it twisted...we both *love* dick." Angelique reassured.

The young waitress arrived with four shots and passed them out. They all clinked their glasses together and toasted to meeting new friends and loving life.

"So I heard you guys wanna get your asses whipped in some pool huh? Dallas flirted. She walked over and grabbed two more sticks, "You don't need to take it easy on us either." Angelique boasted.

The two men ordered another round of tequila for the foursome as the tall one set up the table to begin the game. The party was jumping and overflowing with beautiful women however, none of them could compete with "Monique" and "Kim" who were dressed less to impress. A black see thru mini dress with solid black panty and bra hugged Dallas's curvaceous body and red silk booty shorts with matching low cut blouse squeezed Angelique's body like a boa constrictor. The shoes, earrings and bracelets all coordinated perfectly. Angelique rocked a slightly altered look sporting green contacts, a fake Marilyn Monroe beauty mark, and a honey brown cascading curly weave. She looked like a Brazilian bombshell.

"Hold on Kim." Dallas interrupted. "I don't play with strange men. We don't even know ya'll names." She said folding her arms across her chest.

"Damn, my fault ladies, I'm TJ and this is my partner Lincoln."

Angelique extended her manicured hand with pink

and white fingertips offering it to Lincoln. He gripped her hand softly inside his rough mitt. After Lincoln took the first shot to begin the game, TJ abruptly excused himself. Dallas watched him closely as his dark eyes moved through the crowded club. He disappeared into the bathroom for several minutes then stood at the bar inspecting every corner of the club and the people congregating there. His eyes jumped from person to person, concentrating on their faces. After his inspection was complete, he returned to the table and continued entertaining the ladies. The flirting was moving at warp speed as Angelique and Dallas traded jabs and sexual innuendos with their opponents. Two games and eight drinks later everyone was feeling loose. It was obvious who was feeling who; Lincoln clearly liked Angelique and TJ was staring at Dallas so hard his pupils were dilating.

Beginning to get a little nosey Angelique asked, "Are you guys from LA?"

"*Naw* we from back east…where *real* niggas live." Lincoln bragged.

"*Oh really,* so what ya'll doin' on the west coast with all the fake niggas?" Angelique placed her hands on her hips.

Exchanging a brief glance with TJ, Lincoln answered, "Jus' a lil' business."

Seemingly, on cue TJ left the group and headed to the restrooms. Again, he surveyed the club and then rejoined the group. He sat on the edge of the pool table and looked out into the sea of people. Dallas relocated between his open legs, blocking his view of the dance floor,

"I *hope* you're not looking out for some jealous ex or baby mama. I'm lookin' *to cute* too fight tonight, I'd rather save my energy for later."
She whispered with her lips next to his earlobe.
 TJ palmed her plump ass, "It's nuthin' like that Monique, I'm jus' lookin' for somebody…but it's *definitely not* a jealous bitch and I *don't have any kids.*"

Across from them Lincoln's arms engulfed Angelique's waist as they danced; his dick was as hard as a forehead and it kept head butting her in the stomach.

"Is your friend ok? I mean, he keeps leavin' and lookin' around the club. Did he lose somethin'?" Angelique looked up at him.
"Naw, we jus' tryna mix a lil' business with pleasure; the pleasure showed up tonight but the business didn't. It aint nuthin' tho; look Kim, we stayin' across town and it don't look like we gon be workin' tonight so-" Angelique cut him off.
"I thought you'd never ask daddy." She said

relieved. "Monique baby lets go." Angelique
announced interrupting her deep kiss with TJ.
Dallas turned around and put her ass in his lap,
"That's good with me, but can we jus' hit the
ladies room first?" Dallas requested girlishly.
With their bladders about to burst the ladies
switched back and forth across the dance floor
toward the bathrooms. Lincoln and TJ racked the
pool sticks and prepared to leave the club. They
were pissed that Tyce hadn't made an appearance
tonight. Biz called them earlier in the day and said
one of his boys was in the barber shop today and
told him Tyce would be coming out tonight but
they'd been there for four hours…guess he was
wrong. The night wasn't a total loss; at least they
would get some much needed pussy as a
consolation prize. The lights came on signaling the
end of the party; while they waited on their one
night stands to come out the restroom, they
surveyed the crowd filled with the friends and
family of Flash. The gold treasure chest was
stuffed with cash, checks, and sympathy cards for
Flash's family. Everyone there was mourning and
celebrating his life…everyone except Lincoln and
TJ. They'd gotten as far away from the crowd as
possible, preferring to hang out in the back. They
didn't give a wet fuck about Flash *or* his fucking
family. He was a mistake, and that was all. They

had to put their egos in a straight jacket to keep from grabbing the mic at the DJ stand and announcing, "WE killed his lil' ass, and ya'll aint gonna do *shit* about it!!"

Angelique and Dallas finally emerged from the bathroom and the new couples prepared to leave and regroup in the hotel room. Once outside, the cool night air attempted to sober them up a bit before they all piled in Lincoln and TJ's newly rented "*Maxima.*" The music was turned up, pushing the stock speakers to their limit. TJ shared the back seat with Dallas; his fingers were inside her panties making mini circles around her clit. Her soft moans were drowned out by the loud music as she began to massage her own titties through her black bra. Lincoln's driving duties prevented him from attacking Angelique, but unlike him, her pretty hands were free to roam. She slowly unzipped his baggie jeans and grabbed his dick like a dumbbell; squeezing it gently in her small hand. He licked his lips and leaned his seat back to give her more room to work,

"*Damn girl*…you got my shit as hard as
college calculus right now. I need to speed up;
I can't *wait* to get in that shit!" He confessed as
he merged onto the highway.

Angelique was silent and just smiled at his
honesty. She released his dick and proceeded to

slowly unbutton her blouse, she went braless tonight so undressing would be easy. She took off her shirt; letting her breast come out to play and lazily lit a cigarette. With the window rolled down completely and her seat slightly laid back, she rode the rest of the way topless. Lincoln drifted into the next lane as he tried to watch the show.

"Damn nigga you aint never seen titties
before!" TJ laughed behind him.

As Lincoln straightened out and accelerated toward their destination, Angelique took a long drag from her cigarette…she looked in the side mirror of the car and smiled. 15 minutes later, they pulled up to a quiet tucked away hotel in a suburban neighborhood of Santa Monica. Lincoln parked the car in the back of the hotel and turned off the ignition. He studied her body in the darkness and imagined all the nasty things he was going to do to her. It had been weeks since he had some pussy; all the pent up stress he had from working with no results was about to be relieved by her. Kim was just what he needed to get back on track.

"I'm jus' a lil' curious…are you planning on walking up to the room like that?" He asked gazing at her round titties.

"Like what." Angelique answered winking at him.

She grabbed her small purse, cell phone and opened the door. She hopped out the car and stood up letting anyone who was up at this late hour enjoy the view. Dallas got out the backseat and joined Angelique, the two shared a girlish giggle as the cool breeze made Angelique's nipples perk up.

"What room ya'll in?" Dallas asked looking at the men from across the roof of the car.

"We upstairs on the left, room 224." TJ said walking around to get closer to Dallas.

Everyone walked toward the stairs together; the men purposely let the ladies go up ahead of them so they could be eye to eye with their "backyards" as they climbed the steps. This was an outside hotel only, there wasn't a huge luxurious lobby; there door faced the parking lot and over looked the medium sized pool. The low budget room was warm and smelled like sock scented air freshener; it connected to another room to accommodate two guests. Angelique assumed this was Lincoln's side because he'd opened the door. She looked at her new surroundings, satisfied, she headed straight for the king size bed; laying out on her back. Dallas followed her, crawled like a tiger across the flower printed comforter, and rested on top of her prey. Lincoln and TJ just stood there staring as the two women made themselves real comfortable.

Angelique suddenly sat up on the bed, "Damn I forgot my shirt. Baby could you run down and grab it for me? I promise I won't put it on til' after we leave." She flirted. "Plus I think I'm being held hostage now." She said referring to Dallas who was straddling her.

"Yeah, I'll be right back." Lincoln snatched the keys as he walked out the door leaving it slightly open.

"What you standing there for baby? You need to dim these lights and bring your *fine ass over here*! Like my girl said earlier, we *love* dick and I'm sorry but I don't have one to give her and I *can't fuck myself.*" Dallas spoke to TJ as Angelique began to rub her round ass. TJ wasted no time; he lifted up his long shirt and pulled a silver gun from his waistband. Placing the gun on the dresser next to the TV, he quickly began to unbuckle his belt: he removed his jeans, T-shirt, and boxers. The last item to be taken off was his massive platinum and diamond chain, which he laid next to his gun. His body was nice, not to buff but not too skinny either. It was nicked up and scratched up with old scars and his skin could use a good moisturizer. TJ was completely naked except for his white tube socks; as he strolled over to the light switch near the door, he confidently let his erect dick swing back and forth. Once he was

sure the ladies saw the package he was about to
deliver; he turned off the lights…his plan *was* to
wait for Lincoln but he couldn't pass up the
chance to be the first man in line at a pussy
potluck. He was grinning with excitement and
anticipation as he walked over to the bed, just as
he climbed on the bed to get in on the action the
door to the room violently flew open slamming
into the wall. Lincoln fell through the door
collapsing into a pile on the dirty carpet. TJ heard
the loud boom and spun around, his instinct was to
rush to the dresser to grab his gun, but it was too
late,

    "DON'T MOVE NIGGA!!! A voice yelled from
    the darkness.
Light all of a sudden filled the tiny room and the
owner of the loud voice appeared. Tyce was
standing in the doorway holding two gigantic
black guns, one was pointing down at Lincoln, the
other at an astonished TJ.

    "Stay right the FUCK there!!" He said stepping
into the room closing the door behind him with his
foot. He noticed TJ's gun on the dresser and
moved smoothly toward it; keeping his guns aimed
at their targets. Angelique and Dallas got off the
bed and positioned themselves closer to Tyce.
Lincoln was face down on the floor moaning in
agony, TJ remained as still as statue but kept

shifting his eyes from Lincoln to Tyce. He was obviously concerned for his injured partner but dared not try to assist him.

Breaking the tense silence in the room Tyce said, "Damn…I hope I'm not interrupting anything, looks like ya'll was 'bout to have a party up in here. Especially you boy…you all naked in shit; well you aren't *really* naked if you have on socks…you know that right?"

"FUCK YOU!!" TJ yelled.

"Naw nigga fuck you and this nigga on the floor bleeding. Turn over nigga! I want you to look at me." Tyce commanded.

Lincoln painfully rolled over on his back clutching his stomach. His cream dress shirt was moist with blood and he was coughing and wheezing.

"I heard you been lookin' for me." Tyce said smiling. "I also heard you been lookin' for her too." He said nodding in Angelique's direction. "*Well*…here we are…in the flesh. Sorry we kept you waitin' for so long." He said sarcastically. "Baby reach in my back pocket…I brought you somethin'."

Angelique walked behind Tyce and smiled when she saw her red blouse hanging out his pants pocket like he was a member of the bloods. She gladly put the shirt on and stood at his side, she was all too happy to end the charade. Pretending to be all hot and horny for wack ass niggas was exhausting.

Dallas took her position on the other side of Tyce and just watched the scene like she had a bucket of popcorn in her lap. She loved the way Tyce handled himself, she was turned on for the first time tonight, and he hadn't even touched her.

"Make no mistake about it gentlemen; I'm Tyce, she's Angelique and this is my new friend Dallas. Now that we got that out the way; let's get down to business." Tyce put TJ to work, "pick him up, and get ya ass in the bathroom."

TJ stood motionless and just stared at Angelique in disbelief, he was disappointed that he hadn't recognized her and he was shocked that this nigga had got up on them like that. They had never been caught slippin' like this before. Lincoln was on the floor dying and he was naked...what the fuck happened?

"HURRY UP!!" Tyce boomed snapping TJ out of his confused thoughts.

TJ hesitated but did as he was told. He grabbed Lincoln under his shoulders and moved him toward the bathroom. Lincoln grunted and clenched his teeth in pain as he was being drug across the carpet. Tyce followed the men into the restroom; he was wearing a gun vest and put one in the holster. He ordered the men to climb into the shower.

"Come on man! We was jus' doin' a job nigga,
it wasn't **personal**...it was **business**!! We
thought that lil' nigga was YOU, man I **swear**!!
WE SORRY MAN!!!!" TJ pleaded.

Lincoln was laying against the wall with his legs hanging over the tub while TJ stood up shivering. He balled his fist up as he begged for his life. All the gansta in him was going down the drain, the tables had turned, and it was him who was facing death.

"FUCK THAT, this shit *is* personal for me!!
You snuffed out my lil' brother, was plottin' on
killing **MY** *woman*, and trying to murder **ME**!!
Turn the shower on nigga!!"

TJ finally got some balls and prepared to die like a man; he turned the faucet on and let the cold water spray his naked body. Lincoln's shirt was now soaked with water and blood.

"Fuck this punk ass nigga." Lincoln finally
uttered looking up at TJ.
"That's where you niggas went wrong. You
shoulda *never* fucked with me!

Tyce stepped back and aimed his gun, TJ screamed, "see you in hell muthafucka" before Tyce shot him in the middle of his forehead. The shower wall looked like it was splattered with extra chunky salsa as his brains exploded. Lincoln glared at Tyce and let out a gurgled laugh, Tyce stared back at him and put him out of his misery; he shot him three times in the chest, each bullet rocked his body slightly when it entered. TJ was slumped over next to Lincoln as the cold shower rained down on their bodies…washing away the blood and bodily fluids of the two killers. A powerful sense of relief came over Tyce as he exited the murder scene. In the room, Angelique and Dallas were busy wiping the room down getting rid of any evidence. Even though everyone made sure not to leave a single fingerprint, they left nothing to chance concentrating on every nook and cranny. They picked up hairs and clothing fibers off the carpet and bed spread like a crime crew from CSI.

Walking calmly back into the room Tyce asked, "You two ok?"

The ladies both looked up from their cleaning duties, "Were fine…are you ok?" They questioned showing concern.

"Yeah, I'm straight now. I wanna thank ya'll for helping me out tonight. It can be a little shocking to witness some shit like that; I jus' wanted to make sure you two were alright." He asked putting his arms around them.

"*Yeeaahh* we good Tyce. We jus' happy this

shit is over with and them grimy niggas are dead. I can't believe they was tryna **kill** *my girl!* Fuck them niggas...I'm glad you clipped em Tyce!" Dallas confessed.

"I can't thank you enough," Angelique said holding up an old picture of her she'd found on the nightstand.

Tyce looked at the photo and kissed her reassuringly on the forehead. He was happy to take care of Lincoln and TJ, he didn't care so much about **his** safety; but the fact that Angelique was in danger and Flash died; he didn't have a choice. The trio left the room and quickly walked to Tyce's Benz parked around the corner from the hotel. They got in and sped off, Angelique rode shotgun as Dallas occupied the back seat. His plan was executed perfectly, thanks to Angelique and Dallas. They worked their pussy power on Lincoln and TJ expertly. They had no idea they were being set up or followed to their room the whole time. Tyce was sorry about one thing though-he didn't get a chance to celebrate his little brother's life with his family and friends.

As the Benz cruised down the highway, Angelique stared out the window while little butterflies fluttered inside her stomach. Her heart was dancing the waltz in her chest. She replayed the entire night in her head, especially the part where Tyce said "**she was *his* woman**" That particular part she replayed over and over again.

What's Really Goin On?

Omar was getting restless. All this sitting around not doing shit was starting to get on his nerves. He'd noticed that Tyce wasn't acting the same since Angelique showed up. He just didn't trust that pretty bitch at all, and it seemed that his boy was falling under her spell. He'd expected to see Tyce at the party for Flash but he was a no show, he wished he was there to witness firsthand how that bitch was hanging all over niggas at the club that night. She was wearing colored contacts and a wig but that didn't fool him, he'd know her fake ass anywhere. He started to snatch her ass up but he stopped because he didn't feel like hearing Tasha's mouth. She was tripping at the party and was already not feeling Angelique, she was just itching for a fight that night and it wasn't about to be with him. Shit he'd fuck around and get locked up over that crazy woman. So he chose to play the background...**again**; and sat back watching her hoe ass flirt and flaunt her titties all around the pool table-n-shit. Damn he wished his boy was there to see that shit, but as usual, he was nowhere to be found. Omar finished waxing his truck and

grabbed a cold beer from the fridge. His baldhead
was gleaming in the hot sun so he decided to sit in
the cool shade of the garage. Tasha suddenly
appeared from the house carrying a phone in her
hand, she was grinning extra wide as she
practically forced it in his hand,

"It's Biz!" She said excitedly.

Omar looked a little confused as he took the phone
from her. Why was he calling him? What the fuck
did he want?

"What up?" Omar asked dryly.

"Nuthin' much young blood…jus' wanted to
check in on ya."

"Look nigga, I aint helping you get up on Tyce
aight. I got money to make and I aint about to
let you fuck it up." Omar said taking a sip of
his Heineken.

"Whoa Whoa Whoa. Slow up, I didn't call for
that. I know you won't flip on your
boy…unless you wanna go broke; I mean we
all know he's the brains behind the operation."
Biz instigated.

"Fuck you nigga! You tryna to call me dumb
muthafucka!" Omar shouted.

"Calm down. I don't think that O. I'm jus'
sayin'…that's what everyone else thinks…not
me. Personally, I think he's been holding you
back for all these years. It was him who kept

you from really makin' money; not me. I knew
it was him that fucked up that night…that's
why I didn't fuck with you. I put the hit out on
him and left you out of it." Biz informed.
Omar stood up and really started to listen to the
voice in his ear. It was like he could see into his
thoughts and feelings. Biz was speaking a
language he could understand.

Biz continued, "I heard through a friend of
mine that Tyce is makin' a few moves. Maybe
we could both get what we want. That is *if*
you're ready to go solo?"
Omar took a long swig of his beer and rubbed
his head, "Keep talkin'."
"Well naturally I wouldn't run it to you over
the phone; if you got a little time this evening
we could meet up at my house. Why don't you
come by about seven?"
The timing couldn't have been better for this
phone call. Omar accepted the invitation from his
former boss with a new curiosity. Tasha, who
never left the garage, was on pins and needles as
she waited to be briefed on the conversation. Omar
barely hung up the phone before Tasha put her
hands in the air,
"Well, what he say?"
"He said he wanna talk some business. I'ma go
to his house later and see wasup." Omar

reported trying to remain calm and cool.
"Baby this is what you been waiting on, Biz
aint blind baby, he sees your potential!" Tasha
said tapping his ass playfully.
Omar returned the favor and smacked her ass just
a little harder than she did. This business talk was
like an aphrodisiac for both of them; before he left
to see Biz, they celebrated the good news with a
mid afternoon fuck in the chair...with the garage
still wide open.

#1

It was a Friday night, two weeks after the hotel hit. The crew met up at the warehouse spot before the first job. Everyone showed up on time: Omar, Dallas, Sway, and Angelique were more than ready to get it in. They'd been patiently waiting and Tyce was thoroughly impressed with everyone's poise. He went over the plan for the first job in detail making sure the whole team was on the same page. There was an intense feeling in the dusty air of the warehouse. When Tyce was satisfied each person knew their jobs inside and out they divided into two teams and left the warehouse in separate cars. Tyce secured all the cars and one van for the hits, he stole license plates from other cars and put them on the vehicles they'd be using over the next few days. Tyce, Angelique, and Sway lead the way, followed by Omar and Dallas. Tyce purposely put Dallas in the car with Omar; he knew his friend was anxious and he had no doubt that Dallas could handle his temper and keep him in line. It was ten o'clock on the dot when they pulled up to the Catholic Church. Tyce swooped the car around to the back of the enormous cathedral looking building. All the lights were off in the parking lot but dim lights glowed from inside. Tyce cautiously scanned the parking lot, searching for any uninvited guests. Right on cue, Dallas and her partner in crime exited their car, walked around to the front of the church, and went in. Dallas looked different wearing a *"Tina Turner"* wig and sporting professor style prescription glasses. Omar had a dark blue baseball cap on coupled with black shades. When they entered; Dallas and Omar split up and checked the back room for any unseen people; next, they moved toward the front of the vast room by the confessional booths. Omar opened the door to the side the priest normally occupies and found him sitting on a small bench taking a late night nap.

"Time to wake up Pope!" Omar nudged him in the ribs with his gun.

The gray haired priest looked like he'd seen a ghost as his drowsy brain registered what was happening. With his red eyes wide with fear he stammered,

"*Wha wha* what's going on, *what do you want*!"

"Don't have a heart attack on me pops...jus' get your ass up and walk slowly to that back room in the corner."

The gun remained snuggled in his rib cage as he obeyed orders and stood up real slow. Omar backed up a bit so his new prisoner could step out the undersized booth. He made sure to grab his Bible before he left the booth; his hands began to shake slightly when he saw Dallas leaning against the door of the other booth holding a silver gun by her thigh. No doubt his legs were shaking as well, but they weren't visible under his huge black robe.

"*In the name of God*, please don't hurt me!
What do you want…we *have no money here!*"
"Keep walking pops. We want the key to the
basement door." Omar told the confused man.
"What key…what door?"

Omar and Dallas steadily ushered him toward the back room, once inside Dallas got real serious,

"Look granddaddy, playin' fuckin' dumb is
gonna get your ass speeding down the highway
to heaven! Come up off the key nigga!" She
put the barrel of her gun in his hairy ear and
glared at him.
He lost his breath for a second before he
answered,
"**Ok, ok, ok**…just stay calm, stay calm."

The elderly priest started to put his hand inside his robe, Omar and Dallas tightened the grip on their guns in reaction to his sudden movement.

"Easy easy…I'm just retrieving my keys from

my pocket." He said holding very still.

"Move *real* slow." Dallas pushed the barrel further into his eardrum.

Their captive put his bony hand inside his robe and fumbled around; he produced a key ring crowded with ancient keys. He pointed to a key that had the letters "B D" scratched into it.

"Was that so hard old timer?" Omar joked, snatching the key ring from him, "Now get your ass in the closet, and kneel down."

The priest did exactly as he was told walking inside the coat closet and getting down on his knees like he was saying his bedtime prayers. Omar put the gun to the back of his head as Dallas searched him for a cell phone; not finding one, she pulled out duct tape and some rope from her backpack. She quickly tied his wrist to his ankles and playfully kissed him on the top of his balding head. Omar moved the gun from the back of his head, turned off the light in the closet, closed, and locked the door. Omar put his gun away; he grabbed a walkie-talkie from his back pocket and signaled Tyce,

"We got it."

"Good, open the back door…we ready." Tyce signaled back.

Moments later, Dallas and Omar appeared at the back door to the church and let Tyce and Sway in.

Angelique remained in the car; she drove gradually to the corner intersection and parked, posting look out. Tyce unlocked the basement door and the three men quickly made their way down the old dusty stairs. Dallas stayed upstairs in the church; she locked the gigantic front doors from the inside and stood by the window spotting Angelique outside. Angelique met her gaze and gave the thumbs up sign silently telling her everything was cool; they exchanged flashy smiles and went back to focusing on their jobs.

Tyce approached one of the dozens of storage rooms in the basement. It was an old room with a thick metal door. This church was over a hundred years old and whoever built this room built it to last. Through Tyce's relationship with Simone not to mention the twenty five thousand in cash he paid her the day he and Angelique dropped by, he'd found out that this is where Diego Alverez hid most of his money and the bulk of his product. Diego chose this incredibly low-key spot because in the constitution there was a separation between church and state. The feds would have to jump through a few hoops before they could organize a raid on this place and by that time, he'd know what was up and move the shit. He'd been hiding his shit here for years, the old heads who ran the church didn't mind; especially since Diego's generous donations kept this place open. They didn't even have a key to the storage room.

Tyce looked at Sway, "Do ya thing boy!" Sway dropped his heavy ass duffle bag in front of the door and examined the locks and hinges carefully. He studied the construction and determined where the weak points were located. This was his specialty in the military...they'd basically trained him how to bypass alarms and get into places that regular people couldn't. He was a member of an elite team in the marines a lot of the shit his unit did was off the record and classified; which made him perfect for this type of shit. Sway put on a pair of black welding glasses and broke out a blowtorch. He hit a switch on the handle while flicking the tip and a bright blue light lit up the dark room. Omar and Tyce stepped back to avoid the flying sparks as Sway began to burn through the thick hinges. Tyce was cool as a fan on high while Sway worked on the door. He pulled out a fresh pack of *"skittles"* and poured himself a handful; he passed the bag to Omar who did the same. The two friends snacked in silence waiting patiently for Sway to finish. The last of the four hinges hit the ground and Sway turned his attention to the locks. He sprayed some sort of chemical inside.

"What's that shit Sway?" Tyce asked while

smacking his lips on the juicy "*skittles.*"
"It freezes the locking mechanisms, once it
freezes it's easy to break the device inside."
Sway schooled. "It makes that shit as cold as a
penguins balls!"
Sway grabbed a long metal tool from his bag of
goodies and forced it into the locks one by one. He
yanked the tool; lunging back with his body
weight. Once the third lock was broke, he finally
pulled out a battering ram.

"Help me out Tyce."
Tyce assisted Sway by grabbing two of the four
handles on each side of the colossal pipe. Omar
just watched as they muscled the tool into position,
it had to weigh at least a hundred pounds, but the
force needed to break through the door required
two strong men working together.

Tyce lead the count as they got the momentum
going. One...two...threee!"
BLAAAMMMM!!!!
The gigantic solid door crashed open and fell back
like a tree in the rainforest.

"Damn! That shit was heavy as a muthafucka!"
Tyce confessed out of breath.
They all walked inside together to search for what
they'd come for. Tyce flipped the switch on the
dusty wall and a bright light made all three men
squint. The large room had shelves along the walls

stocked neatly with medium sized plastic bins and large size plastic bins on the floor. Tyce grinned as he counted the containers,

"Four big ones and ten little ones, how much you wanna bet Diego put the money in the little ones?" He walked toward the bins on the shelves.

Tyce immediately snatched one of the bins off the shelf and peeled of the lid…inside he saw vacuum sealed bags of money filled to the top. He was right; all ten bins contained 500,000 each, he knew the exact amount because Mr. Alverez had graciously labeled all the bags in black magic marker with the correct dollar amount. Tyce took two folded up gym bags from his backpack and began transferring the money. Sway just stood there in a pleasant shock. He couldn't believe what he was seeing. He eventually snapped out of it when Tyce interrupted,

"Sway! Stop fantasizing about what you gonna buy your wife and help me pack man." Tyce said jokingly.

Sway snatched the second bag and began filling it up with the loot; he tried to stay serious but he just couldn't wipe the huge smile off his face. Sway's lips were getting ashy from smiling so hard, he couldn't believe what he was seeing. Except for his wife in her leather bustier, this was the sexiest thing he'd ever seen. Omar on the other hand was busy taking the lids off the larger bins on the floor. His eyes lit up when he saw countless bags of white powder stuffed in each of the four bins. There was no telling how much product was inside...not without a scale and a whole lotta time.

"Yo, this Diego nigga got work for centuries my nigga!" Omar exclaimed holding up two ivory colored bricks in the air.

"Good for him........we leavin' that shit." Omar stared at the back of Tyce's head because he was busy working with the money. It burned Omar up inside but he extinguished the fire but not before he slipped a brick into his jacket without anyone seeing.

"Let's go!" Tyce said zipping up the bag. Sway was already done with his bag and was repacking his equipment. Tyce helped him with the battle ram and prepared to leave. "Don't get to relaxed fellas...it aint over yet, the getaway is greater than the taking. Let's move before we gotta kill some of Diego's niggas on the prowl." Tyce warned as he took the steps holding both bags on his shoulders, Sway followed carrying his weighty bags while Omar lazily made his way up the steps looking back at the room that was decorated with beautiful white mini pillows of cocaine. Upstairs the ladies were nervously waiting. Although they didn't want anything bad to happen, they were both willing to shoot first and ask questions later if they had to. Dallas heard footsteps and turned her head around seeing Tyce walking briskly toward her.

"How we lookin'?" He asked evenly.

"I kept everything warm." Dallas said with a seductive smile.

Tyce took her by the hand and led her to the back door of the church. Dallas gripped his strong hand allowing herself to be pulled where she would have gladly gone anyway. Pulling his walkie-talkie out he signaled Angelique outside in the car,

"We comin' out baby."

"It's all clear out here, I'm on my way." She smiled making her way to the back of the church to pick her man up after work.

They all stepped out into the night, Sway was staying alert now that they were out in the open. He'd been ambushed before and that shit wasn't fun. Angelique swerved smoothly around the corner and pulled up to the curb; Sway threw his bags in the trunk and took one last look around before getting in the car. Tyce tossed the bags of money in the back seat with Sway and jumped in the passenger side. Angelique didn't waste time socializing; she just put the car in drive and rolled away. She looked in the rearview mirror and noticed Dallas and Omar getting inside the second car. The job was done…now all they had to do was make it to the warehouse.

Exactly 26 minutes later the five of them were back at the warehouse gathered around the table as their leader dumped the two bags of money out all over the table. They all just stared admiringly at the stacks and stacks of hundred dollar bills…neither one of them had seen that much money in one place at one time before. They'd done it; job number one was finished. Five million dollars in less than 20 minutes!

"Damn that shit looks good." Sway folded his arms across his muscular chest and grinned.

"Yeah that's sexy aint it?" Tyce added lighting a cigarette.

Angelique and Dallas sat down and enjoyed the moment, Dallas pulled out a fresh pack of "*Djarums,*" and the two friends smoked as they relaxed in the cushions of an old worn out couch.

"Good job tonight girl, I'm impressed." Angelique exhaled the flavorful smoke; she crossed her long legs and shot her friend a pleasing look.

"Who you tellin', you didn't miss a beat when you were under that wheel." Dallas complimented back. "Can you believe were about to split *five million dollars*…that's a

million each baby!!!" Dallas stared at
Angelique with a mischievous grin on her face,
"All this money is kinda makin' my coochie
tingle girl." Dallas uncrossed her legs.
Angelique held in a laugh, "Mine too!"
Breathing normally now Angelique continued,
"Yeah I'm still wrapping my head around the
whole night, it all jus' seems like a dream."
Angelique confessed.
Tyce interrupted their little powwow, "Excuse
me ladies, I don't want to break up your social
session but I have a little gift for you two."
He handed each of them a black leather brief case
filled with one million dollars in cold hard stanky
cash. Angelique's brief case was personalized; it
had an 18kt gold heart with her initials engraved in
it dangling from the black handle. Tyce had it
made for her on the sly and wanted to surprise her
with it tonight. Little things like that is what
Angelique loved about Tyce. Although he could
buy her anything she wanted, he took the time to
make her feel special by paying her attention. He
was a master at the little things…at home he filled
her bathroom with her favorite soap and
moisturizer cream, he also scratched her scalp at
night when they watched TV; that shit felt soooo
good. Angelique didn't even bother opening her
case; she just placed it between her legs and

continued to enjoy her cigarette. Dallas on the other hand wasn't so calm; she put the case on her lap and flipped it open. There was so much money inside it looked like a square green stoplight. She stopped short of counting it and just closed the case...she trusted Tyce, and not just any man could have her trust, the only other man to earn that was her father. Dallas Mitchell kept her heart guarded, that's why she never had it broken. Her relationships with men outside of work had been fleeting, this was because they all tried to control her and make her change her ways. Disappointment and frustration soon consumed them when she refused to conform and demanded their unconditional love. Dallas couldn't comprehend why she couldn't find a man that loved her for who she was...a sexy, smart, courageous, sensual, independent young woman who would fight and die for her man and the love they built together. Tyce saw something good in her; the night she met him in the hotel she'd felt so respected. Never had she gotten paid to just sit there and listen to a man's ideas and plans. He explained to her that he saw great potential in her and wanted to help turn her life in a new direction. He was interested in her future plans and goals, he said if she would trust him, this would be her last night escorting...and it was. Dallas was starting to get a little too emotional for her standards, a twinge of envy and loneliness was inching up her spine, and she didn't like it. After a night like this envy and loneliness was the last thing she expected to feel, but what good is good news if you have no one to tell?

"Well ladies and gentlemen the night is still young and I got things to do! I can't be sittin' her all night with all you rich folks." Dallas stood up adjusting her jeans.

"Where you going girl?" Angelique looked up at her.

"First I'ma stash this loot, then I'm gonna burn off some of this energy I got bubbling up inside me; I feel like I jus' had two cans of *"Crunk Juice"*! Dallas did a little dance as she spoke.

"Ha Ha Ha Dallas you're crazy girl." Angelique laughed.

Dallas walked up to Tyce and stopped in front of his chest. She pulled another cigarette from the pack, "Will you light me up please?"

Tyce smiled at her as he granted her request. He liked Dallas, there was obviously an attraction between them, shit they both wanted to fuck each other's brains out that night at the hotel but chose to let business override their lust for one another. Angelique didn't know how the two of them met and Dallas wasn't planning on spilling the beans…after all…nothing happened. But Tyce could tell that Ms. Mitchell wanted something more.

Tyce made direct eye contact as he lit her cigarette, "Be careful Dallas."
She took a drag and licked her full lips as she held the smoke in. Looking up at Tyce, she turned her head slightly to the left so she wouldn't blow smoke in his face but kept her eyes locked with his.

She exhaled, "I will, and you make sure you do as well."
Dallas sashayed toward the door swinging her brief case playfully back and forth. Once she was alone outside, she tossed her lit cigarette on the ground and sighed to herself looking up at the stars. She walked slowly to her car, got in and drove off into the night…heading to an empty house. Back inside the rest of the fab five was getting ready to leave also. The money was already divided up and everybody was still buzzing from the night's event…everyone *except* Omar. He hadn't said a word since they got there but his mood seemed casual. He had received his brief case before anybody else; Tyce made sure to take care of his boy first. Omar gave Tyce a manly hug and punched him lightly in the stomach when he gave it to him.

"Now that's what I'm talkin' 'bout my nigga."
Was all he said.

Sway on the other hand was in heaven; he called Renae as soon as he got back to let her know he was on his way home. He didn't tell her what he was doing that night-the less she knew the better. Sway understood that no amount of money could replace him when it came to his family but this was America and love don't pay the bills. You can't send your love in an envelope and pay your mortgage. So he took a calculated risk for the benefit of his family; all he had to do was concentrate on his job and be ready for any surprises. If he could survive five years in the military; then he could definitely make it through this shit. He couldn't wait to get home and show Renae his brief case that was filled with their bright green financial future.

"I wanna thank you Tyce. I mean you don't even **know** how much this money will help me and my family. I was *drowning* in debt the **fuckin' bill collectors** were breathing down my…….." Tyce waived him off.

"Naw Sway…thank you!"*I couldn't have done this shit without you*. I know how much this million means to you and yours. But don't forget, we got some more work to do baby, million won't get you far these days." Tyce nodded at his long time friend.

"Bet!...I'm all in baby." Sway grabbed his keys and gave Tyce a huge bear hug nearly suffocating him.

"*Aight aight aight*, put me down man, save that shit for your wife!"

He released his grip around Tyce's waist and walked over to Angelique who was still sitting down; he stooped his tall frame over and gave her a hug too. She patted his back and lightly kissed his cheek.

"I'll see you later marine." She teased.

Sway was the second to leave; he actually jogged out the room shouting bye over his shoulder. When he stepped outside; he looked at his used 1996 Ford Explorer and grinned widely,

"Hell yeah, no more "*Ford's*" for me baby!" He shouted.

Omar, Tyce, and Angelique started to make their exits as well. Tyce walked across the large room and turned off the beaming overhead lights. The moon illuminated the space and allowed them to see each other faintly. The darkness hid the look on Omar's face but Angelique who had been observing him all night wasn't blind. She could sense something was up with him and the silent alarm in her head was going off big time!

"Let's go." Tyce walked to the door and held it

open.

They all left the building. Angelique rode with Tyce in his rental car while Omar drove his *"Escalade."* The cars they used in the heist were abandoned and burnt to a crisp by now along with all the disguises. The *"Escalade"* and the *"Dodge Charger"* rode off slowly at first stopping at the street entrance. Omar turned left while Tyce made a right turn. Deep in thought; Angelique just stared out the window, she reached for Tyce's hand and held it tight,

"Thank you for my gift." She said quietly.

"You're welcome." He whispered back as he merged onto the highway.

Ten minutes later, the black *"Escalade"* pulled up to the back of the church again. Moments later a black *"Bentley"* coupe crept around the corner and parked. Omar got out and leaned against the door. The black tinted window of the *"Bentley"* rolled half way down and a hand motioned for him to come over. As he approached the vehicle, the door swung open gently and Omar climbed in. Music from *"Miles Davis"* was flowing softly from the speakers as he shut the door and made himself comfortable in the back seat.

"How you doin' young blood?" Biz asked easily from the passenger side.

"I'm good. Who the fuck is this?" Omar faced

the beautiful woman sitting next to him.
"Excuse my manners...this is Simone; Simone
this is Omar. Don't sweat it...anybody with me
you know you can trust." Biz assured.
"I aint sweatin' it, I jus' thought it would be
you and Bruce, I wasn't expecting a third
wheel."
"I'm hardly a third wheel baby, more like a
spare tire, when the other one goes flat...I keep
shit rollin'." Simone leaned into Omar. He
could smell her scent as her sexy fumes filled
the cabin. "If it wasn't for me you
wouldn't be a rich nigga tonight." She
schooled.
Biz cut in, "Like I said, don't sweat her. Now,
did the church answer our prayers tonight?"
Biz angled himself to look directly at Omar.
Omar reached inside his jacket and showed Biz the
little present he stole.
"There's about two hundred or so more in the
basement."
Biz took the white brick from Omar and stuck his
pocketknife in the middle of it. A mini pile of
cocaine sat on the tip of the knife, he carefully
moved it toward Simone as she extended her head
meeting him halfway. She pulled her hair back as
she leaned in and snorted the soft powder.
She closed her eyes as she felt the sugary

substance drip down the back of her throat,
"That's most definitely Diego's shit." She
sighed.
"Good; Bruce, go with Omar inside and load
that shit up. I'll send somebody with the van in
20 minutes to pick it up. You did good my
nigga...I guess you ready to go solo after all."
Biz turned around and faced the front again.
"Yeah nigga I'm ready to go solo but I'm also
ready to get paid...where's my money?"
Simone reached between her ankles and
handed him a leather bag, "There's half a mill
in there...you get the rest when we weigh all
the product." She stared at him flatly.
"And like I promised you young blood...you
scratch my back...I'll scratch yours." Biz lit a
long cigar.
Omar took the money from Simone, "Come on
nigga lets hurry up and load this shit." He told
Bruce waving his hand.
Bruce scowled as he got out the driver's side, he
never liked Omar, he thought he was a hot head;
he would have gladly killed him and left his body
in the basement but his boss wouldn't allow him to
touch his scurvy ass. As Omar walked in the
building with Bruce, Biz drove up beside them
with Simone in the passenger seat this time, she
was taking another sample up her nose as Biz

spoke to him,

"I'll call you tomorrow young blood…good job tonight."

"What time?" Omar asked.

Simone answered as she wiped her nose,

"When your phone rings."

The *"Bentley"* sped from the parking lot as the smooth horn of *"Miles Davis"* escaped from the open windows.

Just Me And U

Tyce pulled the car into the garage; he let out a tired sigh as he put the car in park.

"Long day?" Angelique twirled her hair with her finger.

"Long month." Tyce answered opening the door.

He grabbed the briefcases out the back and headed for the door to the house. Angelique followed him inside, made her way to the kitchen, and took a seat at the table. Tyce joined her leaning up against the counter. He looked handsomely fine as he stood there wearing black cargo pants and a black sleeveless shirt. His face had a light shadow from not shaving for a few days and his lips were moist with a fresh coat of *"Chapstick."* His deep brown eyes were staring a hole in her…after what seemed like an eternity, he asked a question out the blue,

"Do you trust me?" He continued to stare at her.

"Yes." Angelique answered instantly.

Tyce took a briefcase in one hand and grabbed her hand with the other; he walked down the lengthy hallway heading straight to his bedroom.

Angelique offered no resistance as she followed his lead. The two of them stood at the foot of the giant bed in silence. Tyce opened the brief case, dumped the money all over the bedspread, and smiled.

"Don't move, I'll be right back."
He left the room in a hurry and came back with a butcher knife and a blindfold. Angelique raised her left eyebrow with kinky curiosity and smiled seductively at him. The lights were off but she could see him clearly. He slowly approached and kissed her tenderly on her eyelids. He kissed her behind the ears and made little circles with the tip of his tongue along her neck. Angelique let out a quiet moan as she felt the heat of his mouth on her skin. Her neck was tingling and the sensation was traveling swiftly south...it finally reached its destination, landing right on top of her pulsating clit. Tyce backed away from her and smiled sexily. He was still holding both his mystery tools but laid the knife on the edge of the bed. He positioned himself behind her and put the blind fold over her eyes. Angelique bit down on her bottom lip with excitement. Tyce's hands brushed her hair aside and he tongue kissed the back of her neck. Angelique could smell him, she could smell his masculine scent, and she could smell how much he wanted her at that moment. If you could put

passion, the heat from the sun, honey butter, wild flowers and sweet sweat in a bottle; that might be close to what Tyce smelled like. That sexy ass scent wafted pass her nostrils as he moved around to the front of her body and grabbed the knife.

"Don't worry, you can take a stack and buy another outfit." He whispered in her ear.

Angelique was a little confused with that comment but when Tyce grabbed her by the shirt and began to slash it down the middle...she got the message. He cut her shirt down the middle and up the back letting it fall in two separate pieces to the floor. With her sight taken away, she couldn't tell what he would do next; all she could feel was the cool blade of the knife as it glided across her hot skin. Tyce took his time as he worked. He angled the blade inside the button of her jeans and sliced it off. He then let the sharp edge slide down her leg cutting the denim as he went lower and lower. The action was repeated on her other leg, when he was finally finished her extra tight jeans just fell away from her thighs. Tyce paused to remove her socks then carefully slid the knife up her stomach and chopped right through the middle of her satin bra. Her breasts exploded smoothly out of the bra as that piece of clothing cascaded to the plush carpet. He never said a word as he turned his attention to the last thing in his way. Angelique was breathing heavy as she tried to contain her volcanic passion. This shit was turning her on! Maybe it was the element of danger or the surprise of the cold sharp blade on her warm body but she had never experienced foreplay like this before! Tyce ever so carefully inserted the knife inside her panties. He turned the blade outward so he wouldn't hurt her and poked the tip of the knife through the thin pink fabric. Then he strained the edge of the knife against the sides of her pretty panties and severed the stitching on both sides. He kneeled down like a dog, grabbed the flapping fabric with his teeth, and pulled the panties away from her saturated pussy.

Angelique stood there completely naked, blind folded and in heat! She resisted the urge to snatch off the blind fold and just jump on his ass, he was making her wait on purpose, and that drove her absolutely crazy in a good way! Tyce finally removed the blind fold from her eyes and to her surprise...he was standing in front of her entirely naked. She looked him up and down real slow; his body looked like it was sculpted out of caramel. Tyce didn't have a body builder's physique but what he did have fit him perfectly! His arms were muscular and toned; they were the kind of arms a woman could feel secure in. His chest was the sexiest pillow she'd ever seen, absent of any hair, she couldn't wait to lay her head on it and dream about never waking up. Angelique lowered her stare and silently counted the ripples on his sexy stomach: one, two, three, four, five…and six. Before she could really analyze his hardening man hood, he suddenly pushed her on the bed. Her body fell back and landed on a one million dollar mattress.

"Now that's a view." Tyce complimented looking down at her.

Angelique stuck her foot out and played footsie with his dick. His tool was longer than her foot…and she wore a size nine!

"He likes me." She said referring to his throbbing dick.

"He's not the only one." He lowered himself onto her.

His warm body felt good on top of hers. She wrapped her long legs around his thick waist and gripped his broad shoulders. Her hungry mouth was craving his tongue as she grabbed the back of his head; pulling him to her waiting lips. They kissed rapidly…switching positions from side to side and bobbing their heads up and down like they were nodding yes to each other. Low moans and long sighs echoed through the room as the sex starved lovers finally feasted on each other. Weeks and weeks of strong sexual tension between them finally came to a breaking point. Tyce and

Angelique could no longer keep their private parts...*private*.

Angelique reached for his dick as Tyce lightly bit her neck. She guided him inside her wet pussy and they looked into each other's eyes as they both felt the indescribable feeling you get when you make love to your soul mate for the very first time. Tyce kept his hips motionless; her pussy felt so good movement wasn't necessary at first. As his dick grew larger and snuggled against her creamy walls he couldn't resist the urge to explore her deeper. His hips shifted into first gear as he began to stroke her smoothly; his ass muscles flexed when he skipped second gear and grinded into her in third. His toes dug into the bed for support as he slid into fourth gear. Tyce paid attention to her reactions and based on what Angelique was giving back he decided to work her over in fifth. Angelique gasped in passion; her hands gripped his ass tightly as she helped him fuck her. Her heels where resting on the back of his thighs at first but as the pace quickened she spread her legs into a wide V and took his dick like a pro. Tyce took advantage of the open access and started working his dick in an unhurried grinding motion. Angelique liked it deep, and she let him know,

"*Oooooo right there baby...get in that shit.*"

She rolled her hips in rhythm with his.

"Sssssss…yessss…DAMN you feel good baby.
Tyce uttered cupping her left breast in his
hand.
"*Ummmpph hmmmph ummph* yeah."
Angelique muttered with her eyes closed.
Their bodies were damp with sweat; Angelique's
normally straight hair was beginning to curl up at
the edges. Tyce's heart was beating fast as he
continued to dig in her deep dripping pussy.
Angelique decided to give him a break,
    "Lay down baby, let me take over."
Tyce didn't need to be told twice, besides his
favorite position was looking up at a beautiful
woman while she rode him. He rolled over on his
back and waited for his lady to get on top.
Angelique stood to her feet and turned around
showing him her magnificent backyard. Hundred
dollar bills were stuck to her ass cheeks and back
as she lowered herself onto his erect dick. She sat
on his dick backwards. The view was better than
an oasis in the desert. He watched his dick appear
then disappear in her magic pussy as she bobbed
her hips slowly up and down. Never the one to be
outdone she sped up the pace and dribbled her ass
like a basketball in the hands of a "*NBA*" point
guard. She bounced her ass; up and down-up and
down-up and down, never stopping her rhythm. As
her pussy slid off his dick, she tightened her inner

walls and gripped his shaft causing him to call her
name,

"*Shhhiiitt* Angelique."

"You like that shit baby?" She looked back
over her shoulder at him.

"Hell yeah baby...you got my toes curling
girl." He admitted.

Angelique spun around to face her man, keeping
his dick firmly inside of her, that was definitely a
trick you couldn't do to a man with a small dick
she thought to herself. Angelique arched her back;
sitting straight up. The rocking motion of her hips
was making the tip of Tyce's dick tingle. He put
his hand around her neck and choked her making it
a bit hard for her to breath. She loved this kinky
erotic shit...not too many men could go one on
one with her but Tyce was definitely her equal
between the sheets. The harder he squeezed the
closer she got to having an orgasm. He paid close
attention to Angelique's reaction to his tight grip;
the last thing he wanted to do was injure her. But
she seemed to love it; the more he squeezed, the
faster she moved. Angelique laid her head back
and let Tyce choke her harder, she let out a
breathless scream as she climaxed for the first time
in months! Tyce released his hold on her throat
and sat up; he kissed her breast softly while he
held her shaking body close to his. Her body was

momentarily paralyzed but she managed to speak
softly,

"Thank you baby." She said licking her dry
lips. "Now it's your turn."

She lifted her body up and positioned her head
directly above his big ass dick. She sized up her
opponent as she prepared to finish him off.
Angelique clutched his dick in her hand and
placed all of him in her moist mouth. She swirled
her tongue around his dick and hummed slowly
while she sucked him again and again. Tyce laid
back and watched her in amazement; Angelique
sucked his dick like no other woman had
before…it wasn't her skills that was different…it
was the fact that she did it like there was nothing
else she'd rather do. She made love to his dick
with her mouth. It felt so good that when he
exploded in her mouth, it was the most powerful
yet the most comfortable orgasm he'd ever
experienced. He balled his fist up and just enjoyed
the roller coaster ride she was sending him on.
Angelique didn't even flinch as she swallowed
ever drop of her man's cum,

"You taste like sweet milk." She said licking
her lips again after he was done.

"You are amazing." Tyce shook his head.

"Thank you Mr. Adkins…I aim to please. You
sir…are the **BOMB**! You know you're mine

now right?" She said sitting on his chest.
"Jus' try and get rid of me and see what
happens." He gently repositioned her so that
they could stretch out.

The exhausted couple just laid there in silence;
Angelique rested her head on Tyce's smooth chest,
there was a huge grin on her face that she
hid…what she didn't know was that she wasn't the
only one smiling.

Where My Dogs At?

Bruce walked into the empty hotel room and looked around. Everything seemed to be in place at first until he noticed a big blood stain on the carpet. He leaned over and looked a little harder at the deep red circle; it was then that he heard the sound of water running. Bruce reached for his gun and walked slowly toward the sound coming from the bathroom. He cautiously opened the door and seen the two hired guns from Detroit taking a shower together......**DEAD**!

He laughed to himself, "Look at these fools... Big bad niggas from back east. Yeah right." He pulled his cell phone out and dialed Biz,

"What's the word Bruce? Where you at?" Biz asked anxiously.

"Yeah I'm here boss and ummmm...they dead."

Bruce stared at the phone as it went silent; Biz hung the phone up in disgust when he heard the news. Bruce didn't take it personal though, he'd gotten used to Biz by now and knew that his boss was getting R E A L frustrated with this shit. Although he couldn't stand Tyce, he had to admit…he wasn't a punk. Before he left he took one last look at the room, he saw something shining on the dresser. He moved closer and saw TJ's platinum chain curled up like a snake. He smiled as he took it and put it on,

"Shit…Biz aint payin' that much." He said out loud.

Bruce closed the door and jogged to his car; he never touched anything in the crime scene room, he even kept the shower running, washing away the rotting fluids from their decaying bodies.

Dinner Time

Filet mignon, crab legs, lobster tails, roasted asparagus, Caesar salads, and creamy mashed potatoes. Sway and Ranae were enjoying the good life. It had been ages since they'd been out to dinner let alone a dinner like this. Sway had to endure a thousand and one questions from his wife about his mystery job and their newfound wealth. He assured her that everything was fine and she shouldn't worry, but of course, just like all women...*she worried*. Ranae was a good woman; she was the kind of woman who was made for marriage. She had old school values and believed in God. The number one priority in her life was her family. She knew she hadn't married a saint but Sway was a good man to her and a wonderful father to their kids. Her mind told her what he was up to wasn't exactly legal but her heart told her to trust him. Ranae knew that a man is gonna be a man...and Sway was definitely a man. She had to admit-it was nice **not** to have to worry about money anymore, but inside, she was a little scared. When she was alone, she asked God to watch over her husband and continue to bless their family.

Sway relaxed in his high backed dining chair as the young waiter brought the expensive check. Sway pulled out two crispy hundred-dollar bills and slipped them in the black leather folder. Everyone in the restaurant was glancing and smiling at them. They looked good together, both of them sporting a new financial glow. Ranae wore a black mini dress, a maroon blouse coupled with a charcoal colored cashmere shawl; her hair was pulled up in a French roll with two ringlets spiraling down each side outlining her pretty face. She got her make-up done at a spa in *"Beverly Hills"* and the shoes she wore cost more than their mortgage payment. Sway was equally dapper in a grey suit that even *"Steve Harvey"* would ask to borrow. They held hands lovingly as they left the overpriced restaurant and walked outside...the valet took the ticket stub from Sway and dashed off to retrieve the couple's car. Ranae decided to thank her man for an extraordinary date; standing on her tiptoes, she kissed Sway softly on his lips. While they were publicly displaying their affection, a midnight blue *"Denali"* pulled up. The valet driver got out and opened the passenger side door for Ranae to get in. As he closed her door gently, Sway slapped a crispy 20 dollar bill in his hand and patted him on the back,

"Thanks for not scratching it homie." He

walked over and stepped up into the luxury cockpit.

Tonight, they would take the long way home, he wasn't really in a rush to stop driving his brand new ride.

Eyes On The Prize

A few days later Tyce returned to the warehouse to hide his money. He told no one where he kept his stash but recently he debated with himself about whether or not to share the secret location with Angelique...just in case something was to happen to him. Angelique had shown him that he could trust her; after all, he wouldn't be alive if it wasn't for her looking out for him. Years earlier he had a carpenter friend build a small storage room behind a wall in the back of the warehouse. The room was not visible unless you knew where to look and he had the only key. Inside there was a nice size fire proof safe and a custom built closet that housed his numerous guns. Tyce walked to a corner in the back of the warehouse and stepped on a spot located on the floor. A wall slid quietly back revealing a steel door; placing the key in the titanium dead bolt he unlocked his personal vault and stepped in. He immediately went to the safe and opened it; today was a good day to make a deposit; with the new million added to the money he already had, his safe contained approximately

2.6 million dollars.

For some men that would be enough to retire but for him it only served as motivation to keep stacking. Tyce had a severe allergy to being broke, it made him sick—, and he would do anything it took to remain healthy and wealthy. After putting the money in the safe he quickly left the room, locked the door and hit the floor button to slip the false wall back into place. As he walked outside to leave he thought about Omar. He hadn't heard from him since the other night. Once he was rolling down the city streets, he pulled out his cell phone to see what his friend was up to.

Omar answered on the first ring, "Wasup T, I was jus' thinkin' 'bout you?"

"Yeah, I was jus' seeing wasup on your end. You alright?" Tyce asked as he made a left and merged onto the 101 freeway.

"Hell yeah my nigga I'm straight. Shit since the other night a nigga been real busy you know?" He bragged.

"I can dig it…but you know we aint done yet…we got some more paper to get. We need to all be ready for job number two 'cuz it pops off tomorrow night." Tyce reminded him.

"Shit T, you know I'm ready, you aint even gotta go there with me."

Nodding his head Tyce spoke, "That's what

I'm counting on, I'ma hit you tomorrow, be easy."

"Yeah yeah…I got you, I'll see you tomorrow, peace." Omar ended the brief conversation.

Tomorrow night's events unfolded in Tyce's mind as he continued to roll down the blocks of LA. Out of habit, he kept looking for Lil' Flash on the familiar corners but reality set in when the thoughts of his death came rushing at him like a running back. He missed his friend and that was a very unfamiliar feeling for him.

Work Smarter Not Harder

Things were going well for Biz; with the dope he stole from his rival Diego he was making a killing on the streets. Business was booming but he just had two little problems that irritated the shit out of him; *fucking* Tyce and that *bitch* Angelique! Lincoln and TJ proved to be useless…he knew they took Tyce way too lightly and they paid for it with their miserable lives. If he could, he would bring them back to life just to kill them again!

His plan B was working according to schedule. Biz had Omar under his thumb and because of him; he knew every move Tyce made. He still had no clue where Tyce lived though…Omar wouldn't give up that information. He suspected it was because he was greedy and didn't want Tyce to die before he got paid off the last two hits. Biz could respect that although he'd never tell Omar that; he himself would have done the exact same thing if he were in his shoes. A man's gotta put paper over problems if he wants to be rich, but the fact is that he wasn't in Omar's shoes, he didn't give a fuck about Omar. He just used him to regain the dope he'd lost in the first place, now he had no more use for him or Tyce. With that in mind, he picked up the phone on his office desk and dialed a number he vowed never to call.

"Let's see if this pretty bastard can deal with this shit!" He spat out loud as the phone rang in his ear.

"*Bueno.*" A heavily accented voice answered.

"Buenos Dias...how you doin' these days?" Biz asked leaning back in his chair.

"*Hmmm, if thes is the man who I'm theenking it is; I am wundering to myself...why the fuck is he callin' me?*" The voice responded irritatingly.

"This *is* who you think it is...*why* am I calling you ask...now that's the *five million dollar* question."

#2

The room was packed wall to wall with people ready to lose their hard-earned money. I was caught off guard by the crowd and I really didn't expect that many people to be jammed into the basement of a business that operated as cleaners by day and a mini casino at night. There must have been over two hundred people there...at one o'clock in the morning on a regular Tuesday night. My whole team was there, waiting and ready to get it on. I was pleased to see so many people in attendance, more people meant more money; we would just have to wait until the mob thinned out. I instructed the crew to blend in, I told them we wouldn't move until later; there was just too many people there for the five of us to control. So we all fanned out; even though shit wouldn't jump off now, there was still important work to do. I paid strict attention to the money and the men I saw handling it. The gambling dudgeon consisted of eight gaming tables. The owners set up roulette, black jack, poker, and craps tables; there were no noisy slot machines only big dollar tables with 20 to five hundred dollar minimum betting limits. The small bar in the corner was busy filling the glasses of the gamblers with free alcohol as they tried to beat the house. I ordered myself a rum and coke as I watched the pit boss at the craps table discretely take a thick canvass bag to the count room in the back. Two black security guards that looked like they were mixed with grizzly bear stood on either side of the door. I watched as bag after bag made its way to the count room. Angelique and Dallas were at the roulette table, Sway was on a roll at the black jack table, and Omar was stationed at the craps table. The staff was small but well organized: three security guards, eight dealers, two pit bosses, three bartenders, and one owner who floated from table to table checking on things. He was an older mature white gentleman who wore a plain yet expensive blue suit. He could have fit in at any Wall Street board meeting but his business was gambling and I could see why. I estimated the cash on hand to be well over six million. The Club House didn't take in six million a night but the owner only removed the cash once a month so the count room had 30 days worth of profits on hand tonight.

Two long hours later, I walked over to Omar at the black jack table and told him to get the gear and move the van closer to the exit 'cuz it was almost time. The crowd had reduced drastically as

the three o'clock hour approached. Now there
were only about twelve die hard gamblers pressing
their luck. Omar walked up the stairs out the
basement to get the van that parked around the
corner. There were no signs outside that a
gambling spot was operating down stairs; all the
guest entered and exited through the back door of
the cleaners and only one man was in charge of
searching each person and directing them to the
basement. Angelique and Dallas were at the bar
with a couple of dudes but they spotted Omar
leaving and dismissed the interested men politely.
They made their way to the ladies room to powder
their nose and get the guns Omar was going to slip
them through the tiny basement window. Omar
grabbed the guns from the back of the van and
slipped around the back of the building. He crept
in the shadows of the alley staying close to the
wall. A bright light shined through a mini window
close to the ground. Kneeling down he tapped
lightly on the glass to see if Angelique and Dallas
were in position. The window lifted up little by
little as a manicured hand gripped the edge and
began pushing. Omar took the *Mack* 11 and three
black *Desert Eagle* 9 millimeters out the duffle
bag and quickly placed them in the open palm of
Angelique.

"Give me two minutes exactly to drop the door

man." Omar whispered loudly.

"Okay, we gonna wait exactly one hundred and twenty seconds before we jump the shit off." Angelique said taking the last of the tools from Omar.

The husky guard was nursing a cigarette with his back to the parking lot when Omar walked up.

"Hey man can I get another cigarette off you?" Omar asked nicely.

"Yeah sure…honestly you just saved me five minutes off my life, I need to kick this habit you know?"

The security guard chuckled as he looked down reaching inside his black leather jacket to retrieve the pack of *"Marlboro's;"* Omar suddenly pulled out a tazer gun and plugged the dude in the neck, surprising him. His overweight body straightened up instantly as the stinging volts hit him. His body started to quiver and his eyes bulged as he tried to grab at Omar's hands. Omar finished the job by punching the dude squarely in his jaw, knocking him out completely. He zip tied his hands behind his back and drug him down the stairs leading to the basement by his ankles, his unconscious head bouncing off each step. Omar paused at the bottom, quietly waiting for everyone else to get into position. Standing outside the door of the ladies bathroom, Sway and Tyce eyed each other.

"You ready for this?" Tyce asked pulling the sleeves of his tan colored thermo shirt up around his thick forearms.

"Yep." Sway replied non nervously.

The door to the bathroom opened up; Dallas passed Sway a huge grayish silver gun, while Angelique placed Tyce's piece in his open hand. She took a brief moment to stare into his eyes. Without saying it, she told him she was ready and reminded him to be careful. He smiled and gave her a reassuring wink, topping it off with a gentle kiss on the lips. Dallas tried not to notice the kiss; she pretended to inspect her own gun instead, when she was finished she hid it in her purse.

"Don't worry," Tyce said as he slid the chamber of his gun quickly back and forth. The guns were tucked under the front of their long shirts as both men made their way across the almost empty room. Spotting Omar's shiny baldhead in the darkness of the hallway entrance, Tyce took a deep breath and started the party. Sway and Tyce walked swiftly up to the two men guarding the count room and sprayed mace directly into their faces. Instead of reaching for their guns, the two men instinctively started to rub and cover their stinging eyes. Sway took his man down with a devastating right hook; his giant head collided with the wall and he fell to the ground with a loud

thud. At the same time Tyce stiff kicked the man
that outweighed him by a hundred pounds in his
kneecap, breaking his leg. The giant of a man
blindly screamed in agony as he teetered on his
good leg, finally losing his balance and collapsing
to the floor. Tyce spun around and faced the small
crowd in the room pulling the gun from his waist
and pointing it at the frantic gamblers. Everything
happened fast as the team jumped into action.

Omar rushed into the room-stopping to clothesline
a woman attempting to dash up the stairs to escape
the deadly situation. The force of the unexpected
blow made her slam into the ground like a high
jumper landing without a mat. She laid there
breathless with one shoe on; the other shoe was
laying on its side five feet away from her. Anyone
that wanted to leave would have to go through
him. With two guns in his hands, he covered the
12 customers left in the room.

   "GET THA FUCK DOWN!!!" He shouted
   glaring at the wide-eyed patrons.

Everyone hit the deck like an airplane was flying
too low, covering their heads with trembling
hands. Sway finished searching the guards;
relieving them of their weapons and pinning them
down at gunpoint. Joining the festivities,
Angelique and Dallas handled the dealers and
bartenders. They rounded them up like cattle;

making them pile on the floor behind the bar, one on top of the other.

"Don't **fuck** with me ladies and

gentlemen…not tonight."

Angelique warned as she made the last person lay on top of the stack that was already nine people high. Tyce kept his focus on the slick looking owner of the club and rapidly crossed the room to the corner he was standing in. The man tensed up as Tyce approached. He stood perfectly still; keeping his eyes locked on the hammer in Tyce's steady hand.

"You know what I want…don't make me ask."

Tyce said putting the gun in the middle of his

sweaty over tanned forehead. The middle-aged owner licked his parched lips and started to ask a dumb question but thought better of it.

"Get yo ass over there!" Tyce shoved the man. The man moved slowly toward the direction of the count room door. Tyce shifted his gun from the front his head to the back as he followed him closely. The team had the whole joint on lock down. The Los Angeles SWAT team would be proud. You could hear muffled cries and soft mumbles-everyone was on the ground except the boss.

"Shut the fuck up!" Omar ordered. "It sounds

like a muthafuckin' day care center at nap time

in here!"

Angelique scanned the room to make sure nothing was wrong. Dallas on the other hand was trailing Tyce and the owner to the count room door. Tyce wanted Sway and Dallas to be there when the count room door opened in case there were more armed guards inside. They didn't have to worry about the holice responding to any alarms because this was an illegal gambling spot in the first place. What they did have to worry about was armed and ready guards who heard the commotion and were waiting on the other side of that door. So as the boss man punched in the six-digit code on the panel to open the door; Sway, Tyce, and Dallas all prepared to shoot first and ask questions later, after all, you can't kill money so they had nothing to lose. Sway stood to the side of the door as Tyce stayed behind the nervous owner and made him turn the chrome handle. Tyce went in first, slamming the owner into the door to push it open. Omar, and Angelique paid attention to their hostages but they cautiously eyed the entrance to the count room also. Tyce used the man as a human shield to protect himself, when he entered the room there where white counter tops along the wall and two office desks sitting in the back. The empty leather chairs were facing the door so that the occupants could see who came through the only door in the room. There was an island in the middle of the large-sized room with 11 tan canvass bags loaded on top. Electronic money counting machines were sitting on the counter tops with colorful trays of chips and bowls of rubber bands. Once Tyce and his human shield were inside the room, Sway stepped in military style with his gun drawn and a two handed even level grip on the handle. Dallas posted outside the doorway as a last resort just in case they needed her; she also took over Sway's position and watched the still blinded guards. Angelique jumped on top of the bar to get a good view of everybody; she aimed her gun downwards at the people, moving slowly along the top of the L shaped bar counter. Suddenly she heard the sound of gunshots echoing.

"Blam Blam Blam!!!"

She froze in her tracks and whipped her head around toward the count room. She fought the powerful urge to jump down and run to the doorway, she knew she had to stay and cover the other people in the room. Her eyes widened with fear as she held her breath and tightened the grip on her gun. Omar stayed in place as well; Angelique gave him a look of panic which he did not return…he just stared blankly back at her. Dallas was standing up, taking shallow breaths as she poked her head in and out of the room keeping her body safely behind the wall.

"What the fuck is goin' on! What happened!"

Angelique screamed at Dallas.

Dallas was too busy scoping out the situation to answer her. Inside the room, she saw the owner lying on the floor with blood oozing from his chest and stomach staining his expensive suit jacket. Tyce and Sway were crouched behind the island, she couldn't see anybody else. She made eye contact with Tyce who seemed pissed.

"Stay back...stay back!" Tyce said waiving her off frantically.

"Where the fuck did that short ass nigga come from!" Sway asked in between heavy breaths.

"That lil' nigga jus' popped up like a jack in the box from behind the desk! You stay here...put some heat on that desk...pin that mini muthafucka down, and I'ma creep up on him!" Tyce whispered to Sway as he crawled around to the other side of the island.

They'd been surprised by a trigger happy dude hiding behind one of the office desks. He wasn't much taller than the desk itself so he fit behind it easily. He'd been over anxious and started firing before he even looked; accidently shooting his boss in the process. Now he was hiding behind the desk again, waiting for another clean shot.

"Fuck you black motherfuckers! Look what

you made me do! Fuck you…I didn't kill my
brother motherfuckers…YOU DID! You hear
me…YOU DID!" He shouted hysterically.
The crazed gunman punctuated his statement with
four more blasts to the island counter where Tyce
and Sway were hunkered down. BAP BAP BAP
BAP!!!

"That's enough of this shit!" Sway said leaning
out from behind the safety of the island. Sway shut
him up by pumping round after round into the
dense mahogany desk. The wood splintered into
tiny pieces as the bullets dotted the front side.
Staying low, Tyce crept hurriedly up to the huge
desk as Sway was firing. He wasn't worried about
getting hit with one of Sway's bullets because he
was an excellent shot. Sway was lying on his back
like he was getting ready to do some crunches and
firing his silver gun rapidly. The man was stooped
down with his guns on the sides of his ears to
protect his head. He was completely unaware that
Tyce was standing over the top of him. The
undersized assassins head split open from the
single bullet Tyce put in the top of his dome. His
hands instantly dropped to his sides as his bloody
head rested on his left shoulder.

Careful not to use any names Angelique
frantically asked again,
"D, tell me somethin'…are they ok!"

Dallas finally put Angelique out of her misery,
"Yes, yes girl there fine...there ok now!"
Truth be told; the reason she couldn't respond to
Angelique was that they were both sharing the
same deathly concern. Both women were praying
that nothing happened to the man they had both
grown to love. Angelique felt her stomach relax as
she heard the good news. Sway stood up and
walked over to see the man who'd been wildly
cussing and shooting at them. He sidestepped the
body of the now dead owner on the floor without
looking down at him.
"You got the drop on that fool." He said giving
Tyce a congratulating pound.
"Shit, without your help it wouldn't have been
so easy." Tyce complimented. "But yo...we
need to get the fuck outta here."
They started tossing bags of money out into the
room and snatched the last eight bags up carrying
four each. Omar greedily picked up the three bags
that were on the floor before Dallas could get to
them. Angelique turned and looked down at the
terrified mass of people,
"If I see anybody poke their little heads up, I'll
blow em off like I'm hunting prairie
dogs...comprende?"
They answered her with scared silence as she
hopped down off the bar. The five of them made

their way to the stairs. Tyce had one more important thing to do on his way out. He grabbed the logbook that everyone had to sign before they could get in to gamble. The club kept a record of all the people that attended the underground casino. The owner performed background checks on whoever he was suspicious about. Names, addresses, and phone numbers were all neatly printed in this priceless book.

"Look here, we got the names and addresses of every muthafucka in here! Before you leave tonight, be sure to stop by the count room to see the owner of this fine establishment *and* his short ass brother! If you talk about this shit, you'll end up jus' like them! You won't even make it to the witness stand *or* you'll bury all your fuckin' family members long before the trial begins! Look at it this way people; we took the money you already lost…get over it." Tyce said loud enough for all the customers to hear.

They all ran up the steps and dashed out the back door of the cleaners. The van was parked right outside the door. Tyce ran behind his crew as they hustled to the getaway van. He threw his heavy bags of money in the side door as Omar slid it open. Just like they'd practiced, everybody jumped in and was seated in a split second. Sway and

Omar concentrated on the dim door way just in case someone decided to follow them. Tyce then ran around and jumped in the driver's seat; he hastily put the late model Chevy in gear and sped off down the shadowy alley. The van made a sharp right turn onto the street and merged with oncoming traffic. Tyce looked at Angelique who was sitting in the back seat and winked at her. The robbery seemed like it took an eternity but the whole thing only lasted about five minutes; that was two minutes too long by Tyce's standards.

When the van disappeared around the corner, the headlights of a car parked quietly at the opposite end of the alley came on and drove away slowly.

Snitchin Aint Easy

Omar took a little detour before heading back to his house. He had about a million three in cash in the back seat as he pulled up to the massive northern California mansion. He was anxious to leave the warehouse after the robbery. He collected his wages for the night and left in a hurry giving the excuse that Tasha was waiting on him. Omar stepped up to the large double doors and rang the bell. It took a minute but finally after ringing the bell three times a young pretty woman answered the door. She didn't look a day over 18 and her beauty would rival any Hollywood model or actress. Her eyes showed intelligence and she carried herself like she knew she was attractive.

"Can I help you?" She asked sweetly.

"Yeah baby...I'm here to see Biz."

"Oh ok, come on in." She said stepping to the side to let Omar pass.

His young guide led him up the winding staircase to the back office were Biz was waiting. She walked with him to the smoke tinted glass door and knocked softly. Omar heard Biz say "come in" as he stood there staring at her shiny red lips.

Omar regained his composure and prepared to talk business, with his best friend's enemy.

"Omar, my nigga…what's the word young blood? Have a seat." Biz smiled as he gestured to an empty chair directly in front of him. "I see you got the message from Simone that I wanted to see you, thanks for coming on such short notice being that you had to work tonight and all."

"Yeah she said you had the rest of my money. She also said you had a surprise for me." Omar leaned back in the comfortable chair ignoring that last comment.

Biz reached under his office desk and grabbed a brief case. He slid it across the top of the smooth table. Omar immediately pushed the tabs aside and flipped open the lid. It was neatly packed with stacks of hundreds; he chuckled and quickly shut the case, placing it on his lap.

"That's cigarette ashes compared to what you could make with me. I got big plans for you young blood. I want you to run shit up north." Biz continued, "You get the work from me for 18 a brick and you can sell it for 25 to 27 a key. I already got 30 niggas who rock with me now but I jus' killed my lieutenant 'cuz he started sniffing the shit and getting sloppy. They'll cop from you if I tell them to, I'll introduce you as

my new lieutenant, and you can start makin' money instantly. The northern operation moves a hundred and fifty to two hundred keys a month. At a profit of seven thousand a brick that's about a million dollars every 30 days." Biz paused to let all that math sink in to Omar's head.
Omar's mouth began to water as he calculated how much he could make in a year.

"Shit, hell yeah I'll take that shit over! Aint nobody gonna run that shit better than me! When you want me up there?"

"Patience grasshopper, a million a month doesn't come cheap. You gotta finish paying for it first." Biz schooled.

"What you mean pay for it? I got the money to buy the bricks now!" Omar reasoned patting his brief case, "And if that aint enough I got more in my truck."

"That's outstanding young blood, but that's not what I'm talkin' about. I don't want your money...yet. You gotta prove your loyalty before you can work with me." Biz took his time lighting a cigar.

"Man I been snuffin' niggas out for you for almost ten years...what the fuck you mean loyalty?"

"You got one more nigga to snuff out." Biz blew smoke in the air. Omar could sense his growing anger. "This whole Tyce situation is about the principal." Biz jumped up suddenly from his chair. "That nigga cost me millions of fuckin' dollars! He turned his back on me! He threatened my life! That disloyal muthafucka stole my bitch...a bitch I'd groomed since she was a girl! Biz became more agitated with every word. "That pretty punk spat in my face, and in this game you can't let a muthafucka get away with that shit, you gotta make an example outta that nigga...you gotta take his heart out of chest and squish that shit like a bloody sponge!" He shouted; spit flying from his mouth.

Omar stared at Biz; he'd never seen him so worked up before. He was really tripping over this shit.

"What I gotta do?" Omar asked bluntly.

"I want you to put a bullet straight through his weak ass heart. Then I want you to bring Angelique to me kicking and screaming."

Omar was still staring at his boss when he got curious, "Why don't you kill him yourself?" He leaned forward in the chair.

"Young blood, you think I got this old in the game by getting *my* hands dirty? I play the music that makes these niggas dance. I pull the strings behind the curtains." Biz stated proudly walking around his office desk, "Now can you do that for 12 million dollars a year or should I find someone else?"

Omar rubbed his baldhead and pretended to contemplate the question. There was no way he was going to pass up this opportunity for punk ass Tyce. He'd missed enough money fucking with him in the first place, now he had a chance to bust the dope game wide open and start at the top. If Tyce had to die for that to happen…then, so be it.

"Naw you aint gotta get nobody else. Besides, didn't you try that already? Omar said sarcastically. "Tyce is too smart for bitch ass niggas from out of town."

"That's exactly why I need you to get to him." Biz placed a hand on Omar's shoulder.

"I can get to that nigga anytime I want, you want it done tonight?"

Biz thought about that option in silence as he walked back and forth on the gigantic Oriental rug.

"I don't want him dead yet. Like I said before he owes me. According to you, ya'll have hit two places already. I want you to hit the last spot, kill him, and bring me all of the money." Biz instructed looking directly into Omar's dark eyes.

Omar nodded his head in agreement. He noticed

the wild look in Biz's eyes; it was a lethal mix of hatred, jealousy, and pure evil. Omar didn't hate Tyce, he just wouldn't let him hold him back anymore. Fuck Tyce and his penny pinching no dope policy; that shit was history.

"Consider it done." Omar said.

He stood up to leave when Biz grabbed his attention, "One more thing young blood...don't ever tell me how smart he is again." He said coldly.

All The Single Ladies

Dallas needed to clear her head *and* what better way to do that then to spend a bunch of money. She maneuvered her new 745 *"BMW"* into a parking spot at the *"Beverly Center"* and inspected her makeup in the rearview mirror. She rocked an extra clingy peach sundress; her eye shadow and lip-gloss was a shimmery tan and bronze color that matched the highlights in her dress perfectly. She had to give herself props…she looked *good* today. She hadn't been in her car five minutes before she had to dodge two scrub ass niggas trying to spit game. One dude tried to holla at a red light motioning for her to roll the window down and another one was crossing the street and offered "to make her toes tingle." It was true what they said…money can't buy happiness but she was damn sure gonna let the dollars try and cheer her up today. The mall wasn't as crowded as she thought it would have been. That was just fine with her because it gave her more room to shop. For the first time she was shopping without thinking at all about the price tags. It wasn't like she was broke before but this was a whole new level of wealth she was on now. The view looked spectacular from the top and she planned to stay there. Dallas walked to the food court. She enjoyed the free feeling that wearing no panties under your dress brings as she switched her hips from side to side. She spotted the person she was looking for standing in the corner. They noticed each other and did the "hey girl" wave from across the mall. The two friends made their way toward each other through the hungry crowd.

"I'm sorry I'm so late girl." Dallas apologized opening her arms to give a hug.

"Please girl, I jus' got here my damn self."

"Well then I take that shit back...you got me rushing to get here in shit." Dallas whined playfully.

The ladies ended the hug and stepped back to admire each other's outfits and hairstyles; they exchanged compliments like Christmas gifts as male admirers slowed their pace as they walked by.

"Ok, we didn't come here to chat, let's tear this mall up!" Dallas said excitedly. "Girl I need a serious deep tissue money massage to work this stress out."

"Shit you aint the only one Dallas, but put your cash in your cleavage for second 'cuz mine aint her yet."

"What are you talkin' about girl?" Dallas
looked confused.

"Now you know I don't shop with **my** money!"

"Oh excuse me Miss Simone…I forgot who I
was talkin' to." Dallas laughed. "So who's
donating to the (get what you want foundation)
today?"

Simone looked back toward the exit to see if he
was coming in. She clapped her hands together
when she saw him and dashed off to greet her
generous sponsor. Moments later, she returned to
Dallas and introduced the rich man as Biz. He took
Dallas's small hand politely in his and kissed it
softly.

"It's a pleasure to meet you."

"Thank you…it's a pleasure to meet you as
well." Dallas responded.

Simone rubbed his chest lovingly and leaned her
titties seductively into him. She was telling him
without words that she was ready to go shopping.
He must have heard her loud and clear because
after she did that he gave her a black credit card
from his pants pocket. Simone did a little dance as
she tucked the shiny plastic card in her purse.

"I'll be sure to buy all the sexy things you like
to see me in baby." She teased.

"You can be my top model tonight." Biz flirted
kissing her lightly on the cheek. "Well ladies, I

won't hold you up anymore. Simone, call me when you're done and I'll have Bruce pick you up."

"Ok baby…it should be about three or four hours at least."

"Take your time; I got some things I need to do anyway. It was a pleasure to meet you young lady you two have a good time."

Biz said good-bye and strolled casually out the mall the same way he came in. The two ladies walked through the long hallways of the mall trying to decide where to start spending their money first. Simone was talking a mile a minute about what shoes she wanted or what kind of designer jeans she would get but Dallas's mind was on other things. She was still in shock that the man Simone was seeing was none other than Biz.

She had come face to face with the man that was plotting to murder Tyce and her new friend Angelique! Dallas remembered the conversation she'd had with Simone a while back. That day on the phone, Simone mentioned a woman that came too her house with Tyce. Dallas figured she was talking about Angelique but what concerned her more was the favor that Tyce needed Simone for.

Did Simone know that she was working with Tyce?

Did she know that she and Angelique were good friends and partners in crime?

More importantly, did Biz know and was he using her to get to Tyce and Angelique?

Instantly she lost her appetite for new clothes; all she wanted to do now was escape the mall and get a hold of Tyce to tell him the news. Despite her anxiety she had to remain calm and not arouse Simone's suspicions just in case she was playing her, it was better to let her believe she didn't know anything. Simone stopped talking to herself and switched subjects to include Dallas in the conversation.

"Soooo Miss. Thang, what have you been up to lately? If I didn't know any better I'd say you had a new man." Simone teased.

"Why would you say that?"

"Well shit, I talked to Honey and she said you quit about a month ago. I just assumed it was because you had a new man that didn't approve of your job."

"Naw girl, I quit because I wanted to…I can't do that shit forever."

"Is that right? I jus' thought it was odd that Honey said you quit after your date with Tyce." Simone said turning to look at Dallas.

"There's a whole lot of women that would stop what they're doing in a heartbeat to be with that fine ass nigga!" She said playfully pushing her shoulder.

Dallas chose her words carefully, "Girl I gotta admit...he is fine as hell but it was jus' a date...*jus' a date.*"

They made a right turn into a store and Simone continued her inquiry into Dallas's personal life.

"Have you seen Tyce since then?"

Damn this bitch was being nosey Dallas thought.

"I only asked because *I* haven't got a call from him in months. He used to dip his dick in my pussy at least once a week. He must be real busy or maybe he has a new bitch that's taking care of him nowadays." Simone popped a piece of juicy fruit gum into her mouth and chewed slowly staring at Dallas from across a rack of jeans.

"No I haven't seen him around at all...I can't say that I haven't been looking tho." Dallas lied with a straight face.

"Hmmm maybe he's in a relationshit right now? I bet he's fuckin' that chick he brought to my house...what was her name again?"

Simone tapped the side of her forehead trying to remember.

Dallas camouflaged her surprise and just looked at

Simone with a blank stare.

"Why you so worried about Tyce; it seems like
Biz is taking good care of you. Dallas turned
the tables on her.

"Shit, he better, as much as I *do* and *did* for
him. Trust me I earn every dollar he gives me."
Dallas was tired of playing 20 questions and
decided to leave Simone at the rack of clothes and
shop on the other side to the store. She wanted so
bad to run off and call Tyce but she decided
leaving the mall in a hurry would only lead to
more questions. Three hours and five thousand
dollars later, Dallas finally left the mall. She
trotted to her car, tossed the bags in the passenger
seat, and immediately reached for the cell phone
inside her purse. She backed out of the parking
space and dialed Tyce's number at the same time;
the phone rang four times before he picked up.

"Wasup baby girl?" The sound of his smooth
voice instantly brightened her shady mood.

"Not much jus' leavin' the mall, can you talk?"
She asked as she exited the parking lot and
jumped into traffic.

"Yeah wasup…you ok?" Tyce asked curiously.

"Yeah I'm fine; I jus' need to talk to you…it's
important."

"Where you at?"

"I'm leavin' the *"Beverly Center"* now."

"Ok, meet me at my warehouse in 20 minutes;
    I'm on my way there."
Fifteen minutes later Dallas pulled up to the
warehouse not expecting to see Tyce because she
was a little early but his Jeep was parked outside
already. She got out of her car and walked in. Tyce
was sitting on the old couch and stood up when
she walked toward him. He greeted her with a
warm hug and a hot smile.
    "So what's so important baby girl, somebody
    fuckin' with you?" He unwrapped his arms
    from around her tiny waist and led her over to
    his favorite couch.
They sat down facing each other and Dallas took a
moment to look at him. If she didn't witness the
murderous side of him she never would have
guessed from his handsome face that he was
capable of such bloody actions. Dallas didn't
realize she'd missed him so much until she saw
him again. It had only been two days since the
casino hit but it seemed like two months.
    "No it's nothin' like that, I jus' got finished
    shopping with Simone, and you'll never guess
    who showed up." She raised her perfectly
    arched eyebrows and rolled her neck slightly.
    "Who?" Tyce asked lighting a cigarette.
    "**Biz!**" Dallas slapped his knee to punctuate her
    word.

Tyce leaned back on the couch and looked straight ahead. He took a drag from his cigarette and blew the smoke out lazily.

Before Tyce could comment Dallas interrupted, "She was asking all kinds of fuckin' questions about you, me, and Angelique.
She introduced me to Biz and told me she was seeing him. I didn't tell her *shit* I jus' let her keep talkin'."
"Did anybody follow you here?" Tyce asked; his voice seasoned with concern.
"No, I circled the block four times jus' to be sure."
"Good."
Dallas relaxed a little but continued to talk, "I didn't know she was seeing him Tyce. I haven't seen her in a while. If I had known that I would have nev…….."
He cut her off, "You don't even have say that. I trust you Dallas…I trust you with my life."
Tyce grabbed her hand and squeezed gently.
A long awaited feeling of relief and excitement filled up her insides. Dallas was overwhelmed with joy that transformed to an intense feeling of attraction. Ignoring her mind and listening closely to what her body was yelling; she grabbed Tyce's head with both hands like she was catching a football pass and pulled his face into hers. She felt

his neck tense up from the surprise attack but it slowly loosened up as she began to kiss him passionately. Dallas twirled and flicked her tongue aggressively; her kiss became more intense when she felt Tyce's tongue begin to fight back. For a long moment, they were engaged in a passionate lip lock.

Dallas finally released her grip on Tyce's head and stared at him breathlessly. "I would apologize but I'm not sorry. I meant to do that," Dallas said defiantly.

Tyce stood up and adjusted his jeans keeping his back toward Dallas. "You mind sharing that cigarette?" Dallas asked seductively.

Tyce forgot about the cigarette he was holding and passed it to Dallas. He suddenly felt guilty; his mind was going in two different directions at the same time. He didn't expect for Dallas to come at him like that. His conscience was already eating at him because he actually liked it. Ever since he met Dallas at the hotel, he'd had an intense attraction to her. Up until today, he was able to control it and keep it strictly on a business level. He wasn't blind; he knew Dallas wanted more from him but that was something he just couldn't give her. His feelings for Angelique were growing stronger by the day, he couldn't deny that, but Dallas on the other hand stirred something deep inside of him that he couldn't explain.

Snapping Tyce out his daydream Dallas spoke, "Tyce, I'm not a shy girl, you know that about me...I know you're attracted to me...and I know you love Angelique. I don't want you to get the wrong idea, I value Angelique as a friend, and she's an amazing woman." Her eyes began to mist a little, "I'm not trying to come between you two...I jus' don't know what to do with all this shit inside of me. I think about you all the time, when I stop at red lights I fantasize about fuckin' you, I wonder how you're sleeping at night. This shit is driving me crazy! I'm trying to jus' be your friend but that shit *aint workin'*...Tyce, I love you."

I Aint No Joke

I walked into the showroom of the *"Mercedes Benz"* dealership and looked around slowly. My eyes stared at the luxury automobiles taking in every single detail. After about ten minutes, I finally settled on a black on black S500, that shit was sexy as hell. An overzealous sales man made his way over to me wearing a painted on smile,
"I see you have outstanding taste, I couldn't help but notice you checking out the 500."
"Yeah it's a beautiful car." I walked over to get a closer look with him following close behind.
"We have some great financing options available or maybe you'd be interested in a lease package."
I opened the door and slid into the cockpit,
"Now what makes you think I'd be interested in that?"
The 30 something sales man looked at my outfit and shrugged his round shoulders in an "I don't know motion." I was wearing a camel brown suede jump suit and white T-shirt. I guess to him, my clothes didn't match the car.
"No offense buddy...you just seem more like a

"*Toyota*" man." He offered.

"I bet you're one of the top salesmen here…am I right?" I asked looking up at him.

"Well, I did beat my quota last month and it's only three weeks into this month." He bragged.

"Wow." I nodded.

"Hey, I'm not complaining, if other people around here want to slack then that's just more money for me! So what you step on a few toes, I'll gladly be the bad guy to treat my customers right, you know?"

"I know that's right." I got out the car and faced him, "I'm in sales myself and I hate when I have a weak link on my team." I leaned in closer to him, "If you don't mind me asking, who's the weakest link here?"

The man paused for a second, "Well…let's just say that women should stick to selling "*Avon*" not "*Mercedes Benz's*.""

As he said that, a young woman stepped out of a bathroom and walked by us. He looked over at her, then at me and rolled his eyes.

"That's Jessica, just be glad I'm helping you and not her; she only sold one car this month, she probably was in the bathroom crying about it. Sooo ahhh anyway enough about her, let's discuss the financing options. This baby will run you about 1,200 a month with a down

payment of about 20 percent, if the down
payment is a problem we can stretch it out over
four weeks with half due now and the other
half due in 30 days."

As he continued bumping his gums, my attention
was still on the young lady. She appeared to be in
her early twenties and looked like a schoolteacher
with her hair neatly pulled back in ponytail. She
wore a red pencil skirt and white blouse and
sported an unconfident look in her blue eyes.

"Jessica!" I yelled interrupting the man's
speech.

She snatched her head up from some paperwork
she was focused on with a look of surprise on her
young face. I smiled and motioned for her to come
over.

Jessica quickly walked over, "Yes...can I help
you sir?" She asked shakily.

"Yes you can. I would like your opinion."

"Ok, I'd be happy to assist you, what do you
need my opinion on?" She smiled glancing
nervously at her chauvinistic co-worker.

"Do you like this car?" I put my arm over the
top of the door.

"I love this car; I think it's sexy and sleek."

"What do you think is the best way to buy this
car?" I asked looking at the frustrated
salesman.

"Well you could make payments in a buy or lease program or you could just pay good ole' fashion cash and save yourself tons of money in interest."

"Ok last question…do you think I can afford to pay cash for this car?"

Jessica smiled at me, "I never make assumptions on anyone's financial capabilities. I do however notice that you're wearing a twenty seven hundred dollar jump suit, two hundred and fifty dollar sneakers, and I bet your earrings are at least a carat and a half each, and those diamonds run between eight and 17 thousand each. Sooo in my opinion, I would say that you can afford to pay cash for this car." She concluded with a little smirk.

"Jessica, can you please tell Mr. Payment here to leave, so me and you can work a cash deal on this car…I don't think we need him anymore." I kept my gaze on her.

She blushed like a school girl, "Umm Brian, can you excuse us please, I have some work to do. Two hours later, I was walking out the dealership and Jessica couldn't stop thanking me. She handed me a stack or her cards and assured me that anybody I sent her way would be well taken care of. I was happy with her service and I liked the car; shit I already had one myself but this one was being delivered to Omar as a gift. I had the feeling he was a little salty with some of the decisions I'd made recently and I thought this would help repair the minor damage our friendship had suffered. Omar was just funny like that, he didn't like not being included in the shot calling but there could only be one Chief; and that was me. I was still trying to put things together. What the hell was Simone asking Dallas about me and Angelique for? I was also tripping about her fucking with Biz; I didn't know that shit either or else I never would have asked her to get the info on Diego Alverez. I only asked her 'cuz she used to fuck with Diego and knew his whole operation inside and out. He'd dissed her for a younger version of herself and she never got over it…I guess she got up under Biz instead.

Dallas through me for a loop with that kiss action. I didn't expect that shit to jump off like that but I'ma stick to my motto no matter what happens. You never lose women chasing money but you most definitely lose money chasing women and the one thing I hated…was losing. I needed to stay focused on this last job not to mention this muthafucka Biz; I still had plans for his fake ass! Just as I pulled into my driveway, I got a call from a new friend,

"Wasup baby how you doin'?"

"I'm good…I need to see you tonight is that possible?"

"Everything ok?" I asked frowning.

"I'm fine but everything is not ok, I have to see you tonight."

"Yeah that's cool jus' give me a few hours, I'll be in my regular room at the *"Four Seasons."*

"Ok, I'll see you later." She said.

Honey I'm Home

Angelique was lounging out by the pool trying to catch the last few rays of sunshine. She had her I Pod plugged into her ears and didn't hear me coming up behind; I surprised her with a kiss on the top of her head.

"Hey baby." She greeted me taking her earplugs out.

"Wasup...you workin' on that tan huh?" I asked pulling a chair up to sit beside her.

It was like that scene in the movie "*Sword Fish*" where "*Halle Berry*" was sitting naked in a chair. The view was stunning and her body was making my eyes water and my dick jump at the same time. I loved how comfortable she was with her body; I was a sucker for a woman who wore her birthday suit as an outfit.

"Yeah, you know I can't have any tan lines on this body. Oh, I went to the store and got what you needed; it's on the kitchen counter."

"Good, thank you."

"You're welcome, but, you know how I like to be thanked." She said slyly as she opened her legs slightly.

I took the hint she was throwing at me without hesitation. I grabbed her glass of iced tea and took a drink letting a big piece of ice fall into my mouth. I got on my knees and buried my head between her bronze thighs. I put my mouth directly on her moist clit and began tracing small S's with the tip of my cold tongue. Angelique always kept her pussy waxed so there was nothing to protect her from the hot and cold sensations she was feeling from my mouth. I kept the ice tucked in my cheek while I licked and sucked her pussy perfectly. Her legs were now wide open allowing me full access and her back was arching off the lawn chair as she moved her hips slowly to match my rhythm. Angelique was rubbing the back of my head like a crystal ball and moaning softly.

"You're gonna ma make me cum baby." She shuddered breathlessly. "Oooooo baby lick that shit...yeahhh yessss...lick my p pussy." She said biting her bottom lip.

Angelique's body tensed up and she held her breath like she was going under water. She locked my head in place with her thighs while she rolled her pussy on my tongue real fast. She finally came up for a breath of air after she was finished cuming. I kissed her clit softly and took a much needed breath myself. I leaned over and looked at her face; there were tiny beads of sweat on her forehead as she smiled up at me.

"I needed that baby." She rose up from the chair and licked my lips; tasting her own juices, "Are you big enough to ride this ride?" She turned around and got into the doggie style position with her knees resting on the chair, "Get it while it's hot!" She winked.

I pulled my pants down not bothering to get undressed and dove into her wet pussy. We fit together like a puzzle piece, Angelique's insides felt incredible. I pumped her pussy hard but I was careful not to hurt her. When we both felt the internal explosions of mind numbing orgasms we tumbled over the lawn chair landing on top of each other and busted out laughing.

Now We Up In The Big Leagues

The bank job was coming up fast. Omar needed to get a plan together quickly if he wanted to make good on his agreement with Biz. He knew Tyce didn't suspect anything, especially not from him so the element of surprise was on his side. Tyce had shocked him when he had the S500 delivered to his house out the blue, that shit was tight. He almost felt bad that he was about to murder his ass-but not that bad. Tasha was on a money high these days with all the loot Omar was bringing in; which she was spending like crazy. She bought tons of new clothes, piles of shoes, and a candy red "*Corvette*" convertible. Omar was also shocked to see a chef cooking dinner in his kitchen one night. Tasha had hired the West Indian man to prepare dinner for them Monday thru Friday; she chose to let Omar take her out to eat on the weekends. Tasha was behaving like a lady during the day and a straight freak a night. She was doing everything to keep Omar focused on making that money and eliminating Tyce from their lives. Nothing was hidden from Tasha, she knew *everything*. She asked the right questions at the right times to get the true answers. All she had to do was let Omar sniff the pussy and he would sing like a bird. She mastered how to use her pussy power to get the information she wanted and Omar was an easy victim. Nowadays she was rolling his truck **and** her new convertible; since Omar couldn't eject his ass out the new Benz dumb ass Tyce had given him. Tasha didn't mind though, she'd be twisting that shit all around Oakland soon enough; she was looking forward to her new wealthy life up north, fuck these low budget ass niggas down here...she was on her way up!

Ding Dong

Simone answered the door in her pink silk bathrobe expecting to see Biz but she was shocked to see a blast from her past standing in the doorway. Simone's eyes widened as she took a little step back. She didn't say a word and just stared at her ex-boyfriend astonishingly.

"Hola Simone...are yu going tu stare at me or invite me en?"

"Diego...I ahhhh wasn't expecting you...what are you doing here?"

"I jus' stoppt by tu check en on yu...I missed yu." Diego said with a sexy Spanish accent.

Diego didn't wait for an invitation he casually slid by Simone and walked in like he owned the place...well technically, this was the house he'd bought for her two years ago but that was the past. Simone suddenly became worried about where she'd put her cell phone. Her mind was shifting into survivor mode; she didn't know whether to run out the door or just play it cool. There wasn't a doubt in her mind that Diego was there for a reason...but she couldn't appear to be bothered or frightened so she just decided to feel him out a bit.

"What brings you here? I haven't seen you for about...two years?"

Simone strolled toward the couch Diego was sitting on comfortably and stood with her arms folded across her chest. Her hair was still damp from the shower and she was naked underneath her knee-high robe. Diego didn't answer; choosing to take in the beauty of his ex-girlfriend instead. Simone noticed he was still as handsome as she remembered but she also remembered how cruel he could be. The memory of the day he threw her out the house after she caught him fucking a girl half his age was still fresh in her mind.

Diego cut right to the chase, *"Simone did yu tella man named Tyce where my money an my product was located?"* He maintained his cold stare at her.

"What? What the fuck are you talkin' about! She snapped.

"I will ask yu one las time...ded yu tella man named Tyce Adkins where my money an my product where hidden?" Diego remained calm. His jet-black hair matched his eyes as he continued to look directly at Simone.

Simone stood her ground, "No Diego, I didn't and really I don't know what you're even talkin' about! Get the fuck out! I don't even know a nigga named Tyce, where the fuck is

this comin' from…did you get robbed or
somethin'?"
Diego stood up and buttoned his suit jacket. He
wasn't much taller than Simone but he was in
great shape for a 40 something man. He walked
slowly up to her and grabbed her face gently with
both his hands,
    *"I love yu Simone…an I'm sorry fur hurting
    yu."*
After he said that, he walked out the front door.
Simone stood on her porch and watched him get
into the back of a black SUV; she couldn't see
who was driving because it was dark out. She
relaxed when the truck sped off down the street
disappearing into the night. "What the fuck was
up?" She thought to herself as she closed her robe
tighter. How did he know it was her? She knew
Tyce didn't snitch her out…that would be suicide
for him, but who the fuck was talking. Simone
quickly dressed and decided to go over to Biz's
house to see if he'd heard anything. Ten minutes
later Simone walked out her home and jumped
into her car; she sent Biz a text message earlier to
let him know she was on her way. She took one
last look out of her window; checking for any
signs of Diego in the neighborhood. She gave a
little sigh of relief when she saw no signs of her
ex; she then started her car. An old man was

watering his grass two houses over when he saw the explosion that brightened the dark night. He shielded his eyes from the blast as Simone's car was sitting in her driveway engulfed in flames. The car exploded again as the gas tank ignited, lifting it several feet off the ground. Simone never had a chance...the explosion killed her instantly. Her body continued to cook as her car transformed into a huge barbeque grill. Minutes later fire trucks were heard sounding off in the distance but it was useless...they could do nothing to save her, Simone was dead and gone.

I'm Feelin' You

I was on my way to the *"Four Seasons"* hotel to meet a friend but I decided to make a quick stop at Dallas's house. I made it a point to know where each member of my squad lived, the only one I had to ask was Dallas. I didn't call to tell her I was coming over, I just decided to pop up and try my luck. I walked up to the steps leading to her door and found her taking out her trash.

"Damn Tyce, you jus' popped up on a sista, I coulda' had my nigga up in here or somethin'." She joked as she tied her trash bag up.
"Shit, stop playin' girl. How you doin' tho?" I asked taking the bag from her.
"I'm ok, jus' layin' low like you said; gettin' ready for that last job. I'm surprised to see you here…but I'm happy you came." Dallas smiled widely as she walked down the steps toward the dumpsters.

They walked together to the trashcans talking casually along the way. Dallas wore some flip-flops, denim shorts, and a *"Dallas Cowboy's"* T-shirt. She looked casually fine as always with her hair in a ponytail. Dallas took a chance and reached out to grab Tyce's hand as they walked back across the parking lot toward her home, to her surprise, he didn't pull back; he just let it happen and held her hand back.

"You lookin' real good tonight girl."

"Thanks, but I jus' got my house cleanin' clothes on." She said looking down at her outfit.

"Shit, when a woman is chilling at the house that's when she looks the best." I schooled.

Dallas blushed a little as she let the compliment go straight to her head. Once they reached the steps, Dallas stood on the bottom step to be eye to eye with Tyce. This time Dallas didn't have to make the first move, I seized the moment, and since I was craving her something bad...I decided to have her lips as a snack. This kiss was definitely mutual, as we finally parted lips, Dallas asked,

"Do you have some where to be?"

"Yeah I do...I gotta meet someone in a few minutes." I said reluctantly.

"Oh." Dallas said with a forced smile.

"But, I could swing back by later." I offered.

Dallas grinned, "What's your favorite color baby?"

"Black." I said leaning in closer smelling her sexy scent.

Dallas traced her fingertip down the middle of my

chest, "Well I'll put your favorite color on, but…it won't be much to look at." She winked walking back up the steps and giving me a little preview of tonight's main attraction. I shook my head as I walked back to my ride and headed to the "*Four Seasons*" hotel…I had to put my dick on the bench for a while, it wasn't time to put him in the game yet, but I was definitely coming back later on.

I was fucking up big time and I knew it, but I couldn't help it. I was feeling two women at the same time; the trip thing was that each woman was different and that's what I loved about them. I was breaking my own rules and I knew that shit was a no no.

It's Not So Hard To Say Goodbye

Biz was alone in his bedroom watching the late night news when the story broke. A young man was reporting live from the scene of a car fire in the suburbs' of *"Baldwin Hills."* Biz watched with interest as he recognized the house in the background; it was the house that Simone lived in. The reporter said that a young woman was the victim in the mysterious fire; he went on to say that police had no leads and were leaning towards manufacturing malfunctions as the cause of the car explosion. Biz laughed out loud as the inaccurate reporter ended his live coverage on action news,

"Malfunction my ass…Diego killed that bitch."

He snorted.

When Biz called Diego the other night to let him know who robbed him, Diego naturally asked who told Tyce where his shit was…so Biz informed him that Simone had been fucking with Tyce for years and that she told him where the money and dope was. Of course, he left out the part about him and Simone stealing two hundred pounds of his cocaine; he let Diego believe that Tyce stole everything. He figured Diego would come after

Simone first but he did nothing to warn her or protect her. Biz's plan was to sick Diego on Tyce and give that nigga more than he could handle; .and it was working.

"I guess I can go to sleep now that I know
Simone won't be coming over anytime soon."
He laughed as he turned off the TV and rested
his head on the pillow.
He drifted off to sleep remembering the way Simone sucked his dick; she wasn't as good as Angelique but she was a close second. He was sure gonna miss her mouth.

Finally

It was about two O'clock in the morning when I knocked on Dallas's door, I was thinking it might be too late but she opened the door and was wide-awake. Just like she promised, she was dressed in my favorite color and staying true to her word...there wasn't much to look at. She had a black thong on and a black bra that fully exposed her 34c breast. It was the kind of bra that only offered support not coverage, both her supple titties were completely uncovered. Her eyes were accented with dark eye shadow and her lips were outlined in black with a shimmery grey lipstick to fill them in. Dallas had her hair in a spiked mo hawk and finished it all off with six inch black stiletto heels.

"Get your ass in here." She demanded grabbing my belt and pulling me inside.

From the moment the door closed behind me, Dallas was all over me. She tugged and snatched at my clothes and in less than 30 seconds, I was standing in her front room completely naked. I took a moment to look around the room and noticed the blinds weren't closed and the patio door was wide-open, not to mention the lamp was on. Dallas didn't seem to mind so I kept my mouth shut and just rolled with the flow. Dallas lead me outside to the patio...she even took the time to light candles she'd placed on small tables; the kind of candles that kept the mosquitoes from sucking your blood. Shit, we would need that 'cuz both of us were outside naked like we didn't give a fuck. I picked Dallas up and sat her on the top of the wood railing that lined her balcony, Dallas wrapped her legs around my waist and leaned her body all the way back over the edge. She fondled her breast slowly and slid her hands inside her panties; she let out a moan as she fingered herself. I almost got a splinter in my dick as it bounced up against the wood of the balcony like a hammer. I lurched her back toward me and she kept her legs wrapped tight around my waist. I moved her panties aside and inserted my dick in her pussy like a plug in a light socket. My hands palmed her booty like a "*Nerf*" football; controlling her hips as she thrust up and down like a pogo stick.

"I've been waiting for this baby!" She gasped.

"I been wet since you left."

"Damn you feel good as hell." I said in between pumps.

I continued to carry her as we both sat down in a chair; Dallas straddled my thighs, she reached between my legs and guided me inside her creamy tunnel. Her head flew back as she flexed and twirked her pussy on my dick like a true veteran.

"Shit….fuck….damn!" She moaned. "Don't stop, don't stop baby."

"I been waitin' for this dick Tyce…ooohhh I been waitin' baby."

I had to give it to Dallas…she was workin' me out, but I was still giving her something to **work on**. My mind was jumping back in forth; I saw Angelique's smiling face in my head and when I opened my eyes, I was looking at Dallas's sexy sweaty face. I closed my eyes again, seen Angelique licking her lips…I opened them, and Dallas's eyes where closed enjoying the ride she was on. This shit was making me crazy. Dallas and I were in the type of chair that people sat in when they were lounging at the pool, she reached on the side of my thigh and pulled a lever that made us recline backward even more. Dallas straddled the chair as she stood over me and raised her left leg in the air bringing it down next to the right one. She stood with her feet together along the side of the lengthy chair as she slid off her sexy thong.

"I have to tinkle." Dallas said rubbing her clit.

"You mean you have to pee?" I said leaning on my elbows looking up at her.

"That's right." Dallas confirmed.

Three seconds later, she sat back down but this time her plump ass was on my chest. I kissed her perfume scented stomach as she cupped the back of my head in her petite hands.

"Here it comes baby." She moaned softly.
Suddenly I felt warm fluid covering my chest. Before I could react, Dallas slid her pussy down to my stomach and slowly began riding my abdomen and chest while she peed! Dallas stared directly into my eyes while she continued to urinate all over my torso. The warm liquid flowed down the sides of my ribcage and made a small pond in my belly button. I was getting my first golden shower! I'd heard about freaky shit like this, and swore I would never do it…what I look like letting a broad pee on me? But man, I gotta give it to Dallas; she made me discover something entirely new about myself. I liked that shit…that shit turned me on…that shit made my dick as hard as a nightstick!

"Damn girl. That was some freaky porno type shit."
"I know." She grinded her wet pussy into my abs, "You thought you wouldn't like that shit huh?" Her eyebrows raised up a little.
"I jus' thought it was nasty." I responded.
"Urine is sterile baby…but you're right, it is nasty but guess what…so are we."

Dallas leaned into me and grabbed my bottom lip with her teeth. At the same time, she reached behind her and guided my throbbing dick back inside her dripping pussy. Dallas was on top of me but I was working her hard from the bottom. She matched my forceful rhythms with her own aggressive gyrations.

There was something erotic about fucking outdoors; maybe it was the moonlight or the fact that animals fucked outdoors too. Whatever it was, we were both feeling sexually carnivorous as we feasted on each other. The chair underneath us whined and squeaked as we switched to the missionary position. Dallas bit my neck as I bobbed my hips up and down in between her thighs.

"Yes baby yes! I wanna see you cum, I want you to cum all over me, I love that shit!" Dallas said still holding my flesh in her teeth.

I couldn't hold my nut back anymore, the tip of my dick started tingling. I buried it deep inside of Dallas's pussy for a long second before I pulled out. I held my breath as I gripped my dick in my hand and exploded all over Dallas's breasts and throat as she threw her head back. Her body glistened with beads of sweat and sprinkles of cream colored cum. Dallas arched her back and rubbed it all over her body like lotion. I swear I must of lost ten pounds…

"Oooo baby, sssssss, it's so warm." She said smiling delightfully.

"You are somethin' else Dallas." I said shaking my head.

"I'm not like this with everybody, I dish out ground beef to other men, but you get filet mignon…with grilled onions!" She laughed. "I jus' feel like I can be myself with you, and I wanted to please you like you never been pleased before. I wanted to make the most of my time with you and leave you wanting more and more and more." She sat up gazing at me.

I stared back at her, "Well, you definitely accomplished that…but ummm…was that all an act or are you jus' that freaky?"

Her left eyebrow rasied up a little, "Tyce, honey, I hope you can swim, cuz' it gets deeper."

I grinned at her honest response and helped her get up from the low rise chair, we pressed our naked bodies together and shared a tender kiss under the stars. Suddenly we heard clapping sounds echoing in the night. I turned around and was surprised to see a woman standing in the darkness of her balcony giving us a standing ovation.

"My my my…that was the shit! I thought I was

naughty but boy was I wrong; now I'm not bisexual or nothin' like that but I'd fuck either one of you!"

The oversized sleeves on her pink robe flapped as she started clapping again. Me and Dallas looked at each other and laughed as we stepped inside.

"Thanks for the compliment Ms. Peeper." I said over my bare shoulder.

"You're welcome honey." She said in an appreciative tone.

"I guess we have a fan." I said grabbing Dallas's waist.

"I guess so...*now I aint bisexual or nothin' but I'd fuck either one of you!*" Dallas did an impression of our new friend.

We finished the night off by eating turkey sandwiches and Ruffles potato chips while we laid in her bed naked...I loved turkey sandwiches and sex...what a combination.

Dallas and Angelique.......what a combination.

Time To Make A Withdrawal

Everybody showed up to the "*Starbuck's*" right on time. Tyce, Sway, Omar, Angelique, and Dallas all arrived on schedule and ready to take the bank. Sway's mood was all business; he went over the plan with Tyce several times in private just to make sure he had everything right. He was ready; he'd had a taste of the good life and he wanted to eat that for the rest of his life. He was done with being broke and all the low budget bullshit that came with it. Tyce was focused on the task at hand, he didn't let confusing thoughts of Angelique and Dallas cloud his judgment. This bank job was serious shit…any mistakes could get somebody killed or locked up in a prison for the rest of their lives. He didn't want that on his conscience; he'd come to like his crew…he'd come to love two members in particular but he pushed those emotions deep down inside his gut and pressed forward. Omar seemed very calm…almost sedated. This was a big day for him; this was the day he planned to murder his best friend but you couldn't tell by his cool demeanor. After the bank job was over, he intended to get

Tyce alone in the warehouse and shoot his ass in the back of the head. He kept thinking about all the money he was going to make up north and when he fantasized about that, killing Tyce seemed easy. Biz called this morning to check up on him and Omar told him not to worry and to just be ready to make that move.

Angelique got a manicure and pedicure this morning, and then hit the shooting range to practice her aim just in case she had to squeeze off a few headshots this afternoon. She was doing a good job of managing her strong feelings for Tyce and maintaining her position on the team. She knew her job inside and out and she was also ready to lay somebody down if they got out of line.

Dallas was also the picture of professionalism. Her mind replayed snap shots of last night; her coochie would tingle when she remembered rubbing Tyce's cum all over her titties like sunscreen, but no one could tell by her face. She and Tyce showed no signs of lustful intentions towards each other. Dallas was poised and ready to get paid…she would get laid later.

Jade Mutual was one of China town's most popular banks. Tyce chose to hit the bank today because it was the only time during the year when the bank wasn't busy as hell. Asians were some of the hardest working people he'd ever met but today was some kind of Chinese holiday so a lot of business was done the day before, leaving today wide open. The bank had two security guards and several high tech security cameras. The bank vault was set on a timer and too hard to get into but they wouldn't need that anyway. There was a soft vault in a back room that they used to count the money before putting it into the vault. That room plus the stash the tellers hid under their drawers would easily add up to five million or more. Tyce knew everything about the banks set up. He'd been planning this for over a year but he knew he couldn't do it alone...today was the day he'd been waiting for. The team left the coffee shop, which was a few blocks down from the bank. They all made the short walk to Jade Mutual; the getaway van was already parked in the back of the bank in a narrow alley. Everyone made their way to their positions outside the building and waited for the signal.

Dallas was dressed like a man and from a distance, she looked like one. She wasn't going in the bank anyway; her job was to hold down the back door and stay in the alley with Angelique who was behind the wheel of the van. The windows were tinted black but Angelique still wore a wig and sunglasses. Omar and Tyce planned to enter through the front while Sway came through the alley door. It was a hot California day and it was about to get even hotter. Sway walked around to the alley with Dallas and stood off to the side out of the camera's view.

"You ready lil' bit?" Sway asked Dallas lightly.

"Yeah, I'm kinda' nervous though." She admitted.

"Everything's gonna be alright lil' bit, jus' keep your eyes open back here, I won't let nobody come this way."

Dallas nodded in appreciation, "Ok."

Sway nodded at Angelique who was sitting in the driver's seat of the van, he could barely see inside but he saw the thumbs up signal she gave him telling him she was ready to go. Sway looked like a mechanic, wearing grey overalls, a hat and dark shades. He had a fake mustache on which made him look much older than he was. He looked down at his watch; it was one minute until show time. Angelique was snacking on *"skittles"* in the front seat while she waited for the action to start, she'd taken the bag from Tyce at the coffee shop earlier…she could see why he liked these things so much, they were good as hell she thought to herself. She poured the last of the sweet candy pebbles in her mouth and gripped the steering wheel nervously with both hands. She looked just in time to see Sway dash into the bank. Dallas trotted up to the back door and stood in the doorway looking inside. Sway moved like a soldier down the hallway and entered the lobby, Tyce and Omar came in at the same time. Tyce handled the security guard at the front by spraying mace in his face and hitting him the back of the head with the heavy chrome handle of his gun. He fell to the floor rolling around in pain. The other guard at the back of the bank had no time to react to what was happening in the front because Sway had a gun pointed at him before he could reach for his own.

"ON THE FLOOR NOW!! GET THE FUCK
DOWN!!" Tyce shouted.

The bank only had about six people inside the lobby and five tellers; the manager was stationed at a desk off to the side around a waiting area.

Omar instructed the short Asian man to go to the soft vault room in the corner of the bank. The man hesitated at first, until Omar pistol whipped him a few times. After that brief beating, the man scurried over toward a door that looked like a wall. He put a funny looking key in the hidden lock and opened the camouflaged door. Omar pushed the man inside and made him fill his bag up with stacks and stacks of hundred dollar bills.

"Keep that pace up Mr. Lee....move that money nigga!" He commanded. It took the manager about three minutes to empty the soft count room.

Outside Tyce jumped over the counter, "Back away from the counter people." Tyce was keeping them away from any silent alarm buttons that were hidden in the desk. "Give me the keys to the bottom drawers now!"

The tellers obeyed and removed a key ring bracelet from around their wrist.

"Open the drawers and toss out the fake bank money. Don't try anything stupid people, I know you keep a fake bundle of tens and twenties in the bottom of your drawers...so don't act like you don't speak any english."

The frightened tellers all nodded rapidly but didn't speak a word. They each went to their personal drawers and removed the stacks of money being careful not to include any bait money. Tyce threw a bag on the counter,

"Fill it up and pass it along, don't forget that bottom drawer either!"

Tyce did his research when it came to this bank; he knew the real money was in the second drawer under the top one that the customers see. He put the gun to the back of each tellers head as they filled the bag up with money and passed it down the teller line. After that, they all laid down on the floor like it was naptime. Tyce, Sway, and Omar had the bank on lock down and got the money in less than three minutes.

"Let's go...let's go!!" Tyce said hopping back over the counter with the heavy bag in hand.

Tyce threw the bag to Sway and ran over to the soft vault,

"Yo toss me the bag O!"

Omar turned around and tossed the bag to Tyce, then swung around putting his gun to the little man's head and made him get on the ground; he walked backwards towards the exit keeping an eye on the man. When he reached the door way he turned around and was unexpectedly staring down the barrel of Tyce's chrome 9mm. Omar froze in his tracks and just stood very still, his gun was at his side but he knew he couldn't move fast enough to shoot Tyce.

"What, you thought I didn't know about you? Don't look so surprised O...I'm not a dumb ass nigga." Tyce said staring at his so-called best friend.

"Yo Tyce, what the fuck you doin' man I I I...why you trippin' all..."

"Shut the fuck up nigga, what the fuck you tryna to cop pleas now for huh? I fuckin' fed yo ass for year's nigga! What I got you got,

and now you plannin' my death! Fuck you!"
Omar snarled at Tyce, "Naw nigga fuck you,
you think you king shit around here! You aint
got the heart to shoot me nigga…you a soft ass
no money getting ass nigga! I'm tired of being
yo sidekick! You kept me from gettin' paid all
these years, I COULDA' BEEN RICH NIGGA
A LONG TIME AGO!"
"I'll be sure to send your mom some flowers."
Tyce told him as he fired a bullet into the
middle of Omar's forehead.
His body dropped to the floor and blood began to
puddle from the back of his head. The manager
was speechless and was staring at Tyce like he'd
seen a ghost. Tyce put a finger to his lips in a hush
motion and just closed the door, locking him
inside with Omar's body.

Sway understood and knew why Tyce had
killed Omar. Tyce told Sway about his plans
earlier that morning, so Sway knew this was
Omar's last day on this earth and he backed Tyce
up all the way. No one else knew about the
execution; Tyce trusted Sway to get the security
camera tapes from the bank and destroy the
footage. Sway got those important tapes while
Tyce was busy with Omar. Without those tapes,
there was no evidence of the robbery or the
murder. Tyce and Sway grabbed the bags of

money and ran towards the back exit. All the employees in the bank were on the ground crying and screaming at them in Chinese. The two men ignored the foreign pleas, hit the door, and ran across the alley to the van. Tyce snatched the door open and stopped…

"Where the fuck is Angelique and Dallas!" He turned to Sway with a horrible look on his face. They both looked around the alley but they didn't see them anywhere…they were gone.

"What the fuck…**fuck fuck fuck**!!" Tyce punched the top of the roof.

"We gotta go Tyce…we gotta go!" Sway grabbed his shoulder and pushed him in the back of the van. He got behind the wheel and mashed his foot on the gas pedal speeding away from the bank. Tyce jumped in the front passenger seat and shook his head in disbelief, "Were they here when you went in?" He asked frantically.

"Yeah…they both were here…Angelique was in the van and Dallas was by the door!" Sway shouted as he drove.

Tyce looked around the van; searching for any signs of anything…he noticed a wig lying on the floor in the back, it was the wig Angelique was wearing.

"Somebody got em man!" Tyce said holding

the wig. "Fuck!"

"Let's jus' dump the van and get to the warehouse, we'll figure it out from there."

Sway tried to calm Tyce down.

They pulled up to an abandoned lot ten agonizing minutes later and torched the van; Tyce's jeep was parked there already so they hopped in and headed to the warehouse. Tyce's mind was going a mile a minute. He hated to think that Biz had the girls but that was probably true...damn he hated to think about that, 20 minutes later, they were in the warehouse putting the bags of money in Tyce's vault. Tyce didn't even mind that Sway was seeing where he hid his money...shit he was to worried about Angelique and Dallas to care.

"What you want me to do with these?" Sway held up the security camera tapes.

"Damn the tapes, one of those cameras covered the alley." Tyce remembered.

They looked at the labels on the tapes and finally came across a tape that had the initials, B. A. E. They assumed that stood for back alley entrance. Tyce put the tape in the old VCR and TV set he had from years before. Since they stopped the tapes after the robbery, they just had to rewind the video a little to see what happened. Tyce and Sway watched closely; they saw Dallas standing by the back door, they couldn't see the van because the camera didn't pan that far. Everything looked normal until Dallas turned around and ran toward the van pointing her gun. She never came back into the view of the camera and it cut off shortly after that.

"What the fuck was that?" Tyce said out loud. The two men looked at each other blankly. Just then, Tyce's phone vibrated on the table across the room. He raced over to it and picked it up; he looked at the screen...

"Wasup?" He asked agitated.

"Tyce, Angelique and another girl are here, their locked up in a room in the back of the house!"

"Are they ok?" Tyce asked pacing the floor.

"Yeah, their alive...but you better hurry up and get over here! I gotta go...you jus' need to hurry up!"

Tyce put the phone in his pocket and walked quickly toward his vault. He went inside the room and opened the closet that contained his guns. Curiosity got the best of Sway, so he went into the room,

"Who was that?" He asked.

Tyce didn't turn around to answer, "Biz has the girls."

"Damn." Sway balled his fist up, "What you wanna do?"

Tyce turned around this time, "I'm goin' over there to kill that nigga and pick them up."

"I'ma go with you."

"Naw man...I gotta do this shit alone...this is personal."

"What the fuck you want me to do...jus' sit here, man I aint with that." Sway protested.

"I can handle this shit Sway...jus' take your money and go home to your wife and kids...if I need you I'll call you."

Sway reluctantly agreed with the solo plan,

"I don't like it Tyce but I'ma let you go alone; but if you need me I'll be in the area."

Sway was also wondering how Tyce found out Biz had the girls so fast; and who was that on the phone?

Sleeping Beauties

It was dark in the room. Angelique was lying on the floor unconscious; blood was dripping slowly from a gash on her cheekbone. Dallas was slowly coming out of her slumber and her head was pounding with pain. She slowly raised her head and stared into the darkness. Her eyes adjusted to the blackness of the room and she saw Angelique stretched out next to her.

"Angelique, Angelique, baby wake up!" Dallas whispered loudly shaking her friend lightly. Angelique didn't move right away; so Dallas shook her harder this time. Angelique slowly rolled her head to the side and opened her eyes.

"I thought you were dead girl!" Dallas stood up and helped her friend get to her feet. They had been locked in a room with no windows but they knew how they got there. Angelique adjusted her clothes and wiped her bloody cheek with the back of her hand. Dallas went over to the door and tried the doorknob; she jerked on the handle but it wouldn't budge.

"Who the fuck were those niggas?" Dallas turned around, "I was watching the bank door, and all of a sudden I heard you screaming."

"I don't know what happened…I was looking
at you and then the passenger door opened, the
next thing I knew Bruce was jamming a gun in
my face. I didn't have time to react so I jus'
screamed to draw some attention." Angelique
explained.

"Who the fuck is Bruce?" Dallas asked
confused.

"Bruce works for Biz." Angelique said spitting
out blood from her mouth.

Now Dallas understood…Bruce and some thugs
grabbed Angelique for Biz. She'd gotten in the
way when she tried to help and they snatched her
up too. That was the same Biz that Simone was
dating and the same Biz that was plotting to
murder Tyce. Dallas was starting to realize the
deep shit they were in, she remembered running
toward the van when she heard Angelique scream;
Dallas didn't get to far because she got hit by a car
and was slammed into the back of the van.
Luckily, the car wasn't going that fast but the blow
was enough to knock her out.

"We gotta get outta here." Angelique
announced.

"You damn right." Dallas said looking at her
sincerely.

Dallas paced the room trying to figure a way out.

She quickly realized that there was no use trying to look because that door was the only way in and it was secured by three dead bolt locks. Angelique didn't bother to look...she'd seen this room before; it was the room Biz used as a storage area. She knew there was no way out. Dallas sat on the floor in the middle of the room and just stared at the concrete floor. Her head was in her hands when she spoke,

"Angelique...I have somethin' to tell you." She said quietly.

"What is it?" Angelique walked over to her and sat down, "Girl we gon be alright; don't worry, you know Tyce and Sway aint gonna leave us here." She reassured her friend.

"I know I know...but...it's not that...I" Dallas paused.

"You're scaring me girl...what is it?"

Angelique reached for Dallas's hand and held it.

Dallas tried to make eye contact with Angelique in the dark room; she took a deep breath and let it out slowly, "I'm in love with Tyce."

The room was silent. Neither woman spoke for what seemed like ages. Dallas was waiting for Angelique to let go of her hand and slap the shit out of her or something; but Angelique was still holding on to it.

Breaking the silence Dallas spoke, "I…I don't know what happened…I jus' allowed myself to fall for him…I mean at first we were jus' business partners you know…and then I jus'…jus' started to care about him more than I should."

"I know you love him Dallas." Angelique stared at her with watery eyes, "I've known for a while."

"How did you know?"

"I can tell the way you look at him."

It seemed easier to talk about this in the dark for Dallas; she felt guilty for loving Tyce, she felt guilty for fucking Tyce, but she couldn't hide her feelings anymore, the least she could do was be honest with her friend.

Angelique sighed, "Tyce isn't my man technically…we never…I mean he never really asked me to be his woman or anything…he jus' treated me well and cared for me, he was there for me when I needed him. Because of that, I allowed myself to fall into the routine of being his woman…it felt good to be cared about. I'm in love with him too and I'm not gonna let him go."

Dallas licked her dry lips, "I can't jus walk away and ignore my feelings either."

"Did you fuck him?" Angelique asked bluntly. "Yes, but we haven't been fuckin' the whole time tho…it only happened once." Dallas said clearly.

"Dallas you're my friend, I'm not gonna hate you for having good taste and wanting to be loved…shit I wanna be loved too. I respect the fact that you told me face to face. You risked your life today to try and save *my* black ass; and right now, we're in this fake ass cell together. You're my friend girl…and I love you." A tear rolled down Angelique's cheek. "It's hard to be salty with someone who jus' risked their life for you."

"I love you too Angelique, I jus' wanted to tell you in case we never make it out of here. I was gonna tell you after the bank job, I didn't want nothin' to mess that up." Dallas said emotionally. "And now we might end up dead."

"We're in a fucked up situation…but we're not fucked." Angelique said standing up, "We gonna be alright."

Long Time Comin'

I parked my jeep about a block away from Biz's house. I got out and popped my trunk; I grabbed two 45-caliber glocks and a high powered shotgun. I put my new bulletproof vest on and jogged the distance to the mansion where my women were being held captive. The sun was high in the sky, it was broad daylight but Biz's house was secluded, the nearest neighbor was miles away. That was good for me 'cuz some serious shit was about to go down. I laid down in the manicured grass outside the tall black iron gate, I was hyped; my heart was beating in my chest like a bass drum. I wasn't nervous, I was furious. I had to check my emotions like luggage at the airport 'cuz emotions could get you killed in a situation like this. Biz had an electric gate around his entire property that could only be turned off if you drove in or out, so I couldn't jump it.

I took out my phone and dialed, it only rang once when she picked up,
"I'm outside the gate."
"Ok…jus' hold up a sec, I'll be right there,"
She whispered.

About five minutes later, a black *"Lexus ES 300"* slowly approached the gate; it opened up slowly and the car slid through, stopping right in front of me. The windows were tinted so I couldn't see who was inside; just in case it wasn't who I thought, I aimed the shot gun at the front windshield.

The window rolled down, "It's me Tyce."

Bree was sitting in the driver's seat alone so I lowered my gun, "You alright Bree?" I asked walking toward the car.

"Yeah I'm fine, listen; the girls are in the storage room, it's around the back of the house down the stairs. He aint been down there yet but I heard him talkin' to Bruce and he's about to go down there with him." Bree said almost losing her breath.

"Calm down...take a breath...everything's gonna be alright, I'ma get them out. Is there anybody else in there?"

"No nobody." She shook her head side to side.

"Thank you for your help Bree." I touched her shoulder gently.

"No Tyce thank you. I was happy to help you get that motherfucker! He was the reason Flash was killed...I'll never forget that shit...and now he's gonna get his!" Bree began to cry, "It was hell being with him. I had to hide my sadness and pain for Flash and play the girlfriend role. I hate his ass Tyce; please kill that motherfucker…do it for Flash…do it for me."

I wiped the tears from her eyes, "I'ma get his ass don't worry. You better get out of here, I'll call you later."

Bree sniffed a little and smiled weakly, "Ok." She pulled off and headed down the long road to freedom feeling relieved as she looked at Tyce in the rearview mirror. As she drove, she remembered when Tyce asked her to get close to Biz. At first, she rejected the idea but when Tyce explained how he was the one that was responsible for Flash's death she agreed. She knew Biz didn't pull the trigger himself, but he'd sent the men that did and that was enough for her. She told Tyce that she wanted the men that shot Flash dead as well. Ever since that day she held her boyfriend's lifeless body in her arms she was infected with a feeling of emptiness. She missed Flash terribly but on the other hand, her spirit was surging with anger. She wasn't a forgive and forget type of woman…she wanted revenge. The night Tyce told her the hit men who shot Flash were dead, she poured two shots of Hennessey; one for Flash and one for her…she toasted to their painful deaths and drank them both. Next on the list was

Biz…once he was dead, she planned to visit Flash's gravesite and tell him the good news.

I watched Bree's *"Lexus"* roll down the street, I really admired her courage; she was in mourning, yet she still managed to handle herself around the man who killed the man she loved. In addition, thanks to her expert spying abilities, I knew every move Biz and Omar made. She kept me well informed of all the hidden plans between them, and I was planning on paying her handsomely for her efforts and loyalty. It was easy to see why Lil' Flash was so in love with her, Bree was a great woman. I snatched myself out of my thoughts and focused on the task at hand. The gate was closing quickly so I ran in; the property was laced with trees and high shrubs so I used them to hide behind as I moved to the back of the house. I ran quickly across the grass and posted up behind a thick bush. My ears cocked as I heard voices from the inside, it was Biz and Bruce. They were in the kitchen having a heated conversation,

"Why the fuck did you tell em to leave?" Biz yelled at Bruce.

"I thought you wanted em to…plus I can handle Tyce, I wish that nigga would come up in here…I'll plug his ass!" Bruce woofed.

"Nigga that was stupid…don't you know there's strength in numbers? You

thought…you thought…nigga don't think
shit!" Biz shouted. "Call them niggas back
right now!"

I crouched below the window of the kitchen and
by the sound of their voices, they were close to
me. I took a deep breath and jumped up aiming my
gun at the window. I saw Biz and Bruce standing
in the kitchen a split second before they saw me.
Both of their eyes widened as they recognized the
man they were talking so loudly about, Biz dove
on the floor as I unloaded a round through the
glass of the window and into Bruce's chest. The
force of the blast hurled his body backward,
slamming him into the refrigerator. Big bad Bruce
talking all that shit was dead. I turned my attention
to Biz, I looked just in time to see him running out
the kitchen disappearing around the corner. The
bullet shattered the glass of the window and I
cleared the rest out my way as I climbed through
it. Glass crunched under my boots as I stepped on
the floor. The cold dead eyes of Biz's bodyguard
stared at me blankly,

"I'll plug his ass huh…yeah right nigga." I said
out loud.

I put the shotgun down and pulled out my 45. No
doubt by now Biz had grabbed a gun and was
hiding somewhere in the huge house so I was
cautious. I moved slowly past the front room

looking for any place where he could be hiding; this fucking house was big...where the fuck was he at. I slid slowly down the lengthy hallway and came up on the doorway to the formal living room. The all white room was empty...I sighed and moved further down the hallway. I was heading to the theatre room when I heard a loud BANG! It felt like someone hit me in the back with a heavy ass rock...the blast forced air out my lungs and stopped my breath momentarily. I whirled around and saw Biz standing behind me holding a gun, he looked surprised to see me still standing but he fired another bullet at me but missed. I crouched down and shot back at him, the bullet hit him in his thigh making him fall to the ground. Another bullet hit him in the shoulder as I walked quickly toward him. He no longer could hold the weight of the gun because his shoulder had a huge chunk of flesh missing from it.

"Tried to shoot me in the back huh! That's jus' like you bitch ass nigga!" I shouted kicking the gun away from his reach.

"You aint shit lil' nigga, I shoulda left your ass on the corner where I found you." Biz grunted in pain. Blood was soaking the white linen pants he was wearing like spilt red wine. His shoulder was exposed because he was sporting a black wife beater and blood was running

down his dark brown arm. "You came to get
your bitch? Is that what you came for nigga?
Good luck getting the bitch out my cellar...I
hope she rots in there!" Biz was breathing
heavily as he held his bleeding shoulder.
I glared at him and shot him in the knee cap of
his good leg. He howled with pain as he
banged the back of his head against the wall
repeatedly. His body stiffened and shook as he
tried to cope with the immense pain. Biz gritted
his teeth, "Why don't you jus' kill me and get
it over with!"
I smiled, "Patience pops...the devil will wait
for you."
I was satisfied that Biz wasn't going anywhere and
it would be a minute before he bled to death so I
left him laying there and went looking for the
girls. I went outside to the back of the house and
found the steps that led to the cellar. My back was
beginning to get real sore as I came up on a dusty
door and banged on it with the handle of my gun.
"Angelique! Dallas!" I shouted through the
door.
I could hear the excited voices of the girls as
they recognized my voice, "Were in here, were
in here!!" They screamed.
Inspecting the door, I knew I couldn't get them
out; that shit wasn't like the movies, you couldn't

just shoot the locks off and open the door. I needed some help. I grabbed my phone and dialed,

Sway answered on the first ring, "Yo you good?" He asked anxiously.

"Yeah I'm straight…but I need your help my nigga, the girls are locked in a room and I can't get in the door.

"I'm on my way." Sway hung the phone up. Sway was just around the corner biting his nails with worry, he whipped his new *"Denali"* through the blocks heading for Biz's mansion not knowing what to expect. Tyce met him at the gate and let him in. Once Sway drove through the security fence, Tyce jumped inside his truck and they made their way toward the back of the house.

"Good to see you in one piece." Sway said looking me over.

"Shit why wouldn't I be…Biz aint shit; I left that nigga bleedin' on his living room floor. I'll finish his ass off later but first let's get the girls out."

Sway grabbed a black bag from the back of his truck. He'd changed clothes from the robbery and was wearing a blue polo shirt and jeans. His short curly hair made him look like a model for an S curl ad and his shirt showed off his muscular arms.

"Where they at?" He asked looking around.

"Follow me."

I went down the dark steps and stood in front
of the door.

"Ya'll alright in there?"

"Yeah were ok!" Angelique and Dallas shouted
back.

"Ok, jus' hold on, I got Sway out here workin'
on the locks, He'll have you out in a minute."

"Okaaay!" They both sang back.

Sway sprayed the same stuff he used on Diego's
door to freeze the hinges, he also sprayed the cold
liquid into the key holes. After about a minute, the
hinges began to get brittle.

"On the count of three we gon kick this door
down." Sway instructed.

"Alright." I nodded.

"Ay, ya'll stand back!" I yelled through the
door. "One...two...THREE...BLAAAMMM!"
The door cocked and rocked off the hinges. They
could see the black room behind it; all it took was
one more kick to send the door crashing into the
room. When the dust cleared, we saw Angelique
and Dallas standing across the room with their
backs to the wall.

"Thank God." Angelique said stepping
forward.

"We heard gun shots...I...I mean; we were so
worried about you." Dallas confessed relieved.

"Aint nothin' gonna happen to me...especially

not at the hands of Biz or Bruce. Let's get outta here; I got some unfinished bizness to handle."
Before we all left the room Angelique walked up to me and gave me a long hug. Her body felt warm as I embraced her; there was a moment when I thought I would never see her again. The thought of her leaving my life was more than I could handle. I knew that I loved her at that moment...I wanted and needed her close to me. The funny thing is I felt the exact same way about Dallas. I couldn't lose her either. When Angelique and I finally separated, Dallas walked up and stood directly in front of me. We stared into each other's eyes for what seemed like hours before she kissed me. She kissed me like I just came back from being in a war or something, like she hadn't seen me in years. I felt the passion of her feelings for me...the trip thing was she put her tongue all in my mouth right in front of Angelique. Sway just stood there watching the scene like a housewife watching a soap opera. The four of us all left the room in silence; we walked around to the kitchen entrance and proceeded to the living room. Biz was still laying on the floor with pools of blood under each leg and a hole in his shoulder. He was unconscious as we walked up on him,

"Wake up bitch!" I kicked his foot.
His eyes fluttered open as he straightened his head.

He looked at the crowd around him lazily as his brain tried to register the scene.

"Well well well…hey sweet heart…did you miss ya daddy?" He looked at Angelique.

"Fuck you!" Angelique snapped.

"See, you been hanging around this muthafucka to long; you got a new mouth on you." He nodded his head toward me, "But don't you worry, I got a nice fat dick you can suck on that will shut you up. You remember my dick don't you? Yeah you remember…I used to plug all three of your holes night after night after night." Biz spoke sadistically.

Before anyone knew it, Angelique pounced on him and started punching him in the face; her right hand drilling him like a jackhammer. We all watched in amazement as she viciously attacked him; her punches dipped in hatred as she broke his nose and split his lip, cursing him the whole time.

"Fuck you! You piece of shit! You thought you could pimp me out? Fuck you and your old ass dick…punk ass nigga!" Angelique spat in a rage.

Nobody moved to stop her. We just let her get it out; this was between the two of them. Angelique finally quit punching him and stood up to admire her handy work. Biz's left eye was swollen, his nose was bloody, and both his lips were cut.

"Say somethin' now muthafucka!" Angelique
backed up a little catching her breath.
"DAMN, I need to be training with you...you
fucked him up girl." Sway joked.
Angelique was shaking with rage as Dallas
grabbed her gently by the shoulders; escorting her
off to the side. Biz laid there slumped against the
wall taking shallow breaths trying to recover from
the assault and battery he just received.

But he was still talkin' shit, "Fuck that
bitch...fuck all you muthafuckas. I'm Biz
baby...B, I muthafuckin' Z...ya'll aint SHIT!"
I was tired of his ass. I didn't say a word to him as
I walked over to the huge floor to ceiling drapes
that covered the windows. I pulled out my lighter
and lit the bottoms on fire. Sway caught on to my
plan and helped by lighting the couch and
enormous Oriental rugs on fire too. Within
minutes, the flames were spreading all over the
room. I grabbed a bottle of expensive vodka from
the liquor cabinet and took a sip. I poured the rest
all over Biz's head and body.

**"FUCK YOU TYCE!!! FUCK YOU
TYCE!!!
I'LL SEE YOU IN HELL!!!"** He screamed
with all his strength.
I kneeled over closer to him and whispered,
"You shoulda left me, my little brother, and my

woman alone."

I put the flame of the lighter to his alcohol soaked shirt; the flames immediately jumped up toward his face. He began kicking, screaming and rolling around on the floor as the blistering flames burned his flesh. He tried to cover his face with his hands but the fire seared his palms. He was trying desperately to extinguish the flames but the vodka was acting like lighter fluid so there was no use; Biz was burning to death.

The room was beginning to fill up with thick smoke; that meant the fire department would be on their way soon. We had to get out of there fast or else we would be cooking next. So we all ran out to Sway's truck and left Biz to burn alive. I made sure to grab my shotgun off the kitchen counter before I left the house. All four doors closed at the same time as we jumped in the truck and Sway sped off down the long driveway toward the gate. You could still hear the high-pitched screams of Biz as we drove away. A smile was on Angelique's face…a smile was on mine.

Red Light

Sway pulled up to my jeep in a hurry causing a dust cloud to puff up. The clock was ticking, fire engine sirens blared in the distance, and we could see the dark grey smoke from the house rising in the air.

"Yo we gotta go, they'll be here soon." Sway kept his truck in drive.

"The girls will ride with you Sway."

"No Tyce I wanna ride with you." Angelique protested.

"Me too." Dallas cosigned.

I stared at both of them a little confused, "Wasup with ya'll...never mind...look I need you both to go with Sway, I got these guns and shit on me it's better if we ride separate." I continued, "I'll meet you at the warehouse."

"Ok, but hurry up." Angelique whined.

Before I got out the truck, I looked them both in the eyes wondering what the hell was wrong with them, and then I turned to Sway; the look on his face said hurry the fuck up before the cops come. I agreed with him, so I jumped out and ran to my jeep. I watched as Sway peeled off, pushing the

V8 engine of the *"Denali"* to its limits. When he made a right at the corner and disappeared, I put my joint in gear. I started to pull away from the curb but I was cut off when a car pulled in front of me. Another car pulled in behind me boxing me in. Before I could react, I was surrounded,

"FREEZE POLICE…DON'T FUCKING
MOVE! PUT YOUR HANDS ON THE DASH
BOARD NOW!"

There were four undercover police officers pointing their guns at me and more were pulling up; all in unmarked cars. I put the jeep in park and slowly raised my hands and placed them on the dash board. A scowl was on my face and my jaws were clenched.

"One officer snatched my driver's door open,
"DON'T MOVE *"L L COOL J!"* JUST GIVE
ME REASON…GIVE ME A REASON!" He
provoked as he yanked me out and threw me
on the street.

He put his weapon at the back of my head, while the other officers covered him…there were at least ten guns pointed at me. Within seconds, I was handcuffed, jerked up and thrown in the back of an unmarked car. One fat ass cop got behind the wheel of my jeep, while the others searched for weapons. They didn't have to look hard 'cuz all three of my guns were in the passenger seat. I just kept my mouth shut...to many people hang themselves by talking to the holice. One thing I knew; this wasn't an ordinary bust. The officer that handcuffed me was now sitting in the front seat of the car I was in. Just as fast as they came all the cops were now leaving and taking my jeep with them. Every car left the scene, leaving me and the officer alone on the street. He was about 45 or 50 with salt and pepper hair, he could use a personal trainer to help him work off his huge gut. A thick mustache hid his top lip and he stared at me with cold blue eyes.

"Tyce Adkins...you are Tyce Adkins right?"

He twisted his body to face me.

I was silent; I just stared back at him through the metal gate that separated us. My mind was racing trying to put all this shit together but I was as cool as "*Billie D Williams*" on the outside.

"You don't have to talk to me, I know who you are. I'm Detective Walsh." He said cockily. "There's so much for us to talk about...we could start with the robbery at the church or the house that's on fire around the corner with the two dead bodies inside." He smoothed his mustache, "Frankly, I don't give a rat's ass about Biz or Bruce, and neither does my partner. You see Tyce...I guess you could say being a detective is my part time job; my full time job is working for Diego Alverez. So you just did us a favor by killing Mr. Biz...after all he was the competition. Plus Diego figured it was him that stole his dope since you never showed interest in the stuff; you're all about the money aren't you?"

I looked out the window as two fire trucks sped by us, "What the fuck you want with me?" I broke my silence.

He pointed his finger at me, "That's a good question...**we** want the money you and your friends stole from the church. You not only stole from Diego but you stole from me...and I want my money back."

"What money....what the fuck are you talkin' about?" I played dumb.

Detective Walsh let out a hearty laugh that shook his belly like *"Santa Clause,"* "What money...is that the best you can come up with? That's hilarious! Let me break this down for you...I can bust you on a robbery, an arson and four murders, that's enough to get you the gas chamber. Or you can give the money that you don't know about... back...and only go up for the armed robbery and a few other minor chargers. You'd only be looking at 10 to 15 years; that's the deal. By the way...your old boss Biz is the one who snitched on you, he

told Diego you stole his five million dollars."
He pointed his filthy finger at me.
"Armed robbery, arson and four
murders…again what tha fuck are you talkin'
about?" I wasn't giving up shit.
"Do the names Lincoln and T.J. ring a bell?"
He smiled widely.
I shook my head, I had to play it smart, and being
in the back of this car with him was dangerous.
Detective Walsh was just as much a criminal as I
was, but he was much worse. He was a crooked,
bitch ass, greedy cop…and he had me by the balls.
"Take me to jail."
"What?" He squinted at me.
"You heard me…take me to jail." I repeated.
"Make it easy on yourself Jr. just give the
millions you took back and this….."
I cut him off, "Are you deaf? Take me to jail
fool!"
He kept staring at me, "I'm going to take you
to jail and let you think about your options for
a while; I have a feeling you'll change your
mind about cooperating with me."

No Show

Sway pulled up to the warehouse 20 minutes later. He already divided the money up four ways and he'd taken his share home and hid it. Angelique and Dallas's share was already bagged up, Sway had already stashed Tyce's cut in his vault. The three of them went in the warehouse and waited for Tyce to get there.

"Thank you for coming Sway." Dallas said nudging him playfully.

"Yeah thank you, you work wonders with them doors." Angelique winked at him.

"It's nothin'…don't mention it, besides I never liked your ex-boyfriend anyway." He winked back at Angelique.

A half hour passed and Tyce hadn't shown up yet. Angelique tried calling him but it went straight to voicemail, Dallas tried also but it went straight to voicemail again, Sway tried a third time but it went straight to voicemail.

"Something's wrong." Dallas paced the floor.

"Lock everything down in the vault."

Angelique ordered. "Sway, is your money hidden?"

"Yeah." He confirmed.

"Good…we gotta get out of here."

Everybody left the warehouse in five minutes flat. Sway dropped the girls off at Dallas's condo and went home to his family. He was uneasy and irritated; he needed to know if his friend was ok. Angelique and Dallas left the condo and went to an underground sex club that Angelique was part owner of. They stayed in an unoccupied room to hide out and get their thoughts together.

"I'll start calling the hospitals and the jails."

Angelique sat on the bed.

Dallas put her finger in her mouth and leaned against the wall, "Where is he?" She wondered out loud

I Got Him

Tyce was processed and charged with weapons possession. Detective Walsh didn't include the whole host of other more serious crimes....yet. He was giving Tyce time to stew but if he didn't give up the money by tomorrow; he was a dead man and he would be more than happy to attend his execution. Half a million of that money belonged to him; he was hiding it in the church because that's the last place anybody would look, after all, he was a cop. Diego stashed his money there for years with no problems...until now. Detective Walsh had been working for Diego for over five years and he was now a rich man. He and Diego had a good thing going...he kept the feds off his back and looked out for all his workers on the streets. In exchange, he was paid ten percent of the profit every month. Diego was holding him responsible for the robbery and had frozen his money ever since it went down. Tyce's little stick up job was costing him a hundred grand a month. He picked up a secured line and called Diego,

"Yeah, I got him, he's locked up now on a gun charge."

"Muy bueno…did yu esplain tu heem hees options?" Diego said with an accent.

"Yeah, he's playing dumb but he'll wise up over night. I'll bury him with the other charges…he'll never make bail." Walsh assured Diego.

"I wan my dinero. Nobodee steals frum me. I killed that bitch Simone to set an essample…tha sem can happen tu heem. You tellem that frum me." Diego hung up.

The only reason Tyce was still breathing was because if Diego killed him he wouldn't get his money. He planned on having him killed once he was in prison…nice and neat. Diego like Biz; never got his hands dirty.

I Hate Losing

"You have any tattoos?" The female deputy asked dryly.

I reluctantly raised up the sleeves on my orange jump suit so she could get a picture of my tattoos...all seven of them. I took off my orange jail shirt and turned around so she could photograph the tattoo of my name across my back. My black jeans, black Timberland boots, and black T-shirt were all taken from me and stuffed in a plastic bag. They took my underwear, my belt, and my socks too. I got really pissed when they demanded I take the one and a half carat vvs diamonds out of my ears and put them in a zip lock bag; I didn't want them to come up missing. I was finger printed, photographed, and stripped searched, and I hated every second of it. I was too good to be in jail...I didn't belong here, but I would never let them see me sweat...never-and I would never give up my crew either, even if it cost me my life. Another deputy took me deeper into the detention center where all the inmates were being housed. Along the way, I picked up a bin that had mini versions of bathroom products and something that was going to be a mattress when it grew up. I was lead to a cell on the second floor…fortunately, for me it was empty; the last thing I wanted was to be locked up with a funky ass felon all night. The heavy cell door slammed shut behind me and it was official, I was locked up in the county jail. I laid in bed all night pissed off! I was pissed off at Omar; if I could kill his ass again I would. His bitch ass was the reason I was in here; that snitch ass nigga was telling Biz every move I fucking made.

Detective Walsh was giving me til' tomorrow, but I didn't need time to think…fuck him and Diego.

What about Angelique, what about Dallas, what about me?

Tomorrow I'd be charged with murder, arson, and armed robbery. Yeah I *did* all that shit but so what.

I banged the back of my head on the paper-thin mattress…I was fucked.

Lost And Found

Dallas sat on the bed next to Angelique. She couldn't believe what the man on the phone had said. He told Angelique they were holding an inmate by the name of Tyce Adkins without bail. They both were in disbelief. Angelique called Sway to tell him the bad news,

"We found him...he's in jail." She blurted out when he picked up.

"Damn...what's the charge?"

"It's a weapons charge but I got a feeling it's much worse than that. They didn't give him a bond." Angelique stood up and paced the tiny room. "Where's Omar?" She asked suddenly.

"Oh shit...ya'll don't know...I forgot all about that nigga, Tyce canceled his ass." He filled them in.

"What? When?" Angelique asked slightly confused.

"At the bank...that nigga was planning to clip Tyce the whole time.

"How did he find out?" She suspected he was up to no good; he was a jealous ass nigga.

"My guess is he got the proof from the same

person who let him know where you two were being held. He found out Omar was working with Biz all along."

"I knew that nigga was foul!" Angelique pumped her fist.

"Yeah, I didn't like his ass either." Sway agreed. "Listen I'ma call some attorneys I know and I'll get back witcha; he gon need a good one."

"Ok...let me know what we can do to help." She said.

"Alright, peace."

Angelique was glad Omar was dead...she never trusted his ass anyway, but now her man was in jail...and none of this shit made sense. What happened to Tyce after they left the house?

"I feel so helpless." Dallas said falling back on the bed.

"I feel the same way. I'm going to visit him tomorrow...you down?" Angelique knew the question was dumb.

"Hell yeah I'm down." Dallas said slightly offended, "Shit I might try and break is ass outta there if I can." She joked seriously.

Tomorrow they would walk in that jail together with one thing in common....Tyce Adkins.

All Rise

Tomorrow came and so did Detective Walsh. I had a private visit from him about seven in the morning.

"Wake up homeboy." Walsh banged the metal door. "How'd u sleep buddy?"

"I slept good…I had this dream I strangled you with a piece of barbed wire and I woke up with a huge smile on my face." I got up off the bunk and stretched my back.

"Wow…that was a vivid dream but it was just that…a dream." Walsh put his face up to the little window outside the cell.

"We'll see." I sat back down.

"On a more positive note, you ready to tell me about the money?"

"What money?" I said looking down at the cold dirty floor.

"THE FUCKING FIVE MILLION DOLLARS YOU BLACK FUCK!"

I walked up to the cell window and stared into his beady eyes, "What fuckin' five million dollars you pale fuck?"

He turned red, "You wanna end up like

Simone! Is that what you want?" His forehead was pressed against the glass, "That beautiful bitch was burnt alive for helping you Tyce…helping YOU!"

"Who's Simone?" I made my eyes bigger.

"Ok ok, play dumb if you want to…that's only going to get you killed. Now I'll ask you one more time where's my fucking money!"

I sighed, "What fuckin' money, I don't know what the fuck you talkin' about."

"YOU'RE DEAD! FUCKING DEAD!" Walsh stormed off down the long corridor.

The visit only lasted about two whole minutes; that was all the time I needed to tell him to go fuck himself. He wasn't expecting that, he just knew I was gonna roll over and play dead. That muthafucka thought I was gonna cave under the pressure like so many other niggas do. He got it wrong. What I didn't expect was the news about Simone…that shit threw me off. Biz no doubt snitched her out to Diego, and now I had to deal with him. The odds had been stacked against me since I was born. I wasn't supposed to make it out that dumpster, that was supposed to be my coffin, and now the odds were not in my favor again but so what…I liked it that way.

I walked into court and just like he'd promised, they threw the book at me. Detective Walsh made sure I was brought up on as many charges as possible; including murder. I had court that morning to be arraigned and formerly advised of the multiple charges I faced. The bald white judge asked me if I would be hiring private council or if I would like to be appointed a public defender. I chuckled and told him I'd be hiring my own attorney, "this wasn't no jaywalking ticket," I told him. That got me a laugh or two out the crowded courtroom...the judge even smiled a little. He set the next court date for 30 days out and remanded me over without bail. I was taken back to my tiny cell where my gourmet lunch of a dry ham sandwich, a rock hard peanut butter cookie, and a warm carton of milk was waiting for me on the floor. I wasn't hungry enough to eat that nasty shit; plus I don't eat swine.

Visit

I was transferred to pod four, which was a maximum security area for felons. I still had a cell to myself and I was given another orange outfit to change into. I got a few books from the book cart to occupy my time, it's funny how I never had time to read before, but in here, time was all I had. I was taking a nap on my bunk when the guard told me I had a visit. I'd already talked to Sway on the phone and he told me my lawyer would be down to see me first thing in the morning…maybe he was early. A young guard escorted me down to the day room where I waited with the other inmates that had visits. Four other guards kept a watchful eye on things as the visitors were led in. A huge smile spread across my face when I saw Angelique and Dallas stride in. They looked fine as frog's hair; it felt like I hadn't seen them in decades even though it had only been three days. I wasn't allowed to make physical contact with them; there was a thick red line on the table that separated us that we weren't allowed to cross. I was on my side and they stayed on theirs.

"Damn it's good to see you two." I smiled, "I

thought I didn't want ya'll to see me like this
but I'm glad you came."
"It's good to see you too, we would have come
sooner but they said you couldn't have visitors
til' you were transferred to general
population." Angelique said apologetically.
"How you doin'?" Dallas's voice was heavy
with concern.
"I'm ok…it's jus' a lil' rough being locked up,
I aint used to this shit." I rubbed the five-day
facial hair growth on my cheeks and chin.
"How you two holdin' up?"
They looked at each other, "Were fine…we
jus' miss you and were worried about you. We
checked up on the attorney Sway got for you
and he's one of the best in the state. We gave
him fifty thousand for your defense and he's
already working hard on your case. They
haven't touched your house or the other spot
but jus' in case they did we moved *all* your
shit." Angelique stroked her hair confidently.
I knew what she meant by *all my shit*; that's why I
loved her…she was always looking out for me.
Thanks to Angelique, my money was safe and
sound; it was a good move telling her the
combination and giving her an extra key to the
vault. I knew I could trust her. Dallas's hair was in
a ponytail that extended to the middle of her back.

She had a part on the left side of her head and her makeup was soft with subtle tan tones. Angelique wore light purple eye shadow with matching berry lip gloss. They both had cling tight jeans on that made me want to break the no touching rule and just take my punishment.

"Thanks for movin' my things Angelique." I winked.

"You're welcome, but don't jus' thank me…**we** did it." She wiggled her finger back and forth between Dallas and her.

"What's with all this **we** shit?" I raised my eyebrows.

Dallas looked me in the eyes, "I told her about us."

I was stunned; I just kept looking at both of them…one then the other. Did I hear her right? Did she just say she told Angelique about me and her? I didn't know what to expect, maybe they were gonna cuss me out or something. I mean technically I wasn't wrong, I wasn't with either one of them, I was single. On the other hand, I knew they both loved me and I'd finally realized that I loved them also. I was in an awkward and difficult situation…how do you choose between two women that you love equally?

"Ummm…ahhh…I didn't mean no harm…I jus', well both of you are amazing women and

I, I, I ahh I'm in love with both of you." I
finally confessed. "I didn't mean to hurt you
Angelique; that's the last thing I wanted to do.
And Dallas, I'm not trying to hurt you
either...I jus..."

"Stop apologizing Tyce...it's ok, were not mad
at you." Angelique cut me off.

Dallas jumped in, "We've decided that since
neither one of us wants to walk away from this
situation.......we're not."

"Can you handle the both of us?" Angelique
asked with the sexiest grin I've ever seen.

Dallas held the same look on her face as they
waited for my answer. Did I just hear what I
thought I heard? Did they just ask me if I could
handle being with them both in a relationship?

"You mean be with the both of you?" I asked
cautiously.

"Yes. You would have to commit to us and
only us. We're ok with this...we talked about it
extensively. We love you Tyce and we know
you love us. You risked your life to save ours
and we would do the exact same for you. We
belong together...all three of us." Angelique
stated proudly.

"But...I'm in here," I raised my hands up
looking around, "I jus' got charged with
murder and a whole lotta other shit."

"This is jus' a hurdle we have to get
over…together. Were not gonna abandon you
when you need us the most baby." Dallas
looked at me lovingly.
Angelique spoke defiantly, "Fuck what
everybody else says or does, we've broken all
the laws and rules anyway; why stop now, let's
jus' keep doing it the way we wanna do it."
"Yeah I'm not really a traditional chick at
all…I like bad boys…and you're as good as
they come." Dallas licked her shiny lips.
I took a moment to register what was happening in
this small visitation room. The two women I cared
most about in this world were asking me to be
with them in a committed relationship. I'd never
had a girlfriend before. I mean never; and now I
would have two. A part of me didn't trust women
but I'd found two special women that I could
definitely trust…and I wasn't about to lose them.
　　"You're serious." I asked again.
　　"Only if you are." They said at the same time.
　　"Then in that case…hell yeah!" I yelled.
The buff guard in the corner ordered me to
keep it down.
　　"Damn I wish I could touch you two right
now."
　　"Jus' hold on baby…jus' hold on." Dallas
smiled reassuringly.

"For a minute there I thought ya'll were gonna
kill me." I admitted.

My girlfriends looked at each other and
grinned, "Naw, we'd only do that if you cheat
on us…and you know we pack heat"

Angelique said seriously.

The ten-minute visit flew by, the girls left to the
outside world, and I returned to my cell. Damn I
wanted so bad to get the fuck outta this punk ass
fucking cell!!

I Know Something You Don't Know

It was late in the evening and Detective Walsh was sipping on a cup of coffee in his corner office. The police station was nearly empty as the late hours approached. He was finishing the paper work on the trumped up charges; the district attorney wanted all the details of the case finished tonight because Tyce's big time attorney was scheduled to meet him in the morning to pick up the discovery. Walsh would have to burn the midnight oil to make sure all the fabricated evidence was air tight. He paid Tyce a quick visit in his cell earlier in the day to see if he changed his mind and wanted to tell him where the money was hidden; Tyce gave him the middle finger and just rolled over on his bunk. The detective ordered a search and seizure on Tyce's house and warehouse but came up empty; that only pissed him off further. He was making him look real incompetent in the eyes of Diego. His job now was to make sure Tyce was locked up and placed in a California federal prison where Diego could arrange to have him killed. If he did that, business could go on as usual and he could go back to getting paid.

His concentration was broken when a woman walked into his office unannounced and uninvited. He looked up as the stranger just strolled into his office as if her name was on the desk.

"Can I help you?" Detective Walsh asked irritated.

The woman just stared at him for a while

before she answered, "Yes you can James."

Walsh was surprised to hear his first name come out of her mouth. He was even more surprised when she helped herself to a seat.

"What can I do for you miss......?"

"You don't need to know my name James; we can keep this on an informal level for now."

"Look, enough with this mystery shit lady, what the hell are you doing in my office?"

She crossed her legs slowly and pulled her purse off her shoulder. Her hand slid inside and came out with a large envelope. She casually tossed it on top of the desk and crossed her arms across her medium sized breasts. There was a scowl on Walsh's face as he snatched the envelope off the desk.

"What is this?"

"Merry Christmas." She said ignoring the no

smoking sign on the door and lighting a
cigarette.

Detective James Walsh used a letter opener to slice
the envelope open. He turned it upside down and
three 8x10 photographs spilled out. He nearly wet
his pants when he seen the pictures. The delivery
woman took a long drag from her cigarette and
blew smoke in the air. She said nothing as she
watched James study the pictures.

"Where did you get these?" He turned red with
anger.

"That's not important." She responded.

"Don't play games with me lady! I demand to
know where you got these! Who took them!
Who took them!" He pounded his fist on the
desk.

"Easy James...don't have a heart attack; I'm
the only one who's seen them so relax."

Detective Walsh was boiling with anger and
embarrassment. The woman had walked into his
office with pictures of him and a 16 year old boy.
In one photo, he was sucking the boy's dick on a
couch. In another photo, he was fucking the young
boy against a wall. The third showed him pissing
on the same boy as he laid on the floor naked and
the fourth document in the envelope was a printed
copy of the male escort ad where he'd found his
boy toy.

"How the hell did you get these?" He snorted.
"It's what I do detective…you'd shouldn't be too surprised at what an escort will do for money. Getting him to set that hidden camera up was the best five hundred dollars I've ever spent; certainly more than he was getting from you for an hour." She smiled.
"What do you want?" He stared at her menacingly.
"I want you to burn that stack of papers your working so hard on."
Detective Walsh looked down at the stack with a confused expression. "What are you talkin' about?"
"Don't play games with me." She mocked him, "You know what I'm talkin' about."
A long sigh escaped his nostrils, "Let me get this straight…you're here for that little punk Tyce Adkins?"
"You catch on quick James."
"What do you care about him for?"
"Let's just say I hate to see innocent men go to jail."
"He's not innocent!" He yelled.
"Well that's a matter of personal opinion…he's no angel but he's not the devil either. But never mind what you think about him. If you don't make those charges disappear than these photos

and many more will make it to your captain,
the district attorney, your wife, your fellow
officers, your pastor, your family doctor, and
your real boss…Diego Alverez." She finished
off her cigarette.

Walsh sat there in shock as the words sunk in. She
had him by the balls and all she had to do was
squeeze to ruin his life forever. He'd been fucking
with the 16 year old boy for over a year. He
thought he was being discreet by going through a
private escort service but apparently, he was
wrong.

"If I do what you want how do I know you're
not going to use these pictures anyway."

"You don't. But I'm a woman of my
word…I'm not a piece of shit like you." She
stood up to leave, "I'll know if the charges are
not dropped by morning, I don't care how you
do it…just do it. You can keep those photos
James…I have plenty more." The woman
walked out of the office before Walsh could
respond.

The corrupt gay detective just stared at the photos.
He couldn't afford to let these pornographic
pictures get out but the wheels of justice were
already in motion, it was going to be difficult to
stop them. He looked at the pictures and then
glanced at the discovery and his incomplete police

reports. Walsh had no idea how he was going to pull this off but the thought of his wife seeing a picture of him fucking a 16 year old boy in the ass was enough motivation to figure something out.

He also wondered who the hell that woman was.

Love Don't Live Here

Police had no leads on the China Town bank robbery. All the customers and employees could tell them was that three black men stormed inside the bank and only two left. There was no video surveillance to go over and no prints. The police knew it was Omar that was killed but the employees reported that he was one of the bank robbers, so they really didn't care who killed him. As far as they were concerned, he got what he deserved. Tasha on the other hand knew exactly who killed her man. She found it hard to shed a tear for Omar though. A part of her was saddened at the loss of her short time boyfriend but the over two million dollars and her two new automobiles helped to ease the pain. Of course, the police questioned her for several hours about the murder but she kept her mouth closed. She didn't want to end up laying next to him in the cemetery.

A week after Omar's death Tasha relocated to Las Vegas to start a new life. Before she left town, she had a huge garage sale featuring all of Omar's belongings, including the dogs. A car shipping company transported Omar's *"Escalade"* and

"Mercedes" to Vegas while Tasha and Ace made the three hour drive in her new convertible with two million in cash hidden in the trunk.

Face The Funk

30 days passed as fast as a turtle on crutches. I was going crazy in that jail. I had a new cellmate that talked way to much and took a shit like every 15 minutes. Angelique and Dallas made sure my commissary was stacked up. I had *"Snickers,"* *"Ramen"* noodles, *"Doritos,"* *"Tang,"* all the snacks I could eat and sell. It wasn't as good as the chicken alfredo Angelique cooked for me or some fried fish from Shabazz...but it was better than nothing.

The night before my court date, I couldn't sleep. I was nervous, and I don't get nervous. My lawyer told me he hadn't got the discovery yet because they were stalling. The plan was for him to make his official appearance as my attorney and enter a not guilty plea but he told me to be prepared for the worst and he would find out what the holdup was. The deputies came and got me at seven in the morning for my court appearance. I was lead into the overly air conditioned room with four other inmates. All the inmates sat on the side of the judge's bench while the attorneys and free folk's sat on hard ass wooden pews. I smiled at Dallas and Angelique who were seated in the front row trying not to look worried. I spotted my mouth piece who was busy huddled up in a corner with the district attorney assigned to my case. They were nodding their heads back and forth and whispering loudly but I couldn't make out what they were saying. The D A looked over at me with an evil glare and scribbled something on a note pad. The punk ass judge took forever to bring his fat ass out and he didn't look like he was in a good mood. He kinda looked like he had heartburn when he glanced at me.

"All rise!" The deputy announced.

I reluctantly rose from my seat to show some non-deserved fake ass respect to the judge. Two minutes into the proceedings, my attorney requested a counseling session with me through the deputy. He wanted a chance to meet with me before my case was called up. The hallway was the special meeting place where me and my expensive attorney had our brief conference with the deputy standing close by. The lawyer stared at me through two thousand dollar prescription bi focals.

"Wasup?" I shrugged my shoulders.

He chuckled a little, "Man O man, can I get your autograph?"

"What?" I looked at him closer.

"I want to get your autograph. I mean you have to be a celebrity or royalty to get the kind of deal you just got offered." His eyes were wide.

"What deal...what are you talkin' about?"

He cleared his throat, "How does 60 days on a brandishing a weapon charge sound? You'll get credit for the 30 days you already served and be released in eight days."

I looked at him blankly, "Are you playin' with me?"

"No sir Mr. Adkins...I most certainly am not. I just spoke with the district attorney and I have the disposition paper work all here for you to sign."

He pulled some legal papers out of his brief case and passed them to me. I looked them over while my mouth piece used his manicured finger to point out all the important parts. I read the weapons charge info and the jail time stint. There was no mention of any murders or arson. My lawyer advised me to sign the deal before my luck changed....and I agreed. I couldn't believe it; what the fuck happened? Where was that bitch ass Detective Walsh? How in the hell was this happening? I signed my name like my hand was on fire and my lawyer patted me on my back vigorously. Shit, he was happy he was getting paid without having to earn it. I was taken back into the courtroom and my case was called up next. Me and my newest fan stood at the podium across from a pissed off district attorney.

"Your honor this is case number FR48759, the state vs. Tyce Adkins. Your honor there has been a change of course in this case. We are no longer pursuing additional charges in this case and the people have reached a disposition agreement in this matter. All previous felony charges have been dropped by the people in favor of a misdemeanor weapons charge. The documents have been signed by both parties and the defendant has been advised by his counsel." The D A spat the words out of his mouth like spoiled milk.

The judge read a copy of the document and he couldn't believe what he was seeing. He asked me if I was entering this plea of my own free will blah blah blah blah...and after he was done bumping his gums, he banged his gavel and made it official. "Yesssss!" Angelique screamed.

Dallas was grinning from ear to ear. She didn't say

a word, but her huge *"Kool-Aid"* grin spoke volumes.

"You hold on for eight more days Mr. Adkins."
My lawyer said cheerfully shaking my hand
vigorously.

"No problem." I shot back.

I winked at my girlfriends as I was led out the courtroom…before I walked through the doors I looked over my shoulder and mouthed the words "I love you" to both of them.

"We love you too!" They shouted out not
caring that they were disturbing the calm of the
courtroom.

Now, I really aint talk much to God but I had to give Him a shout out on this one.

Hello Again

I was ecstatic! I walked back to my skinny cell wearing a full figured smile on my face. My celebration breakfast was *"Ramen"* noodles a *"Kit Kat"* candy bar and a glass of *"Tang."* For some reason the snacks tasted like a three course meal from a five star restaurant…*maybe* it was knowing that I'd be out of there in eight days that added the special seasonings to my simple meal.

The afternoon rolled around and brought with it a surprise visit announcement. A jail guard named Cecil who looked like he played nose tackle for the *"Broncos"* informed me that I had company. I suddenly got impatient because I was itching to see Angelique and Dallas again; I jumped up off my bunk and followed him eagerly to the visitation room.

When I walked in my eyes searched the room for Angelique and Dallas but they were not there.

"Where's my visitors?" I turned to Cecil.

"She's right there." He pointed to a middle-aged woman sitting quietly at the corner table. I gave her a puzzled look and walked over to her,

keeping with the rules of the visitation room I took
a seat across from her and stayed on my side of the
red line. I scrolled through my mental rolodex
trying to place her face but came up blank.

"Hello Tyce." She said in a friendly tone.

"How you doin'…and excuse me for being
blunt, but *who* are you?" I leaned back in my
chair.

"My name is Pamela…Pamela Adkins."
My mind was vacant…the room went
soundless…I just watched her. Neither one of us
moved a muscle.

"*Ummm*…I'm the one who rescued you when
you were a baby." Her eyes began to water. "I
ahhhh…I gave you your name."
The levy finally broke and a flood of tears
streamed down her blush red cheeks. She
smoothed over her hair, which was pulled back
into a neat bun and adjusted her position in the
chair. She took shaky breaths as her emotions rode
up her spine.

"I think I owe you…I mean…I feel like I owe
you an explanation." She stuttered.

I finally spoke, "Thank you for rescuing me."
I stood up and gave her a warm hug, I squeezed
her body tight to mine, and we rocked slowly back
and forth. I was breaking the visitation rules but I
didn't give a fuck. Cecil didn't attempt to break us

up he just looked the other way and let us have our moment, plus I think he overheard the conversation because he had a little grin on his face. For the first time in 26 years; I cried, I let the long abandoned tears descend down my face. I cried because I was *left* in a dumpster, I cried because I was *found* in a dumpster. I cried because I had to kill my best friend, I cried because Lil' Flash was dead, I cried because my soul needed to air out; for years I locked my emotions inside my chest and didn't let them out and now there was no more room in there. Pamela held me close and rubbed my back while she let her emotion filled tears flow out as well. We eventually separated and sat back down; both of us had a case of the sniffles as we wiped the water from our eyes.

"I knew a woman found me in the trash, I had visions of how you would look…to be honest I never pictured you being white."

I was being honest, in my dreams I envisioned the woman who found me as being black. I guess in my head she was the closest thing to a mother I had and when I looked in the mirror I saw a brown face staring back at me so naturally my imagination made her look like me.

"I didn't mean anything by it…I'm jus' surprised…*pleasantly surprised*." I touched her hand.

"I'm glad. To be honest I didn't expect to find you in that back alley either. I believe God sent me there to find you and I'm grateful that He did."

"Shit me too." I blurted out. "I have so many questions to ask you…I don't know where to start. First of all how did you know I was in here?" I put my elbows on the table ready to listen.

Pamela sat up straight in her chair and looked me in the eye, "I've always known where you were Tyce…I've kept tabs on you your whole life. Up until now I've stayed in the background but I saw that you were in trouble so I stepped in."

"What do you mean you stepped in?" I asked curious.

"I ahhh, saw that you needed help so I helped." She squeezed my hand lovingly.

And then it hit me, *"You're responsible for the deal today….for the charges being dropped!"* There was a long pause, "Yes I was." She answered quietly.

"How did you pull that off, I mean what did you do?"

"It really wasn't that hard, it's kind of what I do now, I'm a private investigator, I retired from the police department and went into business for myself about six years ago."

"Ok, so you followed me or something?" I asked somewhat confused.

"No, I followed the man that I knew could bring you trouble…I followed Detective Walsh." She lowered her voice, "You see when you robbed Diego Alverez I knew he would send his pet detective after you, so as an insurance policy for *you* I got some dirt on *him* to get you clean."

"You know about the robbery?" I whispered.

"I was there when it happened." Pamela's eyes narrowed.

"Damn. I guess you still rescuing me from funky situations huh?" I smiled.

"That's what good mother's do." She smiled back.

"Yeah…they do. Thank you so much. What the hell did you have on him anyway, it musta been somethin' real bad."

"Let's just say that he had a weakness for young boys." Her eyebrows rose up.

"DAMN…HE WAS A PETOFILE!" I yelled out.

"Something like that…*whatever* he was he didn't want it to get out in the open."

I just shook my head. All that tough talk he was dishing out and the dude was a fucking freak. He was trying to act all hard and shit.

"Listen Tyce…I may not agree with all the things you do but I know inside you have a good heart. I couldn't stand by and watch you get thrown in jail for the rest of your life…not while I'm still breathing." She said confidently.

"Well I'm glad I have you in my corner."

The ten-minute visit was coming to an end but I had to ask one more question.

I licked my lips out of nervousness, "I wanna ask you somethin'."

"Go ahead." She whispered.

I took a deep breath, "Why didn't you keep me?"

She blinked her eyes rapidly and placed her palms on the table, "Tyce I ahhh, I struggled with that question my whole life, even to this day I ask myself that very question. I wonder if I'd kept you-would you even be in this situation." She continued, "I was in a sad place when I found you. I'd just had a miscarriage and buried my birth son days before you came into my life. I kept you for two weeks but I was still mourning the loss of my child and I wasn't capable of taking good care of you at the time. I ummm…was an emotional wreck. But understand Tyce that I never completely left you, I was always near, and now when you

need me the most, I'm here for you."
I digested what Pamela said and I knew she was
being honest and sincere with me. I respected her
for that.

"Times almost up Adkins." Cecil bellowed
from across the room.
I turned to look at him then I turned back to
Pamela, "Thank you for comin'…and thank
you for answering my questions."
"You're welcome."
"I'd like to talk to you again sometime if that's
ok?"
"I'd very much like that." She said as we both
stood up.
I now really looked at the woman that saved my
life; she was a short woman probably about 5.3.
She had to be about 50 but she didn't look a day
over 35. She was dressed in a dark blue pantsuit
with a cream blouse underneath. Her eyes were an
ocean blue and her face expressed kindness and
warmth.

"Thanks again for lookin' out for me….mom."
"You're welcome...son."
I walked over toward Cecil with some new pep
in my step.
"That's my moms." I told Cecil proudly.
"Yeah I heard." He tried not to show it but he
was happy for me. "You'll get to see her in

eight days but for now I gotta get you back to
your cell."

I turned around, "I'll see you later."

"I'll see you later Tyce…keep your head up
you only have a week left." She smiled and
waved goodbye.

You're Fired

"Wha tha fuck you meen yu cuudnt charg hem?" Diego asked Walsh.

"I mean…th th the case fell apart…it it wasn't my fault…the D.A…"

"I dun gif a fuck about tha D A. I tol you to mek sur he was locked up an you cudnt even du that simpul theeng!" Diego walked over to Walsh and punched him in the face.

Walsh stumbled back and fell on the couch in Diego's office, *"Ged the fuck outta my face!"*

Detective Walsh fumbled out of Diego's down town real estate office and jumped in his unmarked cruiser. He didn't bother to wipe away the blood that was running down his lips; he just sped off from the parking lot. The fact that he was a cop offered little protection from Diego…he was now in fear of his life…and he had good reason to be.

I Can't Wait Til You Come Home

The seventh day was a good day for me. I was finally getting released tomorrow and I couldn't wait. I spent the last week reading and talking on the phone to everyone. I talked to Bree and found out she was back in school working on her bachelor's degree. She was doing better emotionally and getting her life back on track. Sway moved down the street from my home and he and Renae were planning to open a day care center in the inner city. He'd hung up his gloves for good but he still was involved in the fight game...he had his hands in a few upcoming fights. He and Ranae were doing quite well these days and both of them slept like babies in their newly bought beach wood bed.

I was looking kinda rough so I paid for a haircut out of my commissary money in preparation for my visit with Angelique. Even though I was also with Dallas, they still gave each other space when it came to spending time with me. They both would be there to pick me up tomorrow but today I was spending time with Angelique. Once again, Cecil led the way to the visiting room and I followed. I was looking as good as I could considering the jail house cut I was sporting; Angelique on the other hand was looking scrumptious. My mouth actually watered when I seen her sitting there. I didn't want to jeopardize my upcoming release so I restrained myself from taking a bite outta her like a juicy peach.

"Hey baby, how you doin'?" She greeted me warmly. "You lookin' like the old Tyce...*kinda*." She teased.

"Yeah I jus' got a cut...it aint that bad is it?" I rubbed my head a little.

"Naw, I'm jus' messin' with you...you look good."

"Thanks, how's Dallas?"

"She's good...we goin' shoppin' after this. She wanna get a new outfit to pick you up in tomorrow." She snitched.

We sat down in our designated spots and continued our short visit.

"Guess what?" I baited.

"What?" She asked putting on raspberry lip-gloss.

I paused for affect, "I met the woman who pulled me out of the dumpster when I was a baby."

"***For real***? What did she say?" She cocked her

head and opened her mouth in awe.

"It was crazy...I mean I was expecting to see you and Dallas but she was sitting in here. She told me she's always been around keeping an eye on me; then she told me she was the one responsible for getting the charges dismissed."

"***Get tha fuck outta here***!" She slapped the table. "How did she do that?"

"Apparently she's a private investigator and she had found out that the punk ass detective that arrested me was fuckin' with little boys."

"What do you mean fuckin' with little boys?"

I lowered my head, "I mean he was gay and was ***fuckin'*** little boys."

"DAMN, aint that some shit!" She gasped, "That dirty bastard!"

"Yeah that's what I said."

We tried to cram a week's worth of conversation into ten minutes. We talked about me and her, her and Dallas and me and my mom. As usual, the time flew by at warp speed. She ended the visit with a bombshell,

"Me and Dallas were talkin' and we wanted to run this past you." She licked her lips.

"Run what passed me?" I asked watching her tongue hit the corners or her mouth.

"What do you think about all of us living together?"

"Wow…that would be a big step…ya'll think ya'll ready for that?" I shot back.

"Yes we can handle it…the question *is* can you?"

I thought about what she just asked me. I was taking this relationship seriously and I didn't want to fuck it up. The one good thing about jail is that you have plenty of time to think shit out and plan your life. During my time in here I came to realize two things: one was that I never wanted to come back here again, and two was that I wanted to spend as much time with the women I loved as possible, that included Angelique, Dallas and now Pamela. I looked at Angelique who was staring at me waiting for my response,

"I'm gonna fuck the shit outta you when you get home and I'm sure Dallas is gonna do the same…are you sure you can handle all that in house pussy?"

I laughed a little, "Yeah I'm sure *we* can handle it." I looked down at my lap and smiled.

Cecil once again ruined the fun I was having by announcing the end of the visit. I reluctantly said bye to Angelique and she blew me a kiss as I walked away.

"I'll see you tomorrow baby." She said excitedly.

"Ya'll need to start packin' your stuff." I

pointed my finger at her.

"Oh don't worry we will." She laughed.

I went my way and Angelique went hers. I made the familiar trip to my cell while she made the long journey to the parking lot. The moon was beaming down on her as she bounced to her car feeling good about her life and her situation. She took the key ring out of her purse and pressed the unlock button. Just as she opened the door it was violently kicked closed, she spun around quickly to see who was behind her. Angelique turned around and found herself staring down the barrel of a loaded gun. She'd left her gun at home...she never brought it with her to the prison anyway but now she wished to God she had.

"I know you didn't forget about me."

She looked passed the barrel of the gun and focused her eyes on the man that was holding it. She recognized Marcus from the pool house. "FUCK YOU!" Angelique spat back.

"Naw bitch...fuck you. You thought you could carve me up like a fuckin' turkey and get away with it. I told you I'd make you pay for that shit...nobody does that shit to me and lives; especially a bitch like you!"

Angelique held her breath and wondered how the hell she was gonna get outta this one. Her man was locked up, she was alone without her gun, and she was playing one on one with a man that was drunk with revenge.

Damn life was a trip.   **TYCE**

TO
    BE
        CONTINUED...

ACKNOWLEDGEMENTS

ALRIGHT ALRIGHT!! Let's do it, I'm sittin with four pillows behind my back and a glass of grape kool-aid by my side. First of all I wanna give a gigantic one up to Allah for giving me the strength, determination and patience to complete my 2nd book. Big shout out to my parents Rose & Willie for all the love and support. Thank you Thank you! Much love to my siblings Jameelah, Ayesha, Wali & Ameenah. Ameenah, you were there when I first talked about TYCE & you helped me with the story line. GRACIAS. I gotta give a special shout out to my girl Melanie for telling me I should be writing when I wasn't…and for loving me and for being the sexiest nurse I ever had. lol To my good friend and partner in crime Angela: thanks for being a tough proof reader…I needed that, your positivity never stops, it jus keeps going and going and going….
I gotta shout out special friends-Shana, Tamika, Michele, Senobia, Lakisha, Jamila, Candy and Dave. Much love!! I wanna thank my children for being great kids! Karese & lil' Shareef, daddy loves you up to the sky!! I must and need to thank

Locksie of ARC book club who by the way is the best reviewer in New York! Big thanks to Aisha Golden, who helped me get in touch with my feminine side. Thank you for all your advice and book wisdom. An author hopes and prays he or she has a gang of fans...I mean unless you're writing books for yourself you want people to read em. So I wanna thank each and everyone one of my fans and if you're not a fan...thank you anyway for jus reading! Thank you to T. J. of New Vision Marketing and Design, all the design work is fantastic; I couldn't have done it without you. Also to DDK, if this book finds you...I'm very sorry from the bottom of my heart. To all the authors out there I wanna say, keep it up, don't quit and don't be quiet...let your words do the talking. I'm not jus an author, I'm a reader so BRING IT!! I know I will. Now let's see....if I forgot anybody it's not on purpose, there are a lot of people in your life who affect you in positive ways...to many to name here. So I'll jus say THANK YOU EVERYBODY. Until the next book drops....be easy ya'll. PEACE! I'm goin to sleep!!!

FACEBOOK.COM

SEARCH
SHAREEF JAUDON

EMAIL: SHAREEFJAU@LIVE.COM

ALSO BY SHAREEF JAUDON

~RELATIONSHIT~

***

ALL BOOKS BY SHAREEF JAUDON
AVAILABLE ONLINE @

AMAZON.COM